IRISH CHRISTMAS STORIES II

IRISH CHRISTMAS STORIES II

Edited by

David Marcus

BLOOMSBURY

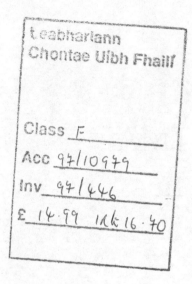
First published in Great Britain 1997

This compilation © 1997 by Bloomsbury Publishing Plc

The copyright of the individual contributors remains with the respective authors

The moral right of the authors has been asserted

Bloomsbury Publishing PLC, 38 Soho Square, London W1V 5DF

A CIP catalogue record for this book is available from the British Library

ISBN 0 7475 3337 7

10 9 8 7 6 5 4 3 2 1

Typeset by Hewer Text Composition Services, Edinburgh
Printed in Great Britain by Clays Ltd, St Ives plc

Contents

CONTENTS

Introduction

The very first story I ever wrote – I wasn't even into my teens at the time – was called *The Truth about Santa Claus*. Just the sort of idea, one would think, to attract a young beginner. But for a fledgling who had been born into an Orthodox Jewish family in a still largely ghettoised micro-community in Cork, whose grandparents had been refugees from Lithuania, who was approaching his own Barmitzvah, and who had never celebrated Christmas? A rather unOrthodox – as well as unorthodox – first venture surely. What interests me now, however, is not what the choice says about me, but what it says about Christmas.

Or should I say 'said'? For Christmas, of course, has changed since then. What hasn't? Yet year after year one apprehends in its celebration an echo of *plus ça change, plus c'est la même chose*. What refrains does that echo carry in this collection of Irish stories about Christmas?

They are many and varied, for Christmas, being almost 2,000 years old, is a theme with countless variations. Parties, presents, Santa Claus, forgotten friends, lost relatives, reunions, nostalgia

– all these are constants. Even snow, more a March visitor than a Christmas guest in Ireland, reprises the Yuletide season for Pádraic Breathnach in *The Snowman*, while in Hugo Hamilton's thought-provoking *Nazi Christmas*, where the driven snow is accompanied not by innocence, but by cruelty and prejudice, it is greeted with the patient courage of Christ's admonition to turn the other cheek.

Nostalgia there is – there must be – aplenty, usually for lost friends and relatives. But often it is through Christmas that relations and relationships are rediscovered and renewed, as in Sean O'Faolain's *Two of a Kind* and Benedict Kiely's *Homes on the Mountain*, and sometimes, as in Colum McCann's *The Year of the Green Pigeons*, the rediscovery has a curative promise.

On occasion, for some people there is a watershed Christmas in their lives, one that comes to be seen as akin to a rite of passage. In Elizabeth Bowen's *The Tommy Crans* it is a certain Christmas party, in Maeve Binchy's *Be Prepared* it is the visit of an unwelcome guest, in William Trevor's *The Time of Year* it is a Christmas swim, and in Clare Boylan's *The Miracle of Life* it is a special Christmas present.

Christmas presents – ah yes, they are the stuff of more than one story in this collection. But one particular such story has for me a special appeal. That is Frank O'Connor's *Christmas Morning*, for its culmination is how a young boy discovered the truth about Santa Claus, and the lesson of that truth. Which is where I came in – came into Christmas, I mean. For my discovery wasn't only that Santa Claus was my father; it was also that if my father – a mature, devout, adult Orthodox Jew – could pretend to be Santa Claus for his young son, then Christmas could mean something for everyone.

David Marcus

FRANCIS MacMANUS

Family Portrait

If you're ever round our side of the country and if you drop in at my uncle's, you'll be sure to find yourself alone in the parlour, for a little while anyway, while there's a fuss and a rattle going on down in the kitchen for the stranger. Take a look around the parlour. On a little table on one side of the fireplace, and among a few fine seashells and a piece of glass containing a coloured view of a foreign city, you'll notice an album of photographs. Be sure to open the album – oh! they'll be proud to show you who is who, and which became a nun and which a priest, and they'll tell you the age of the faded, bearded, stiff-collared gentlemen, when they married and how many smiling children they had and how far they were scattered, still smiling, over the face of the earth. There's one photo, though, that you'll be sure to remark.

Take a good look at that before my aunt catches you and cries: 'Oh! put that thing away out of my sight. Put it away. Do you mean to tell me it's not burnt yet? Put it away.' And then she'll blush to the roots of her hair and laugh with her hands clasped under her chest. If my uncle is there, he'll take the picture in his hand and chuckle, saying, 'Did you ever see such a miserable collection of unChristian snipes in your life? They have beaks on them with the hunger. Look at herself wallfalling.'

Of course, he and she are there in the picture with all the children, besides my brother and myself; for it's a family portrait, taken in the concrete yard with the porch of the house as a background; and on the back, the name of the photographer is stamped over his city, Waterford.

Take a good look at the picture. Some of us are sitting on chairs, and some of us are standing, and there's not a sign of life in the whole lot of us. Our shoulders and heads are drooping, like hounds moping in the rain, and we look petrified with the cold and famished; but in the eyes there's a fire of anger. We appear as if we were ready to jump out of the picture in a wild charge.

As a matter of fact, that's exactly how we felt, for the picture was taken one Christmas Day just before dinner; indeed, just at the time when we should have been all sitting down decently around the table.

'Bad luck to him and his black box,' says my aunt. 'The long string with the grand talk. And it was your fault, too!' she adds to my uncle.

'Go on, woman. You were more anxious than the man himself to have the picture taken. Who delayed us titivating herself?'

'Titivating myself? Did you ever hear the like? Look at the cut of me in the picture. And good God, look, I never noticed this before. I have a big smudge on my chin. Put it away. Put it away.'

That's the way arguments start, and arguments will be going on about that photograph till Tibb's Eve. And yet, nobody will attempt to destroy it, because it was taken on a rare day.

Dinner on Christmas Day is a serious event in my uncle's house. I don't mean that everybody sits down with long, solemn faces to eat like sanctimonious heretics. Far from it. The celebration is too strenuous for heavy hearts. Preparations begin after first Mass and breakfast. While my aunt and the girls are baking and basting themselves alive in the kitchen, where the fire is usually fit to roast a fair-sized horse, the rest of us take out the dogs and go off across the country. The hunting, if you can call it hunting, continues till my uncle says, 'I think we'll be making for home, boys. The women may need a hand. It's a hard day for them.' Nobody says no, and so we turn homeward. By this time we're not anxious to let the dogs wander far, although the hares might be starting up out of every ditch. In fact, when my uncle says, 'I wonder now if that turkey is turning out all right; it was the pick of them anyway,' we are all solicitous for the fate of the same bird. One of my cousins will say, 'The plum pudding is safe anyhow. I saw it this morning hanging in the dairy with the other ones.' 'Do you remember the one we had last year?' another one asks, but only to remind himself. We're all thinking the same thoughts.

On the Christmas Day on which the photo was taken that you'll find in the album, we went over the entire dinner we should eat by hints and suggestions and questions. It would be the same as any other year, but that did not matter to our memories which, apparently, needed to be refreshed. There would be the turkey, of course, plump, brown, bursting with stuffing, a bird specially reared for the sacrifice. Then there would be, maybe, half-a-dozen small tender fowl on the side, roasted with thin slices of bacon on top; a ham roasted in a case of dough so that it would be rich with its own juices and flavours; a bit of roast beef; a bit of spiced beef; a special brawn; baked and boiled potatoes; and sauces and gravies to match. Without much pause for breath, there would follow baked apples, smothered in whipped cream, custards, jellies, a pie perhaps, and then, naturally enough, the plum pudding, the big one that would make my aunt gasp and groan as she lifted it. By this time my uncle, you might notice, would be drinking your health till you wondered if you'd ever have a day's sound health again.

Well, when we hurried into the yard with the dogs on this Christmas Day, the odours and scents of the kitchen were floating out across the porch. It was a bitter day, dry, with a north-east wind, the kind of a day on which you must keep moving to prevent your blood from freezing under your skin. We trooped into the kitchen, slipping in quietly one by one, to see how things were progressing, for it is surely a heavy day for the women. My aunt met us half-way, crying, 'What brought you home so early? We're not nearly ready. Out the whole lot of you. Out. We want room.'

We retreated to lounge against the gates and to take an interest in the sky. My uncle sat dejected, and said, 'We'll be all stretched out stiff if they don't hurry on.' He crossed to the barn and returned, munching an apple ravenously, and we were about to follow his example, when a tall man, with a large black box strapped to his back, entered the yard from the road.

'God save you,' said my uncle. 'A happy Christmas to you.'

The stranger was as tall and as thin a man as I ever saw. His clothes just hung from him, hung and drooped like the ends of his grey moustache, and the bedraggled black bow he had knotted under his chin. His eyes were watery with the north-east wind, and there was a bluish tinge on his narrow face and knobby hands. He swept off a large, wide-brimmed black hat with a vast sweep of his arm, and said, 'May I, sir, return you, whom I presume to be the master of the house, the compliments of this festive season, and may I extend them to your flourishing kindred.' Then he bowed twice, or rather swayed.

'Holy Jerusalem,' said my uncle under his breath, as he eyed the black box and listened. Aloud, he remarked, 'It's a cold day to be trapesing around empty roads, Mister.' And as an afterthought, 'A queer day, too, it is.' We gathered closer.

4

Family Portrait

The tall man rubbed his hands and smiled icily. 'Mother Nature,' he declared, gesturing towards the sky, 'has sent weather which custom more or less deems seasonable, although she has not quite fulfilled the expectations of those genial folk who sigh for the icicles by the wall, the pervading fleecy snow, and the colourful, gentle robin languishing for charitable crumbs at the door of the humble cot. Nevertheless, if one such as myself may be sufficiently venturesome as to express a discordant opinion, I must say she has not tempered the wind to the shorn lamb. Yes, it's damn cold, sir.'

We were stunned. After a moment, my uncle asked, breathlessly and timidly, 'Will you have a little drop of something to warm you?'

The tall man bowed, unsmiling. 'Sir,' said he, 'while I cannot be designated with exactness as a fanatical disciple of those who regard the juice of the grape and the distillation of barley accursed, and while I may be defined as an evangelist of the human conviviality which is moderated by the queenly virtue of prudence, permit me to thank you profoundly and to refuse regretfully . . .' Here he bowed, while my uncle backed away in bewilderment . . . 'and to inform you,' the tall man went on, 'that your neighbours in this hospitable countryside have already shown their appreciation of the festive season by taxing my capacity to the utmost. Sir, I pray you, no more. However, I will trespass on your kindness and generosity by . . .'

At that moment my aunt's long-wished-for call came from the kitchen. 'Dinner. Don't stand there all day gabbling in the yard.'

'Will you eat a bit of dinner, Mister?' my uncle inquired.

The thin man bowed. 'Once more, your hospitable neighbours have forestalled your . . .'

'Will you tell me, then, man, what I can do for you?'

The thin man unstrapped the black box from his back, opened

it dexterously, extracted a collapsible tripod which he rigged up, and a camera which he set on top; and then, standing beside his apparatus, with his hat in the crook of his elbow, he said, 'Here, sir, you behold an instrument which is the happy product of the combined genius and inventiveness of multitudes of scientists and artists who have unselfishly devoted their lives to the cause and advancement of . . .'

'Dinner,' cried my aunt. 'Dinner. You were like a pack of cannibals five minutes ago.'

The tall man bowed in the direction of her voice.

'Do you want to take a photo?' my uncle asked brusquely. 'Yes or no, do you want to take a picture?'

'That, sir, is the purpose of my peregrinations from Waterford to these hospitable parts. Had I the pencil of a da Vinci or the brush of a Rubens, I should be happy . . .'

My uncle cut him short by disappearing into the house where he was heard to say loudly, 'Do you want your photo taken?'

'Are you gone daft?' my aunt inquired shrilly. 'Christmas Day! The dinner nearly on the table! Who's going to take it?'

'A long eejit in the yard. For God's sake make up your mind or he'll talk us all to death.'

My aunt, the girls and my uncle came to the porch where they were met by a flourish of the big black hat and another speech: 'Ladies, it is my practice, be it meritorious or blameworthy, to take photographic representations of human families on Christmas Day at their various domiciles, for on this day of all days, father and mother, brother and sister, and other relatives, are joined together, to partake . . .'

The girls giggled. My aunt moaned, sniffing the air, 'O my lovely turkey! O my lovely turkey!'

'Get out the chairs,' barked my uncle. 'Get out the chairs. Come on, gather together. We'll get it over. Now, where are you all going?' he cried after the womenfolk. 'Off to titivate yourselves. With vanity and oratory and photography and hunger, we'll be all . . .'

'These photographic representations,' the tall man was saying, 'are absolutely unique in that they are taken on Christmas Day when sundered families are joined together, when countenances are wreathed with natural cheerfulness . . . and they are absolutely unique in that they may be had for the meagre sum of six shillings and sixpence per half-dozen. Here, sir, is my card, my Christian name, surname, designation of business, address, and city of residence.'

'I beg you,' pleaded my uncle, 'take the picture. Take the picture.'

The odours and fragrances were floating out from the kitchen as we arranged the chairs and ourselves. Then, the final torture began.

The photographer eyed us and shook his head sadly. 'Permit me,' said he, striding into our midst. One by one he took us, placed us in positions, bent our elbows, crooked our fingers, cocked our heads, draped our clothes, and moulded us like putty. The north-east wind was playing with razors.

'O my dinner, my lovely dinner,' murmured my aunt, hardly daring to move her lips.

The photographer stepped back to contemplate the general effect. We waited. He shook his head despairingly. 'Now, ladies and gentlemen,' he said, holding up one gaunt finger, 'it would be to the advantage of the portrait which, I assure you, will be a magnificent example of this art, if the subjects realised that this instrument is not a lethal weapon of execution and relaxed the controlling muscles of their faces to produce an effect of cheerfulness, nay, even of risibility. Thank you.'

My uncle muttered. We smiled savagely, almost feeling the skin of our faces crackling in the wind.

'At last, thank God,' said my aunt, as the tall man crouched behind his camera. The petrified smiles were held, wrath was suppressed, and we prepared to hear the click.

'Pray, what is that?' inquired the photographer, straightening up again.

One of the dogs had wandered right in before the group and stood shivering, a symbol of our misery.

'Do not move,' the tall man commanded us. And to the dog, he said, 'Please remove yourself from the foreground lest you mar what is strictly intended to be a portrait of a human family.'

The dog sat down.

'For the sake of Christmas,' shouted my uncle, still maintaining the unnatural crook which the tall man had imposed on his elbow, 'for the sake of Christmas, will you take the so-and-so picture, dog and all?'

'Yes, sir. At your service, sir,' breathed the photographer.

The interruption had disarranged us. Once more he organised his picture; once more, drooped heads were elevated, bone-cold fingers crooked artistically.

He stepped back to survey us, smiled, rubbed his hands together, and said, 'Excellent.'

He paused behind his camera, glanced diffidently at my uncle, and said, 'Smile everybody.'

No smile came.

'Please,' he repeated. 'Nothing conduces more to a happy effect in photographic representations than a slight . . .'

At that moment we must have all assumed the murderous, wrathful, malevolent glint of eye which is the only sign of life in the album photo.

The tall man ducked behind his camera, sighed, and the

instrument clicked. Once, once only. There was a rush for positions while my uncle thrust silver into his hand and waved towards the road gate. As we swarmed in around the table, and as the oven doors swung open to release the imprisoned dinner, we heard, dying away down the road: '. . . and may I wish you and yours, in farewell, sir, and in thanksgiving for a privileged moment, a happy Christmas which will be remembered by . . .' The voice faded.

SEAN O'FAOLAIN

Two of a Kind

M axer Creedon was not drunk, but he was melancholy-drunk, and he knew it and he was afraid of it.

At first he had loved being there in the jammed streets, with everybody who passed him carrying parcels wrapped in green or gold, tied with big red ribbons and fixed with berried holly sprigs. Whenever he bumped into someone, parcels toppled and they both cried 'Ooops!' or 'Sorree!' and laughed at one another. A star of snow sank nestling into a woman's hair. He smelled pine and balsam. He saw twelve golden angels blaring silently from twelve golden trumpets in Rockefeller Plaza. He pointed out to a cop that when the traffic lights down Park Avenue changed from red to green the row of white Christmas trees away down the line changed colour by reflection. The cop was very grateful to him. The haze of light on the tops of the buildings made a halo over Fifth Avenue. It was all just the way he knew it would be, and he slopping down from Halifax in that damned old tanker. Then, suddenly, he swung his right arm in a wild arc of disgust.

'To hell with 'em! To hell with everybody!'

'Ooops! Hoho, there! Sorree!'

He refused to laugh back.

'Poor Creedon!' he said to himself. 'All alone in New York, on Christmas-bloody-well-Eve, with nobody to talk to, and nowhere to go only back to the bloody old ship. New York all lit up. Everybody all lit up. Except poor old Creedon.'

He began to cry for poor old Creedon. Crying, he reeled through the passing feet. The next thing he knew he was sitting up at the counter of an Eighth Avenue drugstore sucking black coffee, with one eye screwed-up to look out at the changing traffic lights, chuckling happily over a yarn his mother used to tell him long ago about a place called Ballyroche. He had been there only once, nine years ago, for her funeral. Beaming into his coffee cup, or looking out at the changing traffic lights, he went through his favourite yarn about Poor Lily:

'Ah, wisha! Poor Lily! I wonder where is she atall, atall now. Is she dead or alive? It all happened through an Italian who used to be going from one farm to another selling painted statues. Bandello his name was, a handsome black divil o' hell! I never in all my born days saw a more handsome divil. Well, one wet, wild, windy October morning what did she do but creep out of her bed and we all sound asleep and go off with him. Often and often I heard my father say that the last seen of her was standing under the big tree at Ballyroche Cross, sheltering from the rain, at about eight o'clock in the morning. It was Mikey Clancy the postman saw her. "Yerrah, Lily girl," says he, "what are you doing here at this hour of the morning?" "I'm waiting," says she, "for to go into Fareens on the milk cart." And from that day to this not a sight nor a sound of her no more than if the earth had swallowed her. Except for the one letter from a priest in America to say she was happily married in Brooklyn, New York.'

Maxer chuckled again. The yarn always ended up with the count of the years. The last time he heard it the count had reached forty-one. By this year it would have been fifty.

Maxer put down his cup. For the first time in his life it came to him that the yarn was a true story about a real woman. For as long as four traffic-light changes he fumbled with this fact. Then, like a man hearing a fog signal come again and again from an approaching ship, and at last hearing it close at hand, and then seeing an actual if dim shape, wrapped in a cocoon of haze, the great idea revealed itself.

He lumbered down from his stool and went over to the telephones. His lumpish finger began to trace its way down the grey pages among the Brooklyn Ban's. His finger stopped. He read the name aloud. *Bandello, Mrs Lily.* He found a dime, tinkled it home, and dialled the number slowly. On the third ring he heard an old woman's voice. Knowing that she would be very old and might be deaf, he said very loudly and with the extra-meticulous enunciation of all drunks:

'My name is Matthew Creedon. Only my friends all call me Maxer. I come from Limerick, Ireland. My mother came from the townland of Ballyroche. Are you by any chance my Auntie Lily?'

Her reply was a bark:

'What do you want?'

'Nothing at all! Only I thought, if you are the lady in question, that we might have a bit of an ould gosther. I'm a sailor. Docked this morning in the Hudson.'

The voice was still hard and cold:

'Did somebody tell you to call me?'

He began to get cross with her.

'Naw! Just by a fluke I happened to look up your name in the directory. I often heard my mother talking about you. I just felt I'd like to talk to somebody. Being Christmas and all to that. And knowing nobody in New York. But if you don't like the idea, it's okay with me. I don't want to butt in on anybody. Good-bye.'

'Wait! You're sure nobody sent you?'

'Inspiration sent me! Father Christmas sent me!' (She could take that any way she bloody-well liked!) 'Look! It seems to me I'm buttin' in. Let's skip it.'

'No. Why don't you come over and see me?'

Suspiciously he said:

'This minute?'

'Right away!'

At the sudden welcome of her voice all his annoyance vanished.

'Sure, Auntie Lily! I'll be right over. But, listen, I sincerely hope you're not thinking I'm buttin' in. Because if you are . . .'

'It was very nice of you to call me, Matty, very nice indeed. I'll be glad to see you.'

He hung up, grinning. She was just like his mother – the same old Limerick accent. After fifty years. And the same bossy voice. If she was a day she'd be seventy. She'd be tall, and thin, and handsome, and the real lawdy-daw, doing the grand lady, and under it all she'd be as soft as mountain moss. She'd be tidying the house now like a divil. And giving jaw to ould Bandello. If he was still alive.

He got lost on the subway, so that when he came up it was dark. He paused to have another black coffee. Then he paused to buy a bottle of Jamaica rum as a present for her. And then he had to walk five blocks before he found the house where she lived. The automobiles parked under the lights were all snow-covered. She lived in a brownstone house with high steps. Six other families had rooms in it.

The minute he saw her on top of the not brightly lit landing, looking down at him, he saw something he had completely forgotten. She had his mother's height, and slimness, and her wide mouth, but he had forgotten the pale, liquid blue of the eyes and they stopped him dead on the stairs, his hand tight on the banister. At the sight of them he heard the soft wind sighing over the level Limerick plain and his whole body shivered. For miles and miles not a sound but that soughing wind that makes the meadows and the wheat fields flow like water. All over that plain, where a crossroads is an event, where a little, sleepy lake is an excitement. Where their streams are rivers to them. Where their villages are towns. The resting cows look at you out of owls' eyes over the greasy tips of the buttercups. The meadow grass is up to their bellies. Those two pale eyes looking down at him were bits of the pale albino sky stretched tightly over the Shannon plain.

Slowly he climbed up to meet her, but even when they stood side by side she was still able to look down at him, searching his face with her pallid eyes. He knew what she was looking for, and he knew she had found it when she threw her bony arms around his neck and broke into a low, soft wailing just like that Shannon wind.

'Auntie! You're the living image of her!'

On the click of a finger she became bossy and cross with him, hauling him by his two hands into her room:

'You've been drinking! And what delayed you? And I suppose not a scrap of solid food in your stomach since morning?'

He smiled humbly.

'I'm sorry, Auntie. 'Twas just on account of being all alone, you know. And everybody else making whoopee.' He hauled out the peace offering of the rum. 'Let's have a drink!'

She was fussing all over him immediately.

'You gotta eat something first. Drinking like that all day, I'm ashamed of you! Sit down, boy. Take off your jacket. I got coffee, and cookies, and hamburgers, and a pie. I always lay in a stock for Christmas. All of the neighbours visit me. Everybody knows that Lily Bandello keeps an open house for Christmas, nobody is ever going to say Lily Bandello didn't have a welcome for all her friends and relations at Christmastime . . .'

She bustled in and out of the kitchenette, talking back to him without stop.

It was a big, dusky room, himself looking at himself out of a tall, mirrored wardrobe piled on top with cardboard boxes. There was a divan in one corner as high as a bed, and he guessed that there was a washbasin behind the old peacock-screen. A single bulb hung in the centre of the ceiling, in a fluted glass bell with pink frilly edges. The pope over the bed was Leo XIII. The snowflakes kept touching the bare windowpanes like kittens' paws trying to get in. When she began on the questions, he wished he had not come.

'How's Bid?' she called out from the kitchen.

'Bid? My mother? Oh, well, of course, I mean to say . . . My mother? Oh, she's grand, Auntie! Never better. For her age, of course, that is. Fine, fine out! Just like yourself. Only for the touch of the old rheumatism now and again.'

'Go on, tell me about all of them. How's Uncle Matty? And how's Cis? When were you down in Ballyroche last? But, sure, it's all changed now I suppose, with electric light and everything up to date? And I suppose the old pony and trap is gone years ago? It was only last night I was thinking of Mikey Clancy the postman.' She came in, planking down the plates, an iced Christmas cake, the coffeepot: 'Go on! You're telling me nothing.'

She stood over him, waiting, her pale eyes wide, her mouth stretched. He said:

'My Uncle Matty? Oh well, of course, now, he's not as young as he was. But I saw him there last year. He was looking fine. Fine out. I'd be inclined to say he'd be a bit stooped. But in great form. For his age, that is.'

'Sit in. Eat up. Eat up. Don't mind me. He has a big family now, no doubt?'

'A family? Naturally! There's Tom. And there's Kitty, that's my Aunt Kitty, it *is* Kitty, isn't it, yes, my Auntie Kitty. And . . . God, I can't remember the half of them.'

She shoved the hamburgers towards him. She made him pour the coffee and tell her if he liked it. She told him he was a bad reporter.

'Tell me all about the old place!'

He stuffed his mouth to give him time to think.

'They have twenty-one cows, Holsteins. The black and white chaps. And a red barn. And a shelter belt of pines. 'Tis lovely there now to see the wind in the trees, and when the night falls the way the lighthouse starts winking at you, and . . .'

'What lighthouse?' She glared at him. She drew back from him. 'Are ye daft? What are you dreaming about? Is it a lighthouse in the middle of the County Limerick?'

'There is a lighthouse! I saw it in the harbour!'

But he suddenly remembered that where he had seen it was in a toyshop on Eighth Avenue, with a farm beyond it and a red barn and small cows, and a train going round and round it all.

'Harbour, Matty? Are ye out of your senses?'

'I saw it with my own two eyes.'

Her eyes were like marbles. Suddenly she leaned over like a willow – just the way his mother used to lean over – and laughed and laughed.

'I know what you're talking about now. The lighthouse on the Shannon! Lord save us, how many times did I see it at night from the hill of Ballingarry! But there's no harbour, Matty.'

'There's the harbour at Foynes!'

'Oh, for God's sake!' she cried. 'That's miles and miles and miles away. 'Tis and twenty miles away! And where could you see any train, day or night, from anywhere at all near Ballyroche?'

They argued it hither and over until she suddenly found that the coffee was gone cold and rushed away with the pot to the kitchen. Even there she kept up the argument, calling out that certainly, you could see Moneygay Castle, and the turn of the River Deel on a fine day, but no train, and then she went on about the stepping-stones over the river, and came back babbling about Normoyle's bull that chased them across the dry river, one hot summer's day . . .

He said:

'Auntie! Why the hell did you never write home?'

'Not even once?' she said, with a crooked smile like a bold child.

'Not a sight nor a sound of you from the day you left Ballyroche, as my mother used to say, no more than if the earth swallowed you. You're a nice one!'

'Eat up!' she commanded him, with a little laugh and a tap on his wrist.

'Did you always live here, Auntie Lily?'

She sat down and put her face between her palms with her elbows on the table and looked at him.

'Here? Well, no . . . That is to say, no! My husband and me had a house of our very own over in East Fifty-eighth. He did very well for himself. He was quite a rich man when he died. A big jeweller. When he was killed in an airplane crash five years ago he left me very well off. But sure I didn't need a house of my own and I had lots of friends in Brooklyn, so I came to live here.'

'Fine! What more do you want, that is for a lone woman! No family?'

'I have my son. But he's married, to a Pole, they'll be over here first thing tomorrow morning to take me off to spend Christmas with them. They have an apartment on Riverside Drive. He is the manager of a big department store, Macy's on Flatbush Avenue. But tell me about Bid's children. You must have lots of brothers and sisters. Where are you going from here? Back to Ireland? To Limerick? To Ballyroche?'

He laughed.

'Where else would I go? Our next trip we hit the port of London. I'll be back like an arrow to Ballyroche. They'll be delighted to hear I met you. They'll be asking me all sorts of questions about you. Tell me more about your son, Auntie. Has he a family?'

'My son? Well, my son's name is Thomas. His wife's name is Catherine. She is very beautiful. She has means of her own. They are very happy. He is very well off. He's in charge of a big store, Sears Roebuck on Bedford Avenue. Oh, a fine boy. Fine out! As you say. Fine out. He has three children. There's Cissy, and Matty. And . . .'

Her voice faltered. When she closed her eyes he saw how old she was. She rose and from the bottom drawer of a chest of drawers she pulled out a photograph album. She laid it in front of him and sat back opposite him.

'That is my boy.'

When he said he was like her she said he was very like his father. Maxer said that he often heard that her husband was a most handsome man.

'Have you a picture of him?'

She drew the picture of her son towards her and looked down at it.

'Tell me more about Ballyroche,' she cried.

As he started into a long description of a harvest home he saw her eyes close again, and her breath came more heavily and he felt that she was not hearing a word he said. Then, suddenly, her palm slapped down on the picture of the young man, and he knew that she was not heeding him any more than if he wasn't there. Her fingers closed on the pasteboard. She shied it wildly across the room, where it struck the glass of the window flat on, hesitated and slid to the ground. Maxer saw snowflakes melting as often as they touched the pane. When he looked back at her she was leaning across the table, one white lock down over one eye, her yellow teeth bared.

'You spy!' she spat at him. 'You came from them! To spy on me!'

'I came from friendliness.'

'Or was it for a ha'porth of look-about? Well, you can go back to Ballyroche and tell 'em whatever you like. Tell 'em I'm starving if that'll please 'em, the mean, miserable, lousy set that never gave a damn about me from the day I left 'em. For forty years my own sister, your mother, never wrote one line to say . . .'

'You know damn well she'd have done anything for you if she only knew where you were. Her heart was stuck in you. The two of you were inside one another's pockets. My God, she was forever talking and talking about you. Morning noon and night . . .'

She shouted at him across the table.

'I wrote six letters . . .'

'She never got them.'

'I registered two of them.'

'Nobody ever got a line from you, or about you, only for the one letter from the priest that married you to say you were well and happy.'

'What he wrote was that I was down and out. I saw the letter. I let him send it. That Wop left me flat in this city with my baby. I wrote to everybody – my mother, my father, to Bid after she was your mother and had a home of her own. I had to work every day of my life. I worked today. I'll

work tomorrow. If you want to know what I do I clean
out offices. I worked to bring up my son, and what did he
do? Walked out on me with that Polack of his and that was
the last I saw of him, or her, or any human being belonging
to me until I saw you. Tell them every word of it. They'll
love it!'

Maxer got up and went over slowly to the bed for his
jacket. As he buttoned it he looked at her glaring at him
across the table. Then he looked away from her at the
snowflakes feeling the windowpane and dying there. He said,
quietly:

'They're all dead. As for Limerick – I haven't been back to Ireland
for eight years. When my mum died my father got married again.
I ran away to sea when I was sixteen.'

He took his cap. When he was at the door he heard a chair fall
and then she was at his side, holding his arm, whispering gently
to him:

'Don't go away, Matty.' Her pallid eyes were flooded. 'For
God's sake, don't leave me alone with them on Christmas
Eve!'

Maxer stared at her. Her lips were wavering as if a wind were
blowing over them. She had the face of a frightened girl. He
threw his cap on the bed and went over and sat down beside
it. While he sat there like a big baboon, with his hands between
his knees, looking at the snowflakes, she raced into the kitchen
to put on the kettle for rum punch. It was a long while before
she brought in the two big glasses of punch, with orange sliced
in them, and brown sugar like drowned sand at the base of
them. When she held them out to him he looked first at them,
and then at her, so timid, so pleading, and he began to laugh
and laugh – a laugh that he choked by covering his eyes with
his hands.

'Damn ye!' he groaned into his hands. 'I was better off drunk.'

She sat beside him on the bed. He looked up. He took one of the glasses and touched hers with it.

'Here's to poor Lily!' he smiled.

She fondled his free hand.

'Lovie, tell me this one thing and tell me true. Did she really and truly talk about me? Or was that all lies too?'

'She'd be crying rain down when she'd be talking about you. She was always and ever talking about you. She was mad about you.'

She sighed a long sigh.

'For years I couldn't understand it. But when my boy left me for that Polack I understood it. I guess Bid had a tough time bringing you all up. And there's no one more hard in all the world than a mother when she's thinking of her own. I'm glad she talked about me. It's better than nothing.'

They sat there on the bed talking and talking. She made more punch, and then more, and in the end they finished the bottle between them, talking about everybody either of them had known in or within miles of the County Limerick. They fixed to spend Christmas Day together, and have Christmas dinner downtown, and maybe go to a picture and then come back and talk some more.

Every time Maxer comes to New York he rings her number. He can hardly breathe until he hears her voice saying, 'Hello, Matty.' They go on the town then and have dinner, always at some place with an Irish name, or a green neon shamrock above the door, and then they go to a movie or a show, and then come back to her room to have a drink and a talk about his last voyage, or the picture post cards he sent her, his latest bits and scraps of news about the Shannon shore. They always get first-class service in restaurants, although Maxer never noticed it until the night a waiter said, 'And what's mom having?' at which she gave him a slow wink out of her pale Limerick eyes and a slow, lover's smile.

BRIAN LEYDEN

Christmas Promise

The day after we got the Christmas holidays we took the bus
to a crowded shopping town with my mother. Her lists made
out, the money carefully rolled in a big black purse with a brass
clip, she walked us to the crossroads in our nylon anoraks. There
was an excited hurry in our step as we trotted a country mile to the
main road. My younger brother swinging his arms to keep up the
pace. My mother watching the time on a small gold wrist-watch.
But we got there a few minutes early, our foreheads hot and our
scalps tingling.

'It's not gone yet.'

'That's if it's coming at all.'

And we worried until we sighted the sun-flash of the driver's
big windshield, the red and white coachwork lurching towards
us, taking up most of the road and pulling up tight against the
ditch as we came around the front to the open door. We stood
on the step up as the driver searched a school exercise book with
the fares written in blue biro. My mother with the right money
ready in her fist.

Down the middle aisle we made our way, minding our paper tickets. Past a small man with his hands in his lap, smiling through plastic teeth. There were several more neighbours we knew by sight or by nickname: Kate the miller, long Tom, Pratie Gallagher, Pat the blower and Pat the twin. Small women in belted coats and printed cotton headscarves. Husbands wearing good suits and cardigans inside their jackets, with topcoats and felt hats, talking about airlocks and shorthorns.

'You're late on it today,' my mother says to a neighbour, and they start to chat as soon as she takes her seat. Everyone who boards the bus is brought into the conversation.

'What have you all the coats for, Mary?'

'They were giving out rain on the radio.'

'You're looking as fit as a fiddle, Jimmy.'

'I could kiss me toes if I had me socks off.'

Smooth-faced women with three chins and coiled barbed-wire-tight home perms holding fur-lined gloves, embroidered shopping bags and tied umbrellas, all gabbing together like market-day turkeys.

The bus made slow progress up through the gears but never made any speed. It was always delayed behind a slow car driven at twenty-five miles an hour by a little man looking out through the steering wheel. Or a tractor with baled hay and a bucket of calf-nuts in the transport box. Then we had to stop to leave the papers off at every post office. It was a full hour before we reached the blue outskirts of the town.

The town lights stayed lit all day in the deep gloom of December. We got off at the traffic lights on the Mail Coach road and took a short-cut into the centre. On the terraced hill above we saw men out in their gardens, smoking cigarettes and waiting for the shopping wives to come home. Chapel spires looming through the blanket of coal smoke and fog. The streets netted with coloured bulbs. Snow-capped cars down from the mountains.

'Where do you want to go first, Mammy?'

'We'll go to the hardware.'

'Do you not want to shop for clothes?'

'Why don't we look in the Market Yard?'

Ringed close about our mother we stood to plot the day. She opened her purse and looked at her money again.

'We'll stay with you, Mammy, until you get the shopping done.'

And we followed her about the shops, adding unwanted items to her shopping basket: cooking chocolate, apricots, walnuts.

'We don't need all that,' Mammy would say. 'And put that bottle back and get me a smaller one.'

She kept us distracted roving the supermarket aisles finding items off her list: tin foil, brown sauce, packets of jelly, sponges for the trifle. But we didn't want to buy all our wants here, where, my mother said, they would stand over you looking for the last penny. The turkey, the ham, the bread and the milk and eggs and loose rashers we would need to tide us over the holiday when the shops were closed, we would get from the local shopkeeper, who always sent up an additional Christmas box of a cake and cigarettes with our order.

Between shops the Christmas shopping crowd elbowed and jostled around each other on the packed streets, everybody clutching a brace of plastic supermarket bags with dodgy bottoms, the sides worn ragged by the extra boxes of all shapes and sizes in bright wrapping paper. We saw small, shabby men in working clothes stagger home after Christmas drinks. Cotton wool-bearded Santies wearing black wellingtons, sitting in red crêpe paper-covered booths, with the shop charging for every visit. Plain women buying little presents for themselves. Loaded family cars, the children messing with the lights, parked outside the supermarkets. Perished young lads selling pine trees in the carpark corner. Tinker children selling holly. Seasonal biscuit boxes and tea-caddies, rich chocolate liqueurs, cards, clementines and tinsel decorations, fairy lights and snow sprayed from aerosol cans in the shop windows, latticed with red insulating tape. The enticements to spend were everywhere.

There are old people in from the country moving in twos: unmarried brothers and spinster sisters, giving out constantly among themselves, clearing a path with their sticks. And carol singers in the arcade, led by a bearded man with a guitar. Passing the rattling collectors' cans we have a coin and a recitation out of memory ready:

'Christmas is coming and the geese are getting fat
Will you please put a penny in the old man's hat
If you haven't got a penny, then a halfpenny will do
If you haven't got a halfpenny, then God bless you.'

Chubby children in hooded coats run wild amongst the big, expensive toy displays. They open boxes, drag down stuffed toys, battery-driven and spring-wound things, and leave them scattered about the shop floor.

'This is what Santy is bringing me,' they shrill.

'If you don't behave Santy won't bring you anything. Now, come on.'

We are taken into the toy department to pick out one special want: a book, a junior mechanical kit, an Airfix model aircraft or a chemistry set.

'They have me robbed,' my mother says to a passing school-master.

'Anything that's educational,' he says.

With our presents parcelled and the shopping bags shared out between us we make it back to the bus ahead of time. We sit watching the stragglers take their seats or stop and stand beside the partition talking to the driver. Then a wild-eyed woman with bright red hair arrives, and she keeps changing seats until she is sitting next to us. She smells of whiskey and clutches a poinsettia to her breast. Her eyes are wet.

'There was a little Mexican boy who cried all night because he had no present to give to the baby Jesus,' she explains to my anxious younger brother. 'But when he got up in the morning the leaves of the green hedge outside his front door had turned a beautiful red, just like flowers, and ever since the poinsettia has grown wild in Mexico.'

Everyone makes a path for her between the shopping bags when she stumbles her slow way off the bus.

Clear skies beyond the lit bus windows. A promise of frost in the pastel dusk. Late crows on the wing. Cattle on the bare hillside, following a man with a load of fodder roped over his back.

We step off the bus into the dark and walk the road again, stopping at the stile where we left our wellington boots in the morning. Then take a short-cut through the fields, carting the shopping bags home. Lights in the house up ahead. Smell of hay on the cold air in the farmyard. And Daddy in his socks by the fire. A lamb chop stewing for himself in the kitchen. A pot of spuds freshly boiled for us, waiting for the mince and beans in our shopping bag for a quick dinner.

We burst into the quiet house and start tearing things out of bags. Even Mammy is in a rush to show Daddy the presents bought for relations and the children of her closest neighbours: toilet sets, children's bright woolly things, ankle-socks, face-cloths, story books, comics, tidy boxes of chocolates.

'They'll do grand,' Daddy says, glossing over the presents. 'Did you remember to bring cigarettes?'

We have our own parcels which are kept out of sight. Stashed away in a bedroom for the time being. Nobody leaves their presents under the tree in our house. We will have the little gifts, the milk chocolates, pairs of socks, paperbacks and ornaments we bought on the quiet today ready to hand over on Christmas Day. As soon as we have changed out of our good clothes we will separate the gifts out on the quilt and search the house for clear tape and a roving scissors to cut and make the wrapping paper go round.

We are as restless as bluebottles after our day out, but we do our level best to keep up this peaceful atmosphere in the house by helping Mammy with the late dinner. Daddy sits back in his armchair, the outside jobs done for the night. We sit watching the television, our feet to the fire, our presents put away until the big day, calm again, the spending fever broken.

Daddy didn't have the right attitude to Christmas. He seemed removed. Unconcerned. We were at an age when we wanted all the details just right. Daddy was awkward. He ate slices from the Christmas cake well before the holiday. He tore bottles out of the six-packs we had bought in town, and he opened the visitors' whiskey before we had any visitors. And one year, when we were old enough to notice, he cut two pine branches, tied them together with string and told us it was a Christmas tree.

I took over the business of getting a Christmas tree soon after that.

Off for holly first. Out the hill fields after the late December rain lets up, the two dogs at my heels. The ground soft, no colour in the short grass where hungry pheasants have left their scrapings in the dead bracken. A bow-saw blade over my shoulder, snug as a rifle strap. Pressing through a hole in the hedge because I know a good holly tree two fields over on a neighbouring farm. The best berries grow right at the top, and I have to climb up through the thorn-protected and hard, green holly leaves to get them. Bite of the saw-blade on silver bark. White sawdust in the wind. A satisfying heavy red-berried weight in the fallen branch.

After the holly branch is carried home I face into a watery, winter evening sunset, the low sun punching a hole in the shower clouds. Reaching the mountain plantation at nightfall. The dogs whine to be lifted over the sheep-wire fencing around the plantation. Then I search the lines of trees in the dusk for a nicely rounded young conifer: prickly stem and the sharp pine smell of Norway spruce after the felling.

I wash my wellingtons when I get back and leave them outside on the street. Then I go up and down and all about the house until the green and red holly hangs in clusters over the pictures and the window frames of every room. Decorating with holly is an ancient ritual to safeguard the house and I know that care has to be taken to see that it is done right.

Out on to the front street again to stand the tree in a galvanised bucket with gravel and stones. Daddy going about the cow-sheds and calves' barns like any other winter's night. Bringing arm-loads of hay to leave at the cow-stakes; while I manhandle the tree into the front room, and then cut the wilder branches down to size using a hedge clippers. Last year's decorations in a cardboard box hauled out from under the bed. Baubles and spare bulbs for the fairy lights; a set of frosted glass bulbs which my mother said cost a lot at the time they were bought, but have worked every year since without fail once the loose bulbs are tightened in their sockets.

This is my favourite moment, a moment more precious than the big day itself: sitting with the table-lamp off and only the flames from the open fire and the fairy lights on the tree to colour the room. The holly over the mirror, the carriage clock ticking and the dog asleep on the rug. Green forest resin smell in the room. A deep, satisfying finish to the ritual and ceremony of Christmas.

The idea of peace and plenty in the world seems so real, so close at hand, drinking a cup of tea and eating from the tin of USA assorted biscuits.

On Christmas Eve the postman always stops for a drink in our kitchen. A clean-shaven, well-kept bachelor who lives with an unmarried brother and loves a chat with the housewives. He gets tea and home-made cake every time he calls with a letter – except when Mammy is out and Daddy is in charge of the house; then he gets bread and jam. He brings more Christmas cards on each of the closing days to Christmas, including Saturdays, in drifts of fresh white envelopes. The envelopes are done up in tight bundles for each townland, held together with fat elastic bands, and he is very careful and exact with the sorting, licking the top of his thumb as he goes through his post.

'A cup of tea, James?' my mother says as he sorts his letters.

'I'll have a drop in me hand, if you have the kettle on the boil.'

Then he reaches deep into his canvas sack and brings out a card for my mother from America. It comes every year from her older sister: a specially bright card with a cheque made out in dollars in its folded middle. The postman smiles when he leaves the big card, with its airmail markings on the envelope, on the top of the bunch on the sideboard. To have this one card for my mother makes him feel part of the house, included in the charmed circle of our family business.

My mother gives him tea, with the blue willow pattern cup set in its saucer, a slice of Christmas cake and a glass of neat, amber whiskey.

'Good health and a happy Christmas to you, ma'am,' the postman says, his peaked cap balanced on his blue-uniformed knee.

It is his reward for bringing our letters and creamery cheques

all year; for waiting in the kitchen with a cup of tea while my
mother sits down to finish another letter for him to post; for taking
messages and animal medicines between my mother and her sister
who lives in the next townland; for telling us we have cattle out
on the road; for letting us know that a removal is at seven, or a
funeral on Friday morning after the eleven o'clock mass.

When he has finished his tea and whiskey he lilts a tune for
us or strums a bar on the Jew's harp, killing another half-hour
of his Christmas overtime. Then he walks up the lane, takes hold
of his push-bike, his sack of letters over his shoulder, his oilskins
tied and his parcels balanced on the carrier, and away he goes.

Christmas night and Daddy is gone to the pub, shuffled out of the
way of mother and children. In the fellowship of all the other
outcasts from the busy home kitchens of the valley he takes his
Christmas drink in the front bar. Buying extra-generous rounds;
spending a bit.

The darkness lies thick as a horse-blanket against the windowpanes. But there is a bright light in the kitchen, where the
Christmas cards hang on a string on the wall; Victorian gentlemen
in black top-hats, winter singing robins and sprays of silver glitter,
coach-and-four carriages and women wearing tied hats, bustles
and ribbons. Snowflakes, candles and pine-cones.

We are Mammy's apron-string helpers, looking for small jobs to
do and mixing bowls to lick. We help her to carry in the enormous,
white, goose-pimpled turkey for stuffing. The kettle is breathing
and the big pots left simmering on the black hob; plum puddings
steaming in pudding cloths and double saucepans. Breadcrumbs
tumble out of the metal grater to make stuffing for the bird. There
is also a round of ham to be boiled, which will be roasted in the
oven tomorrow with a glaze of brown sugar and cloves. We are
a last-minute-with-everything family; one cake already half-eaten,

Mammy has another Christmas cake to bake. She stands busy at the table with little cylinders of mixed spice, cinnamon, ginger and mixed peel. The raisins and sultanas are soaking in porter, and everybody gets a turn at the mixing bowl. Then we have blocks of almond marzipan to soften into a roll and fine icing sugar to wet and blend. My brother and I tussle in complete silence over who should be in charge of the little plastic figures used year-in and year-out, propped up in the icing to decorate the top of the cake.

If we have to go to the back door to throw tea-leaves in the hedge we can hear in the still yard the farm animals making tranquil animal gas sounds, chewing on their fodder as they lie down in the Bethlehem of our barns. Our mother has said it isn't safe to put candles in the windows all night – to light the holy family on their journey; too many fires have started that way. But every electric light in the house is left on, and standing at the back door we can see the hills full of lights, our whole townland and the distant countryside all lit up. Above our heads the stars are winking Christmas candles. Venus shines over the shoulder of the mountain like the guiding star in the East. The warm, spicy air from the kitchen is a premonition of wise Kings bringing strange and exotic gifts of gold, frankincense and myrrh. And the water in the winter drains tinkles like the jingle of bells announcing an old mystery.

The Christmas promise is even more intense when an older brother buttons up his coat to go to the midnight chapel. It is not that long ago since we would refuse to go to bed on Christmas night only we knew Santy was coming. We were past that now, but still close enough in years to be touched by the sensation of those Christmas nights when we lay awake and watched the steady moonlight at the end of the bed until we heard the men coming back from mass, talking and drinking soup in the kitchen. We had a plate of biscuits and a glass of orange juice left out for Santy. And at some hour of this magical night he would creep mysterious, and just a little frightening, into the room when we had tried for so long and failed to stay awake all night; just to hear the hoof-tap and harness-jingle of the flying reindeer on the ridge-tiles of our roof, or the rustle of soot in the chimney. It never happened, and Santy was never caught out. For years he filled us with a sense of never-to-be-matched anticipation. And we woke each year in a state of awe to find our wants at the foot of the bed on Christmas morning.

Over the years we found building blocks and jigsaw puzzles; paint boxes and colouring books. Dinky and Matchbox model cars with doors and bonnets that actually opened. Big bags of green plastic soldiers that were manfully posed with rifles and rocket-launchers, but were eventually left limbless and chewed to pieces – not by the machinery of war, but a new terrier pup. As we grew older and more ferocious there was a hullabaloo of cap-guns that devoured red paper rolls dotted with bumps of reeking gunpowder. Police badges and plastic handcuffs. FBI suction dart-guns and water pistols, and German Lugers that were black, detailed and deadly.

We were up with the sparrows on Christmas morning, and as soon as we had sorted through our presents we were off out the fields, half-dressed but strapped into our jewelled holsters, sheriff's badges, Winchester rifles and vinyl cowboy hats, with enough fire-power between us to rout King Kong out of the lower field.

No callers are wanted at the house on Christmas Day. We scrub and dress for first mass to be home early to start the dinner. The men on the road to mass are out with kettles, defrosting locks and tearing newspaper sheets off the white windshields of the cars. We take our seats in the perishing chapel and sit out a long sermon looking over at the crib in the chilly cross-house.

A Christmas morning fry-up as soon as we get home, and then we clean out the grate and leave the fire set in the front room. Soldiers' requests and second mass on the radio. Every man anxious to guarantee the smooth running of the day. The cattle turned out to the short hours of light, old bedding mucked out of the barns, fresh fodder left in. Logs chopped to work up an appetite for the dinner. Films and favourite programmes noted in the double-edition television guides and the fat Christmas supplement papers.

There are sprouts to be peeled and boiled. Plum pudding to warm in a bowl. Cream to be whipped for the topping to go on the trifle. And Daddy has to be talked into wearing his good suit after he has the outside jobs done.

'Don't be making such a fuss,' he says.

But the real fuss is reserved for the turkey. Getting the heat up in the black-lead polished range and the roasting temperature steady – calculating the turkey weight against the number of hours in the oven. Too much heat and the meat will be dry; too little and the flesh inside the leg will stay pink. Everyone looks into the oven, opening the cooking foil wrapping to baste the bird in its juices.

There is a tussle over whose turn it is to make the brandy butter. And someone has to stand over the big cauldron of boiling potatoes to watch for the skins breaking open.

'Lift and drain them the minute they start laughing,' my mother says to Daddy.

'There's not a smile out of them yet,' he tells her, testing with a fork.

The extra leaf is opened out on the table, and by three o'clock we are ready to sit in, although we have to leave off watching in the middle of the early film.

'Is the turkey all right? I think the breast is a bit dry,' Mammy says again as she serves up the dinner on the biggest plates we have in the house.

'No, it's grand. Stop fussing. The dinner is lovely.'

It does not matter to us if the turkey meat is a little too pink or too dry. What is important is that range of familiar tastes of our traditional Christmas dinner: from the turkey breast or brown meat on the leg, to the brassy taste of Brussels sprouts, gravy and brown sauce. The brandy butter on the pudding, red jelly in the trifle. Tea and iced Christmas cake to finish.

Before long it is dark outside. The cattle are back in the barns, and everybody is stretched out in the front room, stuffed and over-full, talking over the television. Torn ends of wrapping paper and empty boxes are spread about the room after the swapping of presents; new jumpers and socks left aside. A box of milk chocolates is opened to relieve the deepening boredom and the sense of anticlimax. After all the effort and the anticipation Christmas Day is over and done with for another year.

'You won't find Christmas coming round again,' Daddy says to tease us, and we all belly-groan in his direction.

Later in the evening we go to visit a schoolfriend's house to take a hand in a family game of cards. Games of twenty-five for small coins, with best fireside-chair fathers who have a knack of dealing all the good cards to themselves and turning up their own trumps.

'I have a crow's nest,' these canny fathers complain as they raise the pot of matchsticks and pennies, and peer down their nose at a winning Jack of diamonds, a five or an ace of hearts. Familiar, predictable, reassuring. Then the turkey carcass is stripped for sandwiches.

*　　*　　*

On Stephen's Day we dress up as wren-boys and go the rounds of the roads. The sad, skeletal remains of a near dead tradition. We make our masked arrival in baggy coats and old clothes out of parcels. Thinly disguised, with perished hands holding a tin whistle or a flageolet, we are only in it for the pennies, collected in a jam-jar with a slot cut in the lid. The sleet gusts about a windy front street. We shake our pennies in the porch. A dog barks inside the farmhouse door.

'Mammy, Mammy, it's the ramble boys,' an excited child shouts from inside.

We start into a short, tuneless version of 'Silent Night'. It is a relief to everybody when we take the money and immediately move on.

New Year's night. Lace of snow on the ground. Daddy out on the front street with the shotgun. Shots fired into the air. More guncracks echoing about the valley at the stroke of midnight – frightening the witches out of the bushes around the house.

First thing in the morning on New Year's Day I put a new calendar on the nail, and then I have visits to make in the falling wet snowflakes. Visits to houses where it is still thought unlucky to have a red-headed stranger for a first caller. I am brought into council row cottages and two-storey farmhouses alike, to have tea and biscuits, lemonade and shiny shillings pressed into my hand for my dark hair to bring a share of luck into the house. Like the holly over the door, the fairy lights on the pine tree, the shots fired on the street, another magic charm to secure the home, to protect and hold the family together.

There is a cock-step in the days after Little Christmas; a thaw on the slush roads walking to school again. The family box of milk chocolates is long eaten and New Year resolutions melt away like the snowmen with coal-nuts for eyes in the front gardens.

It was back in these schoolrooms and playground that the rumours had started, that doubts about Santy came my way. Suspicions were cast on flying reindeer and letters posted to the North Pole.

'There's no such thing as Santy.'

'Yes, there is.'

'No, there isn't.'

'Prove it.'

And the clues and hints coming up to Christmas led me, after a top-to-bottom search of the house, to the wardrobe in Mammy and Daddy's room. Standing on a chair to look in over the top where the toys lay waiting. My heart might have cracked open at the sight.

I was discovering a world where presents were ordered with a down payment weeks in advance, left aside in the shops, and finally hidden in the house by Daddy – often on the very day we went off shopping on the bus. Daddy had been to a different town while we were out. Our presents were put out of reach until Christmas night, when he crept into our room in his socks and left the presents on the dressing table or at the foot of the bed.

I began to understand something about my parents then; how they worked their own magic to hold the house together. The care and trouble they took to meet our needs, to see that we felt secure, loved.

Every year the promise of Christmas was met. Our needs were discovered early and letters to Santy kept by the postman. A fresh turkey was bought for the table, and on shopping trips into town ends were made to meet. Keeping up appearances until we were old enough to understand. But if there was the pain of losing Santy there was the comfort of finding a different Father Christmas. A man who worked hard to provide for us, but hid his feelings as successfully as Santy could hide our toys until we were asleep.

When it was all out in the open I had to promise not to spoil the Christmas magic for the younger ones. That sense of permanence and security, of family love and gifts conjured out of nowhere. It was my first big adult secret: keeping that Christmas promise.

CLARE BOYLAN

The Miracle of Life

I grew up on a street that was skilled in competitive sameness. All the houses boasted a radiant darkness. Pine green or woodstain doors opened to admit or dispatch men in suits, women in costumes, children with long socks and cumbersome frocks and hairy cardigans. The women were constantly afraid that their children would disgrace them in front of the neighbours, the men feared that their wives would let them down by speaking out or earning money and the children worried that no one would know they were unique.

We knew our street had its share of scandals which were much discussed and used as an inoculation against any serious threat of independence. There was Mrs Galvin who ran off with a man and afterwards her small daughter fell out a window. I always pictured the child arched out the frame for a last disbelieving glance, finally toppling as the sinful couple sprinted around the corner. There was Mrs Beech whose husband died and she had to go to work and this so confused her son that he dressed up as a nun. There was Miss Milne-Evans who was a Protestant and a spinster and went mad behind the cobwebby growths that enclosed her big house. Always it was the women. Men's only flaw was failure – failure to make their name or to combat death or keep their hands off the bottle or the women.

I worried about our mother. For instance, although she never went out without her cherry-coloured high heels and her grey two-piece, there was a line of clothes across the kitchen to air and we often ate eccentric meals, tinned sardines with creamed potatoes or curried eggs.

She was respectful to my father but she said heretical things. While she savagely tackled housework in our gloomy kitchen, where light never entered but remained a wistful onlooker at the one small window, she declared that girls were as good as boys, that sex was no picnic, that the key to a woman's happiness was her own income.

One day she told me the facts of life. She drew sperms on a paper grocery bag and concocted a tale so improbable, so far removed from suits and costumes and fathers and mothers that I knew I could no longer trust her. The telling gave her a hectic energy and she went off to scrub the floor, leaving me to look at the bag of human commas. When the red had receded from her face she made tea and grew sentimental. She said the baby that got born was one of millions of sperms that ran in a race until it reached the safety of the womb. She called it the miracle of life.

Awful, I called it. I believed that I had come from somewhere special; I imagined I had been spirited to my mother's body as a sort of fairy doll.

Afterwards I took a bus into D'Olier Street and stood for a long time at the window of the Gas Company Showrooms looking at the model refrigerator. Food was displayed on its shelves, sausages and ham, a roast chicken, a trifle, a bunch of bananas, a whole cheese. It was not real food. It was made of papier mâché and had a dry and itchy look. I liked it because it was both orderly and exotic. It was part of a new world which ought to be my inheritance. In 1960, apart from Elvis Presley singing 'Old Shep', it was my favourite thing in the world.

It was close to Christmas and ropes of fairy lights swooped over O'Connell Street and the shawlies of Moore Street shouted: 'Penny the sparklers.' I no longer cared for all that. The glitter gave me an uneasy memory of Reenee as she had been. Besides, I was not, any more, a child.

Children grow up in secret. They choose their models from the random assortment of people in their path. We did not have a television, which provides the ideals of fantasy for today's children, nor any modern appliance except a vacuum cleaner the size of a St Bernard dog which sometimes spat fire from its hoses. Parents were used only as models for avoidance. I loved my mother and I stuck close to her, drinking tea and eating Hovis in the kitchen after school, but it seemed vital to turn into a different person. I had flung out a schizophrenic net to cover, at the calm end of the pond, our nun, Sister Sophie, and at its deepest and most dangerous extreme, my best friend Katie's older sister, Reenee.

Katie and I had been Reenee's handmaidens. We ran her bath (one keeping a hand in the water until the temperature was exactly right), backcombed her hair, painted her nails. At least once a week we were party to dramatic scenes such as the following:

Reenee was getting ready for a dance. From her bedroom she sent out a thin shriek, summoning Katie and me. 'For God's sake, I've got a spot!'

She was in her half slip and orangey-tan nylons, her sweater flung on the bed, her breasts overflowing the rigid cones of her bra. Her blue satin dress with the tulip skirt and cut-out back was hanging on a chair. We ran about like blind mice, trying to appease her, trying to discern the flaw.

'On my back, for Christ's sake,' Reenee snapped and we found it and it was quite a big spot too.

Katie boiled a kettle and fetched cotton wool and disinfectant and Reenee's Pan-Stik make-up. I got a darning needle and poised it over a jet of flame on the gas cooker. When the needle was red hot I poked it at the centre of the spot and Katie dabbed at its erupting substance. '*Don't* squeeze!' Renee warned. She began to calm down as we patted in the orangey emulsion that matched her stockings better than her skin. At this stage her eyes narrowed with satisfaction at her reflection in the winged dressing-table mirror and she told us the things she knew. S.A. was what made a woman irresistible. You got it by putting pads of cotton wool, soaked in perfume, in your bra. No girl should go all the way but it was all right above the waist if you were going steady. A married woman must always keep her lipstick and mascara beneath the pillow and put them on before her husband awoke so that he would never have to look on her naked face. She spoke of French kissing, of lurching, of *shifting.*

We knew about French kissing, for it was the fate of all women who were brought to the pictures by their boyfriends. Reenee said it was lousy unless you were crazy about the guy and then it was fab. Lurching was close dancing and an occasion of sin. We never quite found out what shifting was but it concerned couples who rolled about the floor at parties.

We watched Reenee like a hawk. She knew all the rules of life and was confident in their execution. When she spoke on the telephone to her boyfriend, Tom, she leaned back in the chair and stretched out a leg and dangled her shoe. She smiled and made sheep's eyes into the telephone.

We both thought that it was the oddest thing, to smile into that handle of black Bakelite, but we made a mental note of it.

Sister Sophie was entirely different, a pious little stick of a woman who told us of a girl who had dressed up in her brother's clothes on Hallowe'en and afterwards she died and her parents saw her ghost, still dressed in men's clothing, flapping about in the moon. She thought I was a good child and prayed constantly for my vocation. I was not drawn to the nuns' way of life, their gliding blackness and the dull certainty of their salvation, but so far she was the only one who had noticed anything about me.

That year two things happened. The first was that Reenee got a crippling disease. In the beginning it crept up slowly like a bad 'flu and she maintained her glamour, propped up in bed in fluffy layers of her favourite blue. Then all of a sudden, she was an invalid, yellow and shapeless and sour and stale. The mysterious womanly parts of her that had been such a source of envy and admiration to us now became the necessity for odious tasks which Katie, blazing with hatred, had to perform. I was no longer involved; I did not have to be so I retreated. Neither of us felt sorry for her. We considered that she had let us down and we despised her. Katie had to share a room with her, with all that soft, sad, dying femaleness. Sometimes when I walked to school with her I could smell Reenee's smell from her and I imagined her pale, intense face had a yellowish tinge. I thought that Reenee's illness would spread and spread like St Brigid's cloak until it covered us all, so I took to going into school early on my own to help Sister Sophie with her dahlias and I stayed on late, when lessons were over, to polish the blackboard and the desks.

I told Sister Sophie I had got The Call. The nun smuggled in special treats for me, Taylor Keith lemonade, Mikado biscuits, iced fairy cakes from the Eaton. She talked about God. She made Him sound like a brother, impractical and all-powerful. I liked that because I only had sisters, but the cakes caught in my throat.

The second thing to happen was that Betty Malibu came to live on our street. Her real name was Mrs Cahill but she told Mrs Elliot next door that she had once sung in the Gaiety as Betty Malibu and after that the name stuck. She was tall and thin with a mock ocelot coat and blonde hair in long waves. She had a husband, Barney, never seen except as a cigar pointing at the windscreen of a Mercedes car. She herself had a car – an unheard of thing for a housewife – a blue Ford Zephyr, which sometimes made snorting sorties down the street, almost killing people. Most of the time she preferred to walk, pushing a go-car to show off her little girl who was called Lucille and who struggled within a pyramid of pink nylon frills. Sometimes when she walked her daughter, she sang to her. I thought she was like Grace Kelly. She was the most admirable woman I had ever seen.

The other women did not like her. They said her American accent had come out of a packet of Mary Baker cake mix. They laughed when she said she put pineapple pieces in her ice cubes. They said that she had come from nothing.

When she was new on the street they tried to impress her. One told her how she had done all her curtains that day because there was a good breeze and another said that she had finished her whole batch of Christmas baking. A third one had cleaned out all her presses to make way for her new cauliflower pickle.

Betty Malibu smiled her dreamy smile. 'I did bugger all,' she said.

Nothing could reduce her in my eyes. If she had come from nothing, then what a remarkable journey she had made, to bring such glamour to our street. She always seemed dressed for a party. I thought the pineapple pieces in the ice cubes sounded so smart, and they meant she had a refrigerator too.

When I said this to my mother, when I praised her mock ocelot coat and her blue car and her gold hair, Mother turned from her polishing with an angry look and said: 'If you think she's got more to offer than we have, why don't you just take yourself over there?'

I did. I put on my pink coat, handed down by a richer cousin, and went and knocked on our new neighbour's door. She was wearing a nylon housecoat with frills. She apologised for it, calling it a peignoir.

'Can I come in and play?'

She gave a little yawn. I think she had been having a nap. 'Who are you?'

'I live down the road.'

'Sure. Come in, little girl. Would you like to watch some television?'

'I'd like to see your refrigerator,' I said.

There was a pause. 'Sure, honey.' She led me through the house which was full of glittering ornaments and bright pieces of china, like the prizes on a raffle stall. 'Would you like to do a job for me while you're in the kitchen? I'll give you a Bounty Bar.'

The fridge was in the kitchenette, where it took up most of the space. It was both tall and squat and every so often it seemed to give a deep chuckle. I drew back its vaulty door. The cold light inside, the white interior, the rows of ribbed shelves like bars on a coat, reminded me of a hospital ward. There was no trifle. No ham or bananas. There was hardly any food there at all, just some plastic boxes and greaseproof bags and a lettuce squashed under a stippled plastic shelf at the bottom. I frowned into the chill emptiness.

'What's the matter, honey? Did you want a sandwich?'

'There's nothing in there.'

'Sure there is. It's in the bags,' she said. 'You have to cover the food in a fridge or else you get odour.' She wanted me to clean out a chicken. 'My stomach just turns over,' she sighed.

Disappointment lay like a stone on my heart but I clawed chicken guts out on to newspaper. I would never do this for my mother. 'What about the pineapple ice cubes?' I said very quietly.

'Oh, sweet! – They're just for parties.'

'Don't you make ice-pops or ice-cream in the fridge?'

'No,' she agreed amiably. 'But we will someday if you want.'

I forgave her. She made coffee – not Irel, which we drank at home, but proper Nescafé. She gave me a Mars Bar and a Bounty. These were English and we could not buy them.

I came to see her every day. I told my mother I was going to Katie's house and, forsaking the dahlias, led Sister Sophie to believe that my mother wanted me (which was not exactly a lie, but did not merit the specific truth I gave it). Betty Malibu and I sat in her drawing room, which had a red carpet and satinised wallpaper, and watched Armand and Michaela Denis wrestling with blurred black and white lions. When we were not watching television we talked about the stars. She bought all the movie magazines and knew about the personal life of every actor and actress: *Bobby and Sandra's Marriage Crisis! Has Eddie Left Debbie Holding the Baby? Janet and Tony – Together Again?* I learned from these publications that having a bosom was the true secret of S.A. and indeed the root of every female success. At the back of the magazines were advertisements for wigs and false bosoms and even false bottoms so that having savoured the turbulent personal lives of the stars you could send off your cheque (or check, as they called it) and receive in the post a parcel of parts which made you just like the screen goddesses.

I felt at my chest and found that two small softnesses covered the wings of bone. I developed a great longing. 'There's just one thing I want for Christmas,' I confided to Betty Malibu, the only person in the world to whom I could say such a thing. She laughed when I told her. 'Well, that doesn't sound too difficult.'

But it was. Nobody ever bought you the things you wanted and they never liked the things you gave them. If I told the family I wanted a bra for Christmas they would laugh at me and say: 'What are you going to put in it – your scapulars?'

Apart from my new craving I loved books. I knew this addiction to be a dowdy one but still I bought books for everyone at gift-giving times.

I spent hours crawling around the floor under the bargain table in Fred Hannas, where nothing cost more than sixpence. I bought adventure stories for my sisters, an old cookery book for my mother; for Father I found a volume called *Sailing up the Belgian Congo*. As an afterthought I picked up a book of faded photographs about a tame bear for Katie. There was nothing good enough for Betty Malibu. All my usual pleasure at book hunting turned to panic as I flung aside old Protestant Bibles and street directories, tomes of Dickens and Chaucer, smelling of mould.

It was while I was there, under the table with the unwanted Greats, that Reenee, crying out a lament about a hangnail, summoned Katie to her side and died.

The funeral was four days before Christmas. Everyone was there, full of regret and chilled by the nudge of mortality. Katie and her mother cried and cried until they seemed to dry out and I was crying too but my misery had a different source.

At school the day before, Sister Sophie had given me a mission. One of the bold girls in the class – an Audrey or an Alma or Dolores – (good girls were always Josie or Brid or Teresa) had been found with an object of obscenity hidden in her desk. That's what Sister Sophie called it. She held up a bulky grey cardboard folder. Concerning its contents, she said, she would leave our innocence undisturbed. All that remained was to dispose of the dirty work and she would give this task to a good child whom she could trust. I stepped forward without being asked. She put the book in my hands.

'Promise you won't look,' she said.

'I swear.'

I did not look – not really look – but as the folder slipped into the waste bin its pages parted and my eye was drawn to the flickering show of Hollywood stars. It was a home-made film album, not just with magazine cut-outs but proper glossy photographs of the kind that fan clubs supply. Before I could think my hands had plunged into the dank cavern of refuse and the album was safe in my grasp. It had suffered only a little in the bin and a quick peek assured me that Alma or Dolores had not identified ownership with the usual: 'This book belongs to . . .' I could feel my heart juddering like an old motor engine as I ran back into school and hid the album in the cloakroom, underneath my overcoat.

I brought Betty Malibu her present after school, wrapped up in a sheet of shop wrapping paper, which cost twopence. She was as excited as I was. 'Oh, you sweet child, wait till I tell them all that you went to the trouble of getting me a Christmas present.' I was pulling ribbons away from the box she had given me – too big for a bra alone so I knew there must be other things as well and I kept my fingers crossed for a stiff slip and nylons.

It was a dress – pink Vyella with blue and green smocking on its flat, flat chest. It was what my mother would call a good item, with spare buttons on a card and little loops inside the shoulders to keep your slip straps in place. I recognised it from an expensive children's shop called The Gay Child.

'Isn't that the cutest thing, honey?' Betty Malibu was delighted. 'I chose it specially to go with your pink coat. Won't you be the smartest kid on the street?'

I nodded bitterly. That was just what I would be.

She was still smiling as she tore the wrapping from her gift. When the folder was revealed she got a puzzled look. She flipped through it and I saw that her fingers were as stiff as Sister Sophie's when she had held it up in class. 'Hey!' She gave a funny little laugh. 'What is this?'

'It's your present.'

When I looked at her she had withdrawn from the album and sat quite still, tears gathering in her eyes. 'Is this what you call a joke?' She said it very softly. 'It's not even new. It's garbage. It's dirty!' Her shining nails brushed a scar of grease which clung to the cover where it had been dipped in the bin. 'I thought you were getting me a book. I thought you were buying me a new book.'

'I didn't think you'd read a book,' I protested. 'You were going to buy me a bra.'

'You shouldn't judge a person by where they come from,' she said with intense feeling. 'I thought you would have something written on the inside and I would show everyone how you had bought me a book and written in it for me. A bra!' She pulled the rags of the wrapping paper around the gift for decency. 'What would your mother say?'

After Reenee's funeral service the mourners seemed drawn by a need for comfort to the Christmas crib, with its real straw and its nice little plaster donkey.

There had been hymns and inspiring passages of scripture and these helped to wipe away the yellowness of Reenee's illness. We all saw her as she had been, blonde and backcombed and full of S.A., but now with the addition of her heavenly crown, like a seaside beauty queen. In the end it seemed that she had simply got bored with us and gone off to look for more exciting company. It made us sad. We thought we would never laugh again. Then Betty Malibu leaned into the crib and looked at the baby Jesus with interest. 'It just goes to show,' she said; 'you should never judge a person by where they start out from.' Everyone gave a little titter.

My mother made me wear the pink dress on Christmas Day. She inspected all the seams and fancy stitches and marvelled at the good taste of a person like Betty Malibu. A funny thing had happened. Mother called around to the house to thank her for the gift and after that she couldn't stop saying what a nice person she really was and how clean her house was and in a day or two all the neighbours were flocking around Betty Malibu and they even began calling her plain old Mrs Cahill. I didn't care any more. I was feeling so rotten I didn't even mind putting on the dress. If someone had told me to, I would have dressed up in the back half of a pantomime horse. All the books I had bought and disguised with pads of newspaper underneath the wrapping ended up as more signposts to my oddness. 'We know!' my sisters teased as I arranged the nicely bumpy packages beneath the Christmas tree. 'They're only old books, aren't they?'

I took the dress out of its box and looked in misery on its neat round collar, the tweaking puffs of the sleeves. I pulled it over my head and felt behind my neck to slide the buttons into their perfect holes. After a long time I looked.

What I saw was something remarkable. The dress did not change me. Wearing it did not turn me into a kid. It did not alter me at all. Inside it, I was still me, a girl with thin plaits and a heart-shaped face on which intelligence sat like a blight, like spectacles; with the beginnings of a bust showing determinedly beneath the flattening bands of smocking.

If it was so, if a child's dress could not turn me into a child, then a bra or a false bust or even a false bottom could not turn me into a woman. I was uniquely myself and the only one of my kind. I had swum in a race with millions but I was the one who had won the race. I could learn from the experience of others without having to share the perils of their fate. My life was mine, whether I learned to smile at the telephone or sing to my children like Grace Kelly, with or without S.A.

'Look at her!' my sisters jeered when I sat down to dinner in the dress. 'Who does she think she is?' My father looked up from his carving with that vague dismay that love of daughters meant. His eye registered my new dress, or something that it suggested. 'She needs a bra!' he told my mother crossly and then went back with relief to his virtuoso solo upon the Christmas turkey.

PÁDRAIC BREATHNACH

The Snowman

Translated from the Irish by Gabriel Rosenstock

He got up from his knees, put out the light and climbed onto
the bed that stretched close to the wall along the window. On
his knees again, on the bed, he looked out at the night outside,
the darkness, the shrouded countryside, the lamps. Which houses
had lamps? Were there stars in the sky, myriads of stars? A great
yellow moon? He might hear a dog bark. He did. You didn't have
to put out the lights in the room to hear the dogs, but you did
to see the lights. He loved looking out, imagining who was still
awake, who had gone to bed. This ritual extended the day that
little bit extra.

He startled. It wasn't the night, the darkness or the lamps that
astounded him but the falling flakes. At first he didn't quite grasp
what was happening. That it was snow. It was snowing!

He leaped from the bed and dressed hurriedly. He put on a
pair of slippers. Down the stairs he flew.

'It's snowing!' he cried feverishly. 'I'm going out for a while!'

He wanted to get out before being restrained. Maybe they hadn't heard him. Maybe the television was too loud.

Big white flakes falling, falling; like confetti swirling in the air or bits of paper dropped from an aeroplane. Thousands of them, millions. Softly falling in graceful silence. Down from the vaults of heaven. He looked up. Gently falling on his face, falling on his eyes. On his eyelashes. Falling on his mouth, cheeks, chin. Ever so tenderly. They melted. He caught them in his fist. The warmth of his skin turning them to water. Metamorphosing the dark land. All becoming white. Not yet a covering, but the groundwork had begun. By morning the miracle would be complete, he hoped.

Who opened the door? Who's there? Who called? His mother yelled at him when she saw him outside.

'Óban!' she cried.

She ordered him in at once. The young boy became frisky. He started to gad about.

'Óban!' she cried again.

She had seen this carry-on before, intoxicated by play, drunk with joy, like some half-wit. For a child who was normally so docile she sometimes believed his erratic behaviour signified some weakness, a mental aberration. You wouldn't know what to make of him sometimes. Sudden fits of uncontrollable glee or bouts of sheer pique. Salivating at the mouth at times with unmitigated joy, like a year old babe, pleasure gurgling in his throat. And then boiling with rage, or in a deep sulk, totally impenetrable like a dog protecting a bone. Ten years old now. Was it because he was an only child?

Out she went to grab him. He escaped. Off he goes as frisky as a colt, kicking his heels. Beaming with laughter. Merriment resounding from him. His mother grew cross.

'Wait there till I get the stick!' says she. 'Come in!' says she.

She said she wouldn't go trapesing after him and not to think she would, whatever the fool he was.

But she did catch hold of him and dragged him in after her. She shook him. Whatever class of a buffoon was he?

'Now do you see yourself?' says she. 'Do you see the cut of you? Not a shoe on you. Look at the state of your slippers!'

She smacked his backside.

'Look at your clothes!' says she. 'Do you think I've nothing better to be doing than to be running after you? Do you see your hair? Throw those clothes off you,' she ordered. 'Have I nothing better to do than to be getting dry clothes and pyjamas for you?'

He must be chilled to the bone, she thought. They said boys don't catch a cold, but that's nonsense. Why wouldn't they? Many a boy caught pneumonia. She ordered him upstairs to take a bath and not to be thinking she'd do that for him as well.

He was glad he could bathe alone. If there was enough water – and he'd feel the tank first – he'd send it spouting into the tub as he'd seen his father do. That's something his mother would never do. She'd only take a shower, being sparing with the water. His father would fill it so you could swim in it if the tub were bigger. He often envied his father in all that water, like a playful walrus. That's what he wanted, to splash and cavort in the soft water. On his back and on his stomach and stretching out fully. A fish in water. Water, water, everywhere. He looked forward to it, now that he had to wash his hair as well. He'd baptise himself with water, allowing it to flow down over him. He'd fill the big blue sponge and disgorge the water over him, again and again. He'd have plenty of foam and would remain there, playing, until the water became cool.

He sat in front of the mirror, drying his mop of hair. The new drier was much better than the old one. Stronger, a gust of wind blowing through his hair. They'd bought quite a few gadgets recently. Look how white the skin is on the crown of his head. But not the white of snow.

Oh the snow. Always coupled with Christmas in his mind. Always expecting snow for Christmas, but it rarely fell on time. Now Christmas was over and it would be an eternity before it came round again. People said snow comes mostly in January or February. Those months, too, were gone. It had been very mild this year: grass coming up, flowers coming out. The crocus blossomed, daffodils and primroses in the beds opposite the house, his mother sprinkling poison from a bottle to keep the slugs and pests away from the new growth. He saw the 'pookies' stretched out dead in the morning like slime on the earth. They were saying it might snow yet, that it often snowed in March, April, even into May. They were right. It was March and the snow was coming down. There are places where it is always snowing, in the North Pole and in the South Pole. He found it hard to imagine snow in the South Pole. He associated it with heat. South means heat, France, Spain, Italy, Africa. But he learned at school that the South Pole has as much ice and snow as the North, since each was equidistant from the sun. He also learned of other areas that are snow-covered permanently, that snow remains on high peaks. At first he thought that was odd, since these peaks had to be nearer the sun than anywhere else on earth. But he was told that high peaks are always cold and he saw himself that this was true. Snow could often be seen where Granny lived, patches of snow here and there in mountainy crevices.

His mother came upstairs and asked him was he ready. She brought him warm pyjamas from the hot press. They felt wonderful, fresh, warm, comfortable. She ordered him back to bed, warning him not to turn on the radio. To go straight to sleep. She shoved him under the bedclothes, kissed him on the top of the head and told him to say his prayers.

'I've said them!'

She said he could say a few more. He had no intention of doing so but he did intend to look out once more at the snow. All the snow in heaven was falling. Thanks be to God! He turned on the radio and got under the blankets again. He loved music even when barely audible. With the help of music it was easy to lie under the bedclothes, stretched comfortably. Nice thoughts would come to him then. And it was easy to switch it off if he heard his mother approaching. Unless he fell asleep. His mother often complained that the radio was left on, that she was always turning it off. But her bark was worse than her bite. It was she herself who gave him the radio and allowed him to have it in the room when they bought a new one. The new one could play cassettes and was much better than the Hi-Fi they had in the sitting room. It could even play records.

He hoped the snow would become even denser. Let it fall, fall and cover the house. Let them be snow-bound inside. Not able to go to school or even to the shop. There were places where snow was up to the height of a house, a two-storey house, where snow piled up relentlessly. Where Granny lived, snow often covered the sheep in the hills during the depths of winter. Snow driving its way into their sheltered nooks. They would lie in the snow until it melted or until they were rescued. You'd know where they were from the breathing holes in the snow. If you saw a huge sieve of holes you'd know the whole flock was buried together. The warmth of their breath creating the holes as the snow piled on them. If it didn't go on too long they'd be none the worse after it.

Though his Granny's house was not as comfortable as his own he liked it, especially in summer. They didn't spend much time there in winter. His mother was always giving out how cold it was there, doors and windows open all the time and when they weren't you could still feel draughts coming through the joints.

But he liked the big open hearth and the turf-fire. Sitting by the fire at night. The floors were of concrete though rugs were placed near the beds. It wasn't only his mother who felt the cold. He always had goose-pimples and if it weren't for the hot water bottle Granny gave him he'd be frozen.

He liked his Granny, though she was very old, stooped and bedraggled. She was constantly knitting pullovers for him and giving him tasty morsels to eat, a fistful of coins and always praising him and remarking how clever he was. His mother too would say he was clever, and he believed he was. Didn't he know everything about the ozone layer and the destruction of the rain forests in Brazil, acres of trees felled in one hour – the size of three thousand football pitches. And not only in Brazil, but all over the Tropics, in Africa, India, Australia and elsewhere. He had read in the paper that scientists were predicting great climatic changes, that the fine weather would come in winter and vice versa. There would be massive earthquakes in places where they had never previously occurred, many animals, fish and birds would be doomed. He wouldn't like that to happen, snow falling in summer.

A sheet of white snow. Piled up against the window panes. The plots beyond the lawn, white, as white as the lawn itself. Hills, valleys, glens. The mountain. Each ditch snow-hooded. Every bush under a weight of snow, every branch and limb. Snow on every bramble. Every tree in the coniferous wood a pale sentry.

Over all things a peaceful white reigned supreme. River banks, right down to the water, completely white. The river itself a greyish torpor. Every roof crowned with snow. Only a few remaining areas of shade where the snow had not yet blown in. He looked out at the blanched countryside, as giddy as a child opening a present under the Christmas tree.

He appeared at the door of the house, well fitted out in high rubber boots, overcoat and a scarf around his neck. He had gloves on and a knitted leprechaun cap on his head, covering his ears. Suddenly he picked up a handful of snow and made a snowball. When he threw it out on the snowy lawn a red-breasted bird flew across to the little stone wall. But he hardly noticed it.

There was enough snow to make thousands of snowballs to throw at targets. He went out to the middle of the lawn, the snow crunching underfoot. The traces of his boots remained in the bright deep carpet.

He was going to make a big snowman, the biggest ever built; it would stand like a white giant on the side of the hill and be a source of wonder to all who'd see him, from the road or from further afield.

He began to mould and squeeze the snow. What fun, with so much snow. This great big lump was only the beginning, he'd add to him. Making him the king of all snowmen. The greatest that ever was built.

He discarded his gloves as they had got too wet. Were it not for his mother he wouldn't bother with them at all. The snow felt different in his bare hands. Much nicer. Now he could sense its texture properly. He piled the snow, packing it densely. It was easier now with his bare hands. The grass was becoming visible. Maybe he'd use up all the snow on the lawn. And fetch more. There was no lack of snow about. But his hands were cold. His fingers tingling. Now and again he would squeeze them, shrink them, to bring back the circulation. He was getting tired as well. His back was stiff. But he wouldn't submit. He'd go on slaving. He'd see it through. He'd continue to collect the snow, to pile it on and pack it firmly. The more he worked the better he became. He learned how to roll it, to allow it to form a ball – a rolling mass.

His hands grew leathery. They hurt. Could he stand the pain

much longer? Should he go in and warm them? It was hard work. The joy of it was running out.

He could barely open the door of the house. He was wheezing and panting. Whimpering. He went into the kitchen, almost whining. His mother wasn't there. She was still in bed. How long would the pain last? What should he do? He tried turning on the hot tap. He breathed on his fingers, knitting and kneading them as much as he could. The pain would eventually go – but when?

He placed the head on the snowman. He fixed the hands. He put a hat on the head. Eyes, a mouth and a nose. Black buttons down the front, from the neck to the belly-button. A pipe in his mouth and gloves on the hands. The harder he worked the more oblivious he became to everything else except the snowman. And now it was finished. The numbness in his fingers returned.

He went upstairs. His mother was getting up.

'I made a snowman!' he told her. He wouldn't say anything else until she saw its magnitude with her own eyes.

'Like to see it?' he asked.

He drew back the curtains. She saw the murky sky. A dark threatening sky. Bulging with great leaden clouds. There would be another fall. Already the odd flake was careering down.

'What do you think of it?' he asked.

EDMUND DOWNEY

A Fog Yarn

A bout a week before Christmas, half-a-dozen coasting captains
were assembled in the outer office of Morgans and Todd, in the
Bute Docks, Cardiff. Morgans and Todd were coasting shipbrokers.
Morgans was a Welshman, born in Merthyr, and had never been to
sea. Todd was an Irishman, and had been at sea up to his forty-fifth
year, when he and Morgans went into partnership.

Of the half-a-dozen coasting skippers who were now chatting
and smoking in the cosy little office – for it was dusk, and most
of the business proper of the day had been disposed of – four were
Irishmen, commanding Irish ships, and two were Welshmen, one
sailing out of Barrow-in-Furness, and the other out of his native
Cardiff. The conversation was chiefly of the sea, and its trials and
troubles, as seafarers seldom think it worth their while to talk of
anything purely of the earth earthly, except, perhaps, to indulge in
growls at the delay in getting waggons for loading and unloading,
or the general depravity and chicanery of 'shore folk'.

The most garrulous of those who were enjoying their pipe and
their chat in Morgans and Todd's comfortable office was Captain

A Fog Yarn

Jack Larrissey, master of the Cork brigantine *Redundant*. A stranger would have been impressed with the wonderful daring, energy, and activity of Captain Larrissey, were he to form his impressions solely from the Cork skipper's own statements. In reality, Larrissey was one of the laziest of mortals; and although he knew perfectly well that his present companions were aware of his easy-going, indolent habits, still his tongue rattled along incessantly – a story of an extraordinary rapid passage in the teeth of an adverse hurricane almost swallowed up by another story of a voyage when the canvas had been torn into ribbons, the crew washed overboard, and Larrissey, single-handed, had brought his good ship safely into port.

His audience listened patiently and good-humouredly to his yarns that evening. The office fire was bright, and inspired cheerfulness; every man had his pipe; and there was no temptation to go out of doors, for a cold, raw wind was blowing, and there was a slight fall of snow. About six o'clock Todd, the shipbroker, came from an inner office, and said:

'I'm afraid I'll have to dismiss you, gentlemen; it is time to shut shop. I suppose,' turning to Captain Larrissey, 'you have been keeping them all alive here, skipper.'

'Ah, my lad,' said Larrissey, 'did I tell you about my last passage to Cork?'

'No,' laughed Captain Todd.

'Well, you know how hard it was blowing,' began the story-teller, 'when I started from the Roads, and—'

'Oh, 'tis too late now,' interrupted the shipbroker. 'You're a wonderful man, I know. No wonder the hair is falling off your head. Look here, now, Captain Jack, are you game to take up a challenge?'

'What about?'

'Well, it's just this. There is a fine south-easterly breeze blowing.

Your ship will be loaded tomorrow night, and I'll bet you a ten-pound note you don't eat your Christmas dinner in Cork. You have eight days to do it.'

'Phew!' whistled Larrissey contemptuously. 'I suppose you want to have a laugh at me. Why, there's nothing to prevent me from having my Christmas dinner in Cork, except that I may get over there before forty-eight hours are over, and if I get the coals out quickly, I'll be back to eat it *here*.'

A general guffaw greeted Larrissey's boast – it is easy to amuse coasting skippers when there is a comfortable fire in front of them. Captain Todd, who had at first offered to make the wager merely for a joke, now grew vexed at being laughed at, and, pulling two five-pound notes from his pocket, said:

'Come, I'm in earnest!'

'Done!' replied Larrissey. 'I'll draw ten pounds on my freight tomorrow, and back that,' pointing to the notes.

The following evening the *Redundant* was towed out of the West Dock basin, and, to the shipbroker's astonishment, the brigantine went straight to sea. He had calculated that the commander of the *Redundant* would, as was his wont, spend a couple of days getting out to the Roads, and would then bring his ship to anchor, and remain about a week in Cardiff, until shame and a few telegrams from his wife drove him to sea.

The south-easterly breeze lasted until the *Redundant* was abreast of Lundy, and then the wind died away, and a dense fog crept up.

Captain Larrissey's ship was nearly as old and as lazy as himself, and it had taken her about eighteen hours to travel with a fair wind from Penarth to the mouth of the Bristol Channel; consequently it was about sunset when the fog began to envelop the brigantine.

Larrissey had exhibited extraordinary activity in getting his craft out of dock and to sea; but the strain on his mental and physical energies had been so great that a violent reaction set in ere long, and when the skipper came up from his bunk to interview the fog, he felt too lazy to give any instructions about altering the ship's course.

'I think the wind is from the nor'erd and aistard now, skipper,' said the mate, Flaherty, 'that is, whatever little wind there is of it.'

'Oh, let her rip, bad luck to it!' responded Captain Larrissey in a melancholy tone, as he prepared to descend to his state-room; 'give me a hail when the fog clears off.'

Next day the fog seemed to have increased in density, so the skipper was in a very ill-humour. His crew considered him 'one of the most knowledgeable captains afloat or ashore', and Larrissey would not wish, for worlds, that they should think otherwise. Therefore he was now in terror lest he should have to declare that he had no notion where his ship had drifted to. 'It's bad enough,' he reflected, 'to lose a ten-pound note and a good Christmas dinner at home, but I'd rather lose them a dozen times over than confess to my crew that I don't know my own bearings.'

The next day the fog showed no sign of lifting. 'Did ever mortal man see the like of this?' muttered Larrissey. 'I suppose the next thing we'll hear is the bump of her forefoot on a rock. I'm a persecuted men, I am.'

On the fourth day the atmosphere was perfectly clear, but Larrissey was now almost as badly off as ever. There was neither sextant nor quadrant aboard the Redundant, and even if he possessed either instrument, the worthy but ignorant skipper would not have been able to take the sun.

'What's to be our coorse now, skipper?' asked the mate, entering the captain's state-room.

'Flaherty,' replied Larrissey from his bunk, 'I must confess to you that I don't know from Adam where we are. 'Tis as like as not we're in the Bay of Biscay now; and, judging from the rowl of the sea, it wouldn't at all surprise me if Gibraltar, or the coast of Morocco, was the next land we got a grip of; but, for heaven's sake, Flaherty, don't let on to the crew about my ignorance.'

Then, a sudden inspiration seizing the commander of the *Redundant*, he started up in bed, and cried out:

'Flaherty, rob the harness cask!'

'Arrah, what do you mane?' asked the mate. 'Is it dhramein' you are?'

'Do what I tell you, Flaherty. Stow all the beef and pork here in my state-room – unbeknownst to the men, mind you – and then maybe you'll know what's in my mind.'

''Tis losin' the little bit of sense you have, you are,' muttered the mate, as he left the state-room to execute the orders of his chief.

The sailors were soon afterwards summoned to the cabin, and their skipper addressed them thus:

'It goes to my heart, my lads, to tell you all that we sailed from Cardiff very short of provisions, and Mr Flaherty informs me now that the harness cask is quite empty, so you must only make the best of a bad bargain, and try and get along on vegetables and hard bread until some ship heaves in sight, and then, my lads, we can barter some of our coals for beef and pork. Go on deck now, men, and keep a good look-out for a strange sail, for that's the only chance left to us.'

There was a good deal of ugly grumbling to be overheard after the skipper's speech; but when Larrissey pathetically observed, 'Shure, boys, it's as bad, if not worse, for your old skipper. Don't you all know how fond of my grub I am?' the crew seemed pacified a little, and went on deck to reconnoitre.

During the afternoon a strange sail hove in sight, and about three o'clock the *Redundant* was alongside an American barque, and, after duly relating his sad tale of short supplies, Captain Larrissey exchanged a quantity of coals for a week's provisions.

A Fog Yarn

After the exchange had been negotiated, Captain Larrissey, his arms folded on the top-gallant rail, carelessly asked the Yankee skipper:

'Where are you bound to?'

'Plymouth,' replied the Yankee. 'Guess we ought to sight English land before the sun goes down, eh?'

'How's your reckoning?'

'Well, we calculate we're about sixty miles west of the Lizard, and we're steering east and by south just now. How do you make it?'

'Ah! you're about right – near enough, at any rate,' condescendingly replied Captain Larrissey, after a short pause. 'Near enough; but if you'll be said by me you'll put your ship's head just a trifle more to the s'uth'ard. The sky looks all s'utherly,' waving his hand vaguely, for he wasn't yet certain where the south really lay.

'Much obliged. Where are you bound?'

'Cork, my lad; Cork. It's about square yards for me with a southerly wind – east-south-east is your course, if you'll be said by me; and keep a sharp look-out! You'll soon pick up the land, if you pay attention to what I'm telling you – east-south-east!'

'Thank you. Dirty weather, isn't it?'

'Shocking! We've been knocking about for days in a fog, and I'm fairly choked. Safe voyage! Mind now, east-south-east!'

The ships then parted company, and Larrissey was in high glee. He had obtained the requisite information as to his whereabouts without allowing the crew to perceive that he had ever been confused or alarmed; and his wager with the Cardiff ship agent was almost as good as won.

As soon as he had consulted his compass, and had taken a long look at the sky, he made up his mind that a southerly wind was really brewing, so he ordered the Redundant's yards to be squared. When the men came down from aloft, their skipper informed them that a good supper awaited them in the cabin – in coasting ships the sailors usually get their meals aft – and while the hungry crew were rapidly consuming the welcome victuals, Larrissey remarked:

'What a nice, agreeable fellow that Yankee skipper was! None of your bounce or tall-talk about him – a man quite after my own heart. But wasn't it the mercy of heaven that he fell in with a smart, knowledgeable skipper like myself? There he was, boys, steering straight for destruction – he'd be atop of the Land's End before midnight, perhaps lose all hands and the ship, if the wind freshens – only that I gave him his coorse fair and square. I suppose the poor fellow lost his way in that dirty fog; and you may all thank your stars it is Jack Larrissey that's sailing the old *Redundant*, or maybe you'd be all on your beam ends in the Western Ocean by this time, perishing with cold and hunger.'

'You're a wonderful man, you are, and no mistake,' chuckled Flaherty, the mate. 'And there's your wager with the Cardiff man as good as gold, for the sail is full to bustin' this minute of a dead fair wind.'

'I'll say good-night now, boys,' yawned Captain Larrissey, 'for I am fairly wore out with anxiety of mind. Give me a hail, Flaherty, when Ballycotton is in sight.'

The skipper was hailed about noon the following day, and before nightfall the brigantine had dropped her anchor in the pleasant waters of the River Lee. So Captain Larrissey won his wager, ate his Christmas dinner in Cork, and was deemed by his crew a more 'knowledgeable' man than ever.

TERRY PRONE

Butterfly Christmas

He had marched the Christmas trees out to where she sat in the car. Two by two, thumping their stumps into the pavement and twirling them. The first two she rejected.

'Spacer,' she said decidedly, then shook her head as a wet dog does, two rigid hands rising off her lap to sketch in the air.

'Spacer,' she said again, helplessly.

A couple of passers-by, one clutching two turkeys by the neck in much the same way as her husband held the trees, stopped to watch.

'Bigger around?' her husband asked. She was silent.

'Taller?'

The nod was frantic.

'No problem,' he said, and marched the shorter trees away.

The chosen tree was now anchored in a clever red contraption that held water, and five sets of tiny lights had been threaded all over it. Today, he would put up the decorations. She went to turn in the bed and failed. The reflexes of mobility don't give up easily, she reflected. Nor the dreams, filled with unplanned, unquestioned movement.

'Very fortunate your ribs weren't broken,' he said, sliding out his side of the bed and heading for the bathroom. 'You'd never have managed without the deep sighs.'

Snorting laughter overcame her, alone in the big bed. The snorts had been there since childhood, but in self-conscious adolescence she had developed the habit of cupping a hand over mouth and nose so that her laughter made a drowned noise. Now, neither hand could reach mouth and nose. Thinking about this provoked an itch beside her nostril. She concentrated on it, having been taught that if you tried to make it get worse, rather than better, you could eventually make it go away, because your brain lost interest in paying so much attention to one small irritant.

The itch stayed and worsened, unaware of the sophisticated psychology being applied to it. It took ownership of her as pain never had. In the intensive care unit, staff had driven her berserk by their solicitude for the pain. Pain control was now in fashion. Everybody was geared to stop it before it started, as opposed to the old days when it was allowed to become a raging torrent before the easing needle was employed. Nobody, however, was geared to take an itch seriously. And for her, the itches were worse than the pain.

He was beside her with a rough dry face cloth. He rubbed it impersonally all over her face, scouring the itch away. The cloth then went into the bowl of hot water he had carried in, its coarse terry loops softening so that when he washed her face, it was a warm wet infusion of comfort.

'This is gonna hurt you more than it hurts me,' he said, as he now always did, before cleaning her teeth.

The jaws were locked, leaving only an inch of access. The brush, scrubbing against the enamel, was loud in her ears as he talked to her, the words lost. She looked a question at him, but he seemed contented with her lack of response, and dressed her, buttoning her blouse right up to the collar as if readying her in a school uniform.

'I've solved the problem of getting you downstairs,' he said, looping one of her arms over his shoulder and lifting her. As he carried her across the small landing, she could feel the redness rising in her face for shame at her own heaviness.

'Now, I'm going to lean you against the wall and slide you down,' he said, ignoring her anxious grunts.

The painted wall was smooth and chill against the white blouse as he slid her down into a sitting position at the top of the stairs, where he had laid the single bed duvet. Once she was seated, he pulled the plaster rigidities of her legs out in front of her, pointing down the stairs towards where he was, a few steps below her. He then tipped her forward, so that her head was on his shoulder, and gently pulled the duvet so that her bottom went bump from one step to another, her forehead hitting the soft padded shoulder of his cardigan in an off-tempo echo. She began to laugh at the awkward efficiency of it, sucking in hairs from the cardigan at every in-breath.

Three steps from the bottom he straightened her up as briskly as if she had been a shop mannequin, and hefted her into the wheelchair.

'Now,' he said, kicking off the brake of the wheelchair with enormous satisfaction. 'Now.'

He parked her where she could watch the flames of the freshly-lit fire and went off to the other end of the long oblong room to start making breakfast. She could follow what he was doing just by the sounds. Paper rustling and then a clunk as sliced bread was slid into a toaster.

A fainter click as the kettle went on. Crackling of eggshells and the chatty monologue of an egg frying. He always fried eggs too quickly, so they developed a lacework of bubbles and a black edge.

'Oh, d'you know what . . .' he said, coming over to the stereo and rifling through discs.

'What would you like?'

'Diminished fifth,' she said. Quite clearly. He looked at her in intense silence, a record in one hand, a teatowel flung over his shoulder.

'Minor Detail?' he suggested. She nodded, wondering again at the scrambled brain cells that could so transpose a band's name. He put on the disc and returned to the cooking, swearing to himself as the fat spat at him.

He had developed a way of feeding the two of them, mouthful about, which ensured that both got hot food, but which required concentration on both parts. He got momentarily touchy when she turned her head away from a proffered bite of toast.

She was looking beyond him at the window of the converted eighteenth-century millhouse.

'Butterflies,' she said. The word was muffled but unmistakable. Her husband sat back in his chair and went through his usual routine.

'Butter? No. Marmalade? Birds? Decorations? Music?'

'Butterflies,' she said again, more firmly.

'Jesus, I can't figure . . .' he said, baffled.

She butted her head in the direction she wanted him to look, but he was back with the problem of food.

'I'll work it out in a minute, OK?' he said, and inserted toast in her mouth as if he was a postman delivering a letter. For a moment, she considered shoving it back out with her tongue, but sucked it instead. Next time he arrived with a forkful of black lacy egg, she turned her head as far away as she could.

'OK,' he said, ostentatiously patient. 'OK. Butterflies.'

He stood up, turned to the window, and a coloured cloud of them surrounded him. Some of them settled on him, the elaborate primary colours bright against the grey of his cardigan. He stood in startled stillness.

'Butterflies,' he said again, his accent adding a soft aitch after the T so they became buttherflies. There were at least ten of them. He nudged the one on his shoulder and it shifted to the back of his hand. He brought it to her, placing it on the frame that held her wrist rigid. For a few seconds, the russet and ultramarine wings fluttered anxiously, and then were at peace. She watched it for a long time in silence, rehearsing the words so they would come out right.

'At Christmas?'

The man nodded.

'Never heard of that before. Maybe because it's thatched. Maybe the eggs got laid and the warmth of the fire . . .'

He poked the one on his arm until it flew off and settled on the Christmas tree, and then put a fire guard in front of the flames. The room was warmer now and the butterflies flew high in the rafters as if in the branches of a tree in midsummer. She wanted to look more closely at the one on her wrist, but could bring it no closer.

'Tantalus,' she said aloud.

'Yeah,' her husband said, picking up the plates and heading for the sink.

Not being able to get a proper view of the butterfly tainted the pleasure of it being there at all, she realised. It was like having eye-floaters, those oddly shaped images that stay constantly out of visual range, rising and falling with the pattern of one's gaze. Tantalus and the grapes. Or was it grapes? Water, perhaps? And what had been the offence for which that perverse incarceration was the punishment? Her ideas floated ahead of her like a conveyor-belt clothesline decorated with pegs, but moving too fast for garments to be appended thereto. A moment of misery surged inside her head, pressing against the hard shell of her skull as the traumatised brain had.

'Tantalus,' she said, more exigently.

'I know bugger all about Tantalus,' he said comfortably, clattering clean plates. 'Nothin'. Empty. White sheet.'

Catching the demand in her face, he closed his eyes to dredge for memories.

'I presume Tantalus is the guy who gave rise to the word tantalise,' he speculated. 'Same as yer man that couldn't push the stone up the hill. Sisyphus. Tantalus had some equivalently frustrating exercise that he couldn't quite fulfil. I'll look it up in the library when we go out.'

She sat silently, the front of her legs beginning to be too warm in the fire heat. He would not remember to look it up, she knew, and she would not remember to remind him. And if she later reproached him, he would laugh and tell her he had more important things to be doing.

'Now, tell me where these go,' he said, kicking off the wheelchair brake and pushing her towards the Christmas tree. Her legs cooled down and she nodded her instructions as to where the tinsel baubles should go. Pain was riveting the bones of her face.

'Don't grind your teeth. Makes you look like Desperate Dan in the *Dandy*,' he said.

She watched him open two capsules and empty them into a flat soupspoon filled with yoghurt. He fed the sour mixture to her and a great shudder at the taste ran through her, knocking her plastered legs together and forcing one rigid forearm off the arm of the wheelchair. He lifted the arm back into position without comment. Nor did he make predictions about the painkiller, as her mother would have done.

'You'll feel the good of that in just a few minutes,' her mother would always say. 'You'll never notice the time passing.'

Having dosed her as neatly as a farmer dosing a sheep, he went off to get logs, stepping into wellington boots at the door before heading out into the rainy backyard. For a moment she was filled with fear that the butterflies would follow him out the open door and wilt in the cold outside air, but they stayed where they were. He came back to build up the fire with the sure-handed enjoyment he took in any physical task. He sat back on his hunkers, his hands palmed towards the blaze.

Then the boots were shoved off and he heel-padded in socked feet to wash his hands. One of the butterflies settled on the hot tap, and he tipped it with the back of his hand to get it away.

'Needn't have bothered our arses buying decorations,' he said, half to himself. 'Free butterflies . . .'

The pain was beginning to ease, keeping in time with her pulse as it retreated.

'Here,' he said. 'Hold these.'

The lightness of the box put into her lap mimicked paper. She pushed with her caged hand at the lid until it came up and off and fell to the floor. The sound of it was swamped in a sudden loud rigour of Gregorian chant from the record player. Her husband's voice joined those of the choir.

'*Lumen ad revelationem gentium . . .*'

Six bright silver balls sat, segregated, egg-fashion, in the box, reflecting back six fattened faces at her. Bloated by the convex mirroring, the face was nonetheless different, nose tilted at an angle, forehead dented, the dent rimmed by pale raised scarring. A squealing whimper came through her clenched teeth and the six reflections blurred. Her husband, unhearing, came back to the wheelchair, still singing, and began – deftly – to loop skinny wire hooks onto the baubles.

'Jesus,' he said, breaking off from the male voices. 'Don't dribble on the bloody things. Oh. You're crying. Why're you crying?'

The caged hand thumped against her chin, then onto the baubles. The voices continued to sing 'Nunc dimittis servum tuum, domine'.

'Your face, is it?'

She nodded. He mopped her with the teatowel from off his shoulder.

'Yeah,' he said thoughtfully, taking some of the hooked baubles and beginning to position them on the tree. 'I'd forgotten you wouldn't have seen yourself since the accident.'

His tone was casually observant, as if commenting on a one-degree change in external temperature or the lateness of a newspaper. She roared at him in wordless agony, bubbles forming and bursting in the gap between top and bottom teeth. He finished hanging the baubles, came back and mopped her again.

'You have a thing called keloid scarring,' he said informatively. 'That's why the bump on your head has a kind of a rim on it. If you really want to, later, you can have it sort of filed down. But probably if you just grew your fringe a bit longer . . . Other than that, your face is going to be a bit different. But you'll get used to it. I have.'

He took the now empty box off her lap and replaced it with another one. When the lid came off, it was filled with red balls, crusted with metallic grains and non-reflective. After a moment, he resumed the Gregorian chant. When the track ended, he hummed the notes again.

'Good singer always hits the notes from above,' he said, quoting some college music teacher he had liked. 'Never reaches for them . . .'

You are without sympathy, she thought. You are without

imagination. You lack the capacity to understand the true horror of being behind a strange, distorted face, of knowing that it will never present to the outside world what you are used to it presenting. You have no patience for 'talking out' of problems and your favourite phrase is: 'There's the status quo, and there's worse – which do you want?' You have already got used to my battered face and you will never understand why I should have a problem doing the same. It wouldn't even occur to you to say that you see my face more than I do: you simply don't empathise enough to argue it through at all.

'D'you know what I was thinking?' Her husband was standing over her, dangling a red bauble from its hook. One of the butterflies had settled on it. 'We won't be able to have candles at all. And we'll have to be very careful with the toaster and things like that. I must rig a couple of shields to prevent these lads getting into danger.'

She held out her arms to him and he put his head down on her neck, one arm extended to take care of the butterfly. In a desperation of trust and need, she hugged him awkwardly, hiding her hospital-pale face in the always tanned warm skin of his neck.

'Now,' he said, straightening as if something had been settled and returning to the task. 'Butterflies and Christmas. What more could we want?'

COLUM McCANN

The Year of the Green Pigeons

Everyone knew Rhubarb Wilson's pigeons. They flew their way, rude and green, through the sky. You could point them out instantly over the rooftops of Bray, shafts of colour in flight, spinning their way down along the seafront, dipping and swerving and arguing against the winter skies.

Rhubarb had set up a coop on the roof of his tenement house. When some of the pigeons went missing one night, he took all the birds down to his flat – he owned every inch of the tumbledown house – and he dipped them in green food-colouring so that even the birds emerged shocked at themselves. The dye ran into their feathers, down their legs, colouring the underside of their wings, leaving only their faces untouched. They burst like blades of grass through the air.

'We'll see who steals the little beggars now,' he said, ferreting his way down Main Street, a Bray Wanderers scarf wrapped around his neck, a cage held under his arm.

We called him Rhubarb because he looked like a long thin shaft, with veins striated on his forearms. An absurd blue cap sat awkwardly on his head. He walked along through town, lopsided with his cages, a shyness in the walk. Rhubarb was a caretaker in the Christian Brothers school, and when he slopped out the toilets we used to joke that if he joined the Comprehensive, he'd be able to get himself some tart – and he'd chase us out, swinging the broom through the air.

'Hey, Ruby! Don't forget the custard!'

But there was grief there in Rhubarb Wilson, some sort of unrelenting pilgrimage into misery, with two lines permanently etched down along from his lips as if he'd forgotten to smile. The family had come down from the North years before, to rid themselves of some sort of tortured history – it was said that Rhubarb's two younger brothers couldn't even stand to be in the same room together. It was one of those arguments that had spun so much out of control that nobody could even remember what it was about. The family came down South to see if the gap could be bridged.

Nothing changed. Rhubarb's parents eventually gave up the ghost, lying back in oxygen tents in Loughlinstown hospital, gasping for cigarettes – his father even once tried, unsuccessfully, to light a match in the tent just before he died. After the parents passed away the brothers scattered, leaving Rhubarb to look at his reflection in the floors of school corridors.

One brother became a garage mechanic in an outback station in Australia; the other got a job as a glazier in London. It was an unwritten rule that they would avoid one another for the rest of their natural lives. Over the telephone they each assaulted Rhubarb with their invective, and he held the phone away as he smoothed down the feathers of his birds.

But the strange thing was that the two brothers, unaware of each other, decided to come to visit Rhubarb for Christmas in the year of the bright green pigeons.

It wasn't the fact that they carry messages, or that there's some metallic magic in their bodies that leads them home, or that when they put their heads under water they make the most curious of sucking noises – instead, Rhubarb Wilson was fondest of his pigeons because of their eerie accuracy when they chose to shit down on the world.

The brothers arrived on the same Dart train on Christmas Eve, out of neighbouring carriages, unknown to each other, and they sauntered up to where Rhubarb was waiting, along the railing of the seafront. The tide was long out. Rhubarb said later that there was the strangest of silences, like the quiet that comes with having forgotten something very important.

They hovered on each side of him and simultaneously called him a conniving bastard.

But the tenement house was large and each of the rooms was full of old and bloated sofas which they could sleep on, far away from one another. For a greeting, Rhubarb had let some of his pigeons in, and they flew around under chandeliers that had lost nearly all of their bulbs. The brothers ducked their heads. Little or no decoration had been done since Rhubarb's parents had died, so the glazier decided that he'd spend his Christmas doing some carpentry on the third floor and, if he had the time, he'd wash all the windows.

The other brother spread out on the lower living room floor and hugged a three-bar heater to himself and climbed his way down into a bottle of Jameson. The television rang its banalities around him and out into the rest of the house.

Rhubarb moved between his brothers like a courier with nothing to say and, late on Christmas Eve, he went up to the coop on the rooftop. It was warm for winter and he sat at the coop in a white shirt, staring at some stars agitating their way through the Wicklow night. He felt a strange sort of violence rise up in him –

the sort of violence he'd seen when one day each of the brothers tried to stab each other's eyes with hypodermic needles – and he stood and kicked at the door of the coop. The chickenwire dented into the shape of his boot and then he slid the wooden door across and grabbed two pigeons by the neck. He took them down to the kitchen. Rhubarb had some bottles of food colouring in the kitchen cupboard. He mixed it in two large chipped bowls. He dipped both the pigeons in. The first came out of the bowl, bright yellow. The second was a shade of dark blue. There could be no mistaking the two. They flapped and sprayed their colour onto the kitchen wall.

He weighed them in his fingers and stood at the bottom of the stairs, shouted for his brothers. They each emerged from their rooms of miasmic dark.

'Happy Christmas,' Rhubarb said. 'We'll release these fellas tomorrow on the seafront and see which one of you bastards wins. First one back to the coop wins. Then I never want to hear any more about it, not a word, nothing. Winner takes all.'

I was home from Korea for the season and on Christmas afternoon I went wandering down to the seafront. I went past the closed arcades and along the promenade, strolling through memories of Dodgem cars and choc ices and swimsuits and teenage fumblings under the blouses of nervous girlfriends. It was strange to be home in Bray after the streets of Pusan. I couldn't get the faces of the Korean fishmarket sellers out of my mind, all those old men and women bent over their catch, bent by yesterday's pain and bent into tomorrow's pain, always bent over, and always in repetition.

They knew me well, since the English school where I was teaching was on the edge of the market and each afternoon, when I clocked off, I would walk past the stalls and sometimes buy some squid. They shouted out 'Hello, Irish!' in a slow magnificent fashion as if they'd just gobbled their own tongues. I'd taught them how to say the phrase and, even though they mangled it, they loved those words.

It was the sight of Rhubarb coming along the hard sand that woke me up and I said to him 'Hello, Rhubarb' before I could catch myself. He looked at me for an instant. He could have had a fisherman's face himself – it was already hard and wrinkled and sad and brutal. He held a picnic basket and a white plastic bag.

'School,' he said to me, with a jerk of his hat. 'You're the brat who used to scream at me about the custard.'

He placed the plastic bag on the sand, bent his finger and beckoned me over. 'Have a goo at this, son.' In a picnic basket he had the pigeons, one yellow, one blue. They were tied with string into the wicker of the basket by their legs.

'You're an emigrant,' he said without even a grin, 'which one would you bet on?'

He told me the story of the previous day and I imagined the two brothers standing apart on the rooftop, waiting for some tangible vindication of their pasts, each of them looking to the sky for the yellow or the blue to land down into their outstretched hands, men crucified by their wordlessness, a silence that had dug itself deep into them years and years and years before.

We released the pigeons into the bright Christmas sky as the tide was coming in. Rhubarb handed me the plastic bag – filled with two containers of food colouring – and he began to run along the soft strand. The picnic basket banged at his thigh. I followed behind him. He was panting heavily in his middle age and he kept repeating in staccato over and over that his brothers had each staked £50 on the birds. Rhubarb clattered his way along towards the rocks underneath the promenade. A bead of sweat leaped at his brow when he turned around. 'Fifty bloody pounds, son!'

We ran through surprised families along the beach, parting to let us through; children crying because their new tricycles had stuck in the sand; teenagers working hard at being bored, a girl whose hair was ringed in tinsel; a father who still wore a red hat with a white bobble. In the sunlight, Rhubarb pulled the brim of his hat down to shade his eyes as he looked skyward.

The coloured pigeons broke through the air and I ran, amazed.

At the steps up to the promenade, Rhubarb took off his shoes and kicked out the sand. Wheezing, he didn't bother to lace his shoes and his left foot crunched down on the heel of the leather and he was almost limping up the street with his head cocked to the sky, looking for the birds.

Across the road we went, and a car screeched to a halt and he tapped the bonnet with his picnic basket and waved at the driver. He kept shading his eyes with his free hand and he was so winded by the time he reached his house that all he could do was let out a series of long, harsh coughs. He closed the gate behind us and fumbled madly in his pockets for his keys. He beckoned me in, said he wanted a witness. In the hallway, Rhubarb Wilson ducked underneath the shabby chandelier in the hall and told me to make sure to wipe my feet on the mat. He negotiated the stairs two at a time and emerged at the top of the house, took his cap off, his hair gone wild and astray on his head.

The two brothers stood there on the roof edge, with their Christmas gifts, dumbfounded.

Their hands were spotted with the food colouring, still wet. They carried the pigeons towards Rhubarb, and it was incredible to see him, in the glorious and warm and unusual December sunlight, leaning against his chicken coop, the upturn of the wrinkles around his mouth, the first time I'd ever seen him move from his sadness, the whole of his body tumbling with laughter.

Both birds were absolutely identical, painted half-yellow, half-blue. There was no way to distinguish between the two.

The brothers said nothing, although they each handed over £50 to one another. They stuffed the notes in their pockets as Rhubarb cackled. And then the brothers let the pigeons go free; the birds beating their wings against the gift of the sky. The Wilson brothers all stood with their hands supine. The birds flew around for a moment and then, as if on a whim, simply decided to land.

BERNARD MacLAVERTY

A Present for Christmas

M cGettigan woke in the light of midday, numb with the cold.
He had forgotten to close the door the night before and his
coat had slipped off him onto the boards of the floor. He swivelled
round on the sofa and put the overcoat on, trying to stop shivering.
At his feet there was a dark green wine bottle and his hand shook
as he reached out to test its weight. He wondered if he had had
the foresight to leave a drop to warm himself in the morning. It
was empty and he flung it in the corner with the others, wincing
at the noise of the crash.

He got to his feet and buttoned the only button on his coat.
The middle section he held together with his hands thrust
deep in his pockets and went out into the street putting his
head down against the wind. He badly needed something to
warm him.

His hand searched for his trouser pocket without the hole. There
was a crumpled pound and what felt like a fair amount of silver. He
was all right. Nobody had fleeced him the night before. Yesterday he
had got his Christmas money from the Assistance and he had what

would cure him today, with maybe something left for Christmas Day itself.

Strannix's bar was at the back of the Law Courts about two minutes from McGettigan's room but to McGettigan it seemed like an eternity. His thin coat flapped about his knees. He was so tall he always thought he got the worst of the wind. When he pushed open the door of the bar he felt the wave of heat and smoke and spirit smells surround him like a hug. He looked quickly behind the bar. Strannix wasn't on. It was only the barman, Hughie – a good sort. McGettigan went up to the counter and stood shivering. Hughie set him up a hot wine without a word. McGettigan put the money down on the marble slab but Hughie gestured it away.

'Happy Christmas, big lad,' he said. McGettigan nodded still unable to speak. He took the steaming glass, carrying it in both hands, to a bench at the back of the bar, and waited a moment until it cooled a bit. Then he downed it in one. He felt his insides unfurl and some of the pain begin to disappear. He got another one which he paid for.

After the second the pains had almost gone and he could unbend his long legs, look up and take in his surroundings. It was past two by the bar clock and there was a fair number in the bar. Now he saw the holly and the multi-coloured decorations and the HAPPY XMAS written white on the mirror behind the bar. There was a mixture of people at the counter, locals and ones in from the Law Courts with their waistcoats and sharp suits. They were wise-cracking and laughing and talking between each other which didn't happen every day of the year. With Strannix off he could risk going up to the bar. You never know what could happen. It was the sort of day a man could easily get drink bought for him.

He stood for a long time smiling at their jokes but nobody took any notice of him so he bought himself another hot wine and went back to his seat. It was funny how he'd forgotten that it was so near Christmas. One day was very much the same as another. Long ago Christmases had been good. There had been plenty to eat and drink. A chicken, vegetables and spuds, all at the same meal, ending up with plum-duff and custard. Afterwards the Da, if he wasn't too drunk, would serve out the mulled claret. He would heat a poker until it glowed red and sparked white when bits of dust hit it as he drew it from the fire – that was another thing, they'd always had a fire at Christmas – then he'd plunge it down the neck of the bottle and serve the wine out in cups with a spoonful of sugar in the bottom of each. Then they knew that they could go out and play with their new things until midnight if they liked, because the Ma and the Da would get full and fall asleep in their chairs. By bedtime their new things were always broken but it didn't seem to matter because you could always do something with them. Those were the days.

But there were bad times as well. He remembered the Christmas Day he ended lying on the cold lino, crying in the corner, sore from head to foot after a beating the Da had given him. He had knocked one of the figures from the crib on the mantelpiece and it smashed to white plaster bits on the hearth. The Da had bought the crib the day before and was a bit the worse for drink and he had laid into him with the belt – buckle and all. Even now he couldn't remember which figure it was.

McGettigan was glad he wasn't married. He could get full whenever he liked without children to worry about. He was his own master. He could have a good Christmas. He searched his pockets and took out all his money and counted it. He could afford a fair bit for Christmas Day. He knew he should get it now, just in case, and have it put to one side. Maybe he could get something to eat as well.

He went up to the counter and Hughie leaned over to hear him above the noise of the bar. When McGettigan asked him for a carry-out Hughie reminded him that it was only half-past two. Then McGettigan explained that he wanted it for Christmas. Three pint bottles of stout and three of wine.

'Will this do?' asked Hughie holding up the cheapest wine in the place and smiling. He put the bottles in a bag and left it behind the counter.

'You'll tell the boss it's for me, if he comes in,' said McGettigan.

'If Strannix comes in you'll be out on your ear,' Hughie said.

Strannix was a mean get and everybody knew it. He hated McGettigan, saying that he was the type of customer he could well do without. People like him got the place a bad name. What he really meant was that the judges and lawyers, who drank only the dearest and best – and lots of it – might object to McGettigan's sort. Strannix would strangle his grandmother for a halfpenny. It was a standing joke in the bar for the lawyers, when served with whiskey, to say, 'I'll just put a little more water in this.' Strannix was an out-and-out crook. He not only owned the bar but also the houses of half the surrounding streets. McGettigan paid him an exorbitant amount for his room and although he hated doing it he paid as regularly as possible because he wanted to hold onto this last shred. You were beat when you didn't have a place to go. His room was the last thing he wanted to lose.

Now that he was feeling relaxed McGettigan got himself a stout and as he went back to his seat he saw Judge Boucher come in. Everybody at the bar wished him a happy Christmas in a ragged chorus. One young lawyer, having wished him all the best, turned and rolled his eyes and sniggered into his hot whiskey.

Judge Boucher was a fat man, red faced with a network of tiny broken purple veins. He wore a thick, warm camel-hair overcoat and was peeling off a pair of fur-lined gloves. McGettigan hadn't realised he was bald the first time he had seen him because then he was wearing his judge's wig and sentencing him to three months for drunk and disorderly. McGettigan saw him now tilt his first gin and tonic so far back that the lemon slice hit his moustache. He slid the glass back to Hughie who refilled it. Judge Boucher cracked and rubbed his hands together and said something about how cold it was, then he pulled a piece of paper from his pocket and handed it to Hughie with a wad of money. The judge seemed to be buying for those around him so McGettigan went up close to him.

'How're ye, Judge?' he said. McGettigan was a good six inches taller than the judge, but round shouldered. The judge turned and looked up at him.

'McGettigan. Keeping out of trouble, eh?' he said.

'Yis, sur. But things is bad at the minute . . . like . . . you know how it is. Now if I had the money for a bed . . .' said McGettigan fingering the stubble of his chin.

'I'll buy you no drink,' snapped the judge. 'That's the cause of your trouble, man. You look dreadful. How long is it since you've eaten?'

'It's not the food your lordship . . .' began McGettigan but he was interrupted by the judge ordering him a meat pie. He took it with mumbled thanks and went back to his seat once again.

'Happy Christmas,' shouted the judge across the bar.

Just then Strannix came in behind the bar. He was a huge muscular man and had his sleeves rolled up to his biceps. He talked in a loud Southern brogue. When he spied McGettigan he leaned over the bar hissing, 'Ya skinny big hairpin. I thought I told you if ever I caught you . . .'

'Mr Strannix,' called the judge from the other end of the counter. Strannix's face changed from venom to smile as he walked the duck-boards to where the judge stood.

'Yes Judge what can I do for you?' he said. The judge had now become the professional.

'Let him be,' he said. 'Good will to all men and all that.' He laughed loudly and winked in McGettigan's direction. Strannix filled the judge's glass again and stood with a fixed smile waiting for the money.

At four o'clock the judge's car arrived for him and after much handshaking and backslapping he left. McGettigan knew his time had come. Strannix scowled over at him and with a vicious gesture of his big thumb, ordered him out.

'Hughie has a parcel for me,' said McGettigan defiantly, 'and it's paid for,' he added before Strannix could ask. Strannix grabbed the paper bag, then came round the counter and shoved it into McGettigan's arms and guided him firmly out the door. As the door closed McGettigan shouted, 'I hope this Christmas is your last.'

The door opened again and Strannix stuck his big face out. 'If you don't watch yourself I'll be round for the rent,' he snarled.

McGettigan spat on the pavement loud enough for Strannix to hear.

It was beginning to rain and the dark sky seemed to bring on the night more quickly. McGettigan clutched his carry-out in the crook of his arm, his exposed hand getting cold. Then he sensed something odd about the shape in the bag. There was a triangular shape in there. Not a shape he knew.

He stopped at the next street light and opened the bag. There was a bottle of whiskey, triangular in section. There was also a bottle of vodka, two bottles of gin, a bottle of brandy and what looked like some tonic.

He began to run as fast as he could. He was in bad shape, his breath rasped in his throat, his boots were filled with lead, his heart moved up and thumped in his head. As he ran he said a frantic prayer that they wouldn't catch him.

Once inside his room he set his parcel gently on the sofa, snibbed the door and lay against it panting and heaving. When he got his breath back he hunted the yard, in the last remaining daylight, for some nails he knew were in a tin. Then he hammered them through the door into the jamb with wild swings of a hatchet. Then he pushed the sofa against the door and looked around the room. There was nothing else that could be moved. He sat down on the floor against the wall at the window and lined the bottles in front of him. Taking them out they tinkled like full bells. In silence he waited for Strannix.

Within minutes he came, he and Judge Boucher stamping into the hallway. They battered on the door, shouting his name. Strannix shouted, 'McGettigan. We know you're in there. If you don't come out I'll kill you.'

The judge's voice tried to reason. 'I bought you a meat pie, McGettigan.' He sounded genuinely hurt.

But his voice was drowned by Strannix.

'McGettigan, I know you can hear me. If you don't hand back that parcel I'll get you evicted.' There was silence. Low voices conferred outside the door. Then Strannix shouted again. 'Evicted means put out, you stupid hairpin.'

Then after some more shouting and pummelling on the door they went away, their mumbles and footsteps fading gradually.

McGettigan laughed as he hadn't laughed for years, his head thrown back against the wall. He played eeny-meeny-miney-mo with the bottles in front of him – and the whiskey won. The click of the metal seal breaking he thought much nicer than the pop of a cork. He teased himself by not drinking immediately but got up and, to celebrate, put a shilling in the meter to light the gas fire. Its white clay sections were broken and had all fallen to the bottom. The fire banged loudly for it had not been lit for such a long time, making him jump back and laugh. Then McGettigan pulled the sofa up to the fire and kicked off his boots. His toes showed white through the holes in his socks and the steam began to rise from his feet. A rectangle of light fell on the floor from the streetlamp outside the uncurtained window. The whiskey was red and gold in the light from the gas fire.

He put the bottle to his head and drank. The heat from inside him met the warmth of his feet and they joined in comfort. Again and again he put the bottle to his head and each time he lowered it he listened to the music of the back-slop. Soon the window became a bright diamond and he wondered if it was silver rain drifting in the halo of the lamp or if it was snow for Christmas. Choirs of boy sopranos sang carols and McGettigan, humming, conducted slowly with his free hand and the room bloomed in the darkness of December.

CARLO GÉBLER

Christmas

I

Marie stared at the face in the mirror. Her right front tooth over-lapped the left. At school the other girls had called her 'Rabbit Face'.

Marie was not beautiful, she was pretty, and the best feature was her mouth, with the intriguing freckle which was half-on, half-off her upper lip. When she had her lipstick on, as she had now, the top half of the brown disc stuck up over the red line. It was like the sun rising out of the sea.

She opened her mouth, smiled, and tried to imagine her teeth if they were straight. Her mother could have had them fixed – like her older sister's – only she hadn't. Marie's were just wonky, whereas Rosemary's were proper buck teeth. They stuck so far out over her bottom lip, Rosemary had been able to fit her thumb in the space behind.

Then, about the time Marie was five, and Rosemary was ten, their mother, Angelica, took her sister up to a specialist in the

Royal Victoria Hospital. He provided a brace for Rosemary to wear at night. It was a thing of stainless steel hoops and black rubber bands which fitted over the teeth and attached behind her sister's head.

'It tastes of yuck,' Rosemary had screamed, a few minutes after she had been put to bed with the contraption in place for the first time.

Marie was in the bed with her.

'I'm going to take it off,' Rosemary had roared, 'I can't sleep.'

'Don't,' Marie whispered to her older sister, 'she'll hit us both if you go on, you know she will.'

Angelica was pretty free with her hand; when one sister was hit, the other invariably caught a whack or two.

And now Marie heard the sound of mother's feet, racing up the stairs of their house. Angelica was on the war-path.

'You'll be beautiful one day,' Angelica shouted ahead, 'that's why we are making sacrifices now!'

The bedroom door flew open. Mother appeared in the doorway, her bouffant hair like piled candy floss, her mouth a little round 'O' out of which she fired her words.

'I don't want to hear another word out of you. Do you understand?' Angelica hissed at her two daughters, who by now were rigid with fear in the bed. 'Not one word. Now get to sleep, the two of yous.'

Months passed. The brace reined in Rosemary's upper teeth. Her lower jaw came forward. Rosemary's face lengthened and evened up.

Three years on, Rosemary turned fifteen, and Marie saw that what mother had shouted up the stairs had come to pass. Now that her sister's teeth were straight, Rosemary's physical qualities – always there but hidden before – were suddenly visible; the lovely hair and the clear blue eyes, even the tapering fingers with the tapering fingernails. At weekends, Rosemary was allowed to coat these with red varnish, and when the family watched television, her mother liked to sit with Rosemary on the sofa and to stroke her sister's hands. Sometimes, Angelica whispered, 'You have the hands of a pianist.'

When Rosemary was eighteen, she met Terry at a disco. Terry was a builder by day, a bouncer by night. Terry lived in Andytown. Terry's parents owned their own house. Terry was a catch. After four months of courting, Terry took Rosemary into Belfast, to a jeweller's in Queen's Arcade. The engagement ring he bought that afternoon was a sapphire set with two emeralds.

When Rosemary came home wearing the ring, Angelica cried, and even her father's eyes, Marie noticed, moistened at the sight of it.

It was a Saturday afternoon, about five o'clock. The television was on. Marie's father had been watching the football results which were being read aloud by a lugubrious sports commentator.

'Motherwell 1. Hibernian 2. Kilmarnock 3. Rangers . . .'

In deference to the occasion, her father turned down the volume. Angelica and Rosemary sat beside him on the sofa. Mother and daughter began laughing and crying together; meanwhile, her father waited patiently, secretly hoping they would go into the kitchen. Every now and again, he would glance at the silent television set, at the names of the football teams with the scores at the end of each line.

Marie was on one of the armchairs, looking across at them, and she saw that everything about Rosemary that afternoon was lovely. The long straw-coloured hair bunched into a perfect pony tail with a black velvet band. The way her sister's skirt cinched at the waist. Her long legs with their shiny knees and shiny calves, encased in her shiny tights.

Because she was favoured, Rosemary's potential had been spotted by her mother. Rosemary had been made beautiful. Now, because she was beautiful, Rosemary had found a husband.

Marie was happy for her sister, but sad for herself. Rosemary's good fortune was not to be her destiny. Her teeth were crooked, but not enough to warrant fixing. She had nice hair but it was black not blonde. There was a strange freckle on her lip. Builders from Andytown were not a prospect. Ditto sapphire and emerald engagement rings. The beautiful enjoyed good fortune. The fate of the non-beautiful was something else. It was not going to be bad luck, but it was not to be good luck either.

Marie was only thirteen, yet she knew this as she looked across at mother, Rosemary and her father. The understanding brought a lump to her throat. There was a danger she might cry. She turned sideways.

There was a fish tank on a shelf beside the television. Marie pretended to be looking at it. Then she found that she actually was looking at it.

What intrigued her was a blue fish with black stripes. The fish had put itself in the way of the bubbles which were streaming up from below. As they rushed up, they touched the scaly belly of the fish. A few tears rose in Marie's eyes. She blinked them away. She wondered if the bubbles were giving the fish pleasure.

II

When she was eighteen, Marie left school. She had three 'GCSEs' and an E in English 'A' level. She went to Leicester. Her mother had a sister there.

Auntie Carmel was married to Ron. Carmel had met Ron at the bottom of Broadway in 1974. Ron was a British soldier in the Staffordshire Regiment and he was manning a checkpoint. Carmel had followed Ron to Leicester, and married him there.

Since then, Carmel returned to Belfast rarely, and never brought her husband home.

Carmel and Ron had two sons, both now away at University. Marie was given the older boy's room. There were several pictures of Eric Cantona pinned up on the walls.

Marie found a job in a shoe factory. Her job was to stamp the brass eyes into the uppers of shoes with an hydraulic press.

After she had been in Leicester six months, one of the factory girls got engaged. At the party to celebrate, Marie met Paul, a Greek-Cypriot.

Paul's eyes were darker than hers. His hair was blacker. His teeth were whiter. Marie married Paul. After the birth of their first child – they named him Justin – Marie went off sex. After two years of celibacy, Paul became exasperated. He went back to Nicosia and the marriage ended.

Marie came home. The Housing Executive put her in a new development in the west of the city. The Executive said the houses on the estate were the best houses built that year anywhere in the United Kingdom. Marie did not dispute this.

The fire drew beautifully. There was hot water all day. There was not a patch of damp. The windows did not rattle when the wind blew. The difficulties began when she stepped outside her front door.

The trees which had been planted along the street had all been snapped in half by young delinquents.

In one of the houses opposite, there were all night drinking parties. The revellers would vomit in her front garden, and worse. Marie had to keep tongs and a spade in a bucket of disinfected water beside her front door all the time. She used these to pick up the turds.

Then, there was the matter of the wind. It always seemed to be blowing in this raw new place, as it never seemed to blow anywhere else in Belfast. It blew very hard, all day, every day, and it always bore a cargo of grit, it seemed.

She and Justin could not venture out without it stinging into their faces. She knew better than to rub her eyes, but her son couldn't stop himself. Of course, this only made the problem worse. Then, he would cry. By the time they got home, his eyes would be bloodshot. She would bathe his eyes with *Optrex* and Justin would scream . . .

However, in the scale of things which could go wrong, the grit was only a small difficulty, and of course Marie recognised this. For instance, she could have been one of the girls who lurked in the burnt-out petrol station, drank *Special Brew*, and tore around with their men in stolen cars. Marie had to pass this petrol station where the joyriders hung about every day, when she made her way through the wind, to and from the shops. It consisted of a filthy, bare concrete forecourt, a row of charred lock-up garages, and two rusting stumps. These had once been the pumps. Marie loathed the place, her superstitious fears focusing on her son.

In ten or twelve years time, she imagined, he might become one of them. He might start stealing cars and racing them around the streets. It would end unhappily because, eventually, they would take him up an entry and punish him, as they had always done, ceasefire or no ceasefire, and she knew about punishment. It was why she had left . . .

The night of her eighteenth birthday – it was the late nineteen eighties, the Troubles were still going – she had been in a bar, celebrating, when two men dressed in boiler suits and balaclavas had come in. It took them less than a minute to find the one they were looking for. He was eighteen, with a little moustache, a thin body, and he wore a back-to-front baseball hat with 'No Problem' on the front. He seemed not unsurprised when the men appeared, and he let them lead him away without complaining.

The bar fell quiet. She heard the shots outside. Everyone heard the shots, and that way everybody knew, the youth with the baseball hat had been done.

Then everyone went out to look and Marie went too. He had got one in each knee. He was bleeding. Someone brought out a couple of towels from the bar with *Guinness* printed on them. These were used to staunch the blood. A barman went to telephone for an ambulance and the youth screamed as he lay on the ground, 'My mother' – he sounded like a little boy to Marie – 'I want her, my mother . . .'

Marie saw his red blood seep through the brown *Guinness* beer towels. She went down the entry and out into the street. She was sick in the gutter. She had been drinking crème de menthe and cider all that evening and her sick was green. Two months later, she sat her 'A' levels, then left the north . . .

And now, every time she passed the burnt-out petrol station, the memory of this evening was always vaguely in her mind. It wasn't that she was actually thinking about it. It was just with her, like a stone in her shoe, pressing against her foot.

In fact, the memory was so compelling, even if there were no thin-bodied moustachioed men in trainers standing around a fire drinking *Special Brew*, even if the forecourt was completely deserted, except for a rook pecking at a styrofoam cup, Marie would always push Justin in his buggy across the road, just in order to put as much space between that place and themselves as possible.

Marie did not like this life she had come back to in Belfast, even after the ceasefires which followed her return. Sometimes she even hated it.

III

Marie stared at the face in the mirror. Her right front tooth over-lapped the left. At school the other girls had called her 'Rabbit Face'.

The hair which framed her face was hennaed black.

She pursed her lips. There was a little spot of lipstick on the end of the right tooth where it overlapped the left. She rubbed it away with the tip of her tongue.

She went downstairs to the sitting room. The Christmas tree was in the front window. Justin was playing on the floor. Early that morning he had been excited when they had opened the presents. What happened then had puzzled her, but at the same time, she had not been surprised. Justin had abandoned his presents – the walking-talking robot, the garage with a car lift, the box of Duplo bricks – and returned to his favourite toy. This was a white plastic car made by Fisher-Price. There were four round holes inside the seats into which four round figures fitted. The figures had the faces of clowns and wore clown hats. Oh yes, she thought, precisely the sort of toy a future joyrider would favour. The car was a present from Justin's father.

Marie went to the kitchen and poured out a small tumbler of Bailey's Irish Cream. Normally, there was never drink in the house, but she made an exception for Christmas. She looked at the kitchen clock. It was two o'clock. Where was her father?

She carried the glass back into the front room and sat down. She took a drink. She saw her lipstick left a smudge on the rim of the glass. She would have to put more lipstick on. Two thoughts now began to war in her mind. One, she wished she had got some brandy in. She would have liked to have offered father a drink, and brandy was his favourite. Two, she was angry. Why hadn't he collected her by now? It was past two o'clock, and when she had spoken with her mother very early that morning, Angelica had said, 'Your father'll be up to you, twelve midday, latest.'

When one o'clock came and there was no sign of him, Marie had rung home again, and her mother had said, 'He's just going out the door. We've been a bit held up.'

Now it was after two and it didn't take an hour to drive the three or so miles from her parents' house to hers. No, it did not.

Marie took another sip of *Bailey's* and looked across at her son. He had piled up some of the needles which had fallen from the Christmas tree, and he was driving his car through them. The needles were soft and the wheels left their imprint on them.

When she was a child, Marie thought her father was amazing. He drank but he was never drunk – never. He never quarrelled with his wife, Angelica, and he was always back from the car plant where he worked at the time he said he was coming back. Always.

With all the other families who lived around them when she was growing up, it was different. All the men drank, and all the couples quarrelled. Husbands and wives would often shout at each other in the street; on rare occasions, they would even fight out there. And when husbands got roaring drunk, their wives would lock them out. The husbands would spend the night wandering up and down the Andersonstown Road or the Falls, until their wives had cooled down and would let them back into their homes again . . .

Marie took another sip. No, she thought, her father was never late, other than when mother made him late. And this Christmas afternoon, she knew that her mother was making him late.

Marie took yet another drink. She wasn't certain what made her angrier? Was it mother's overbearing, domineering manner? Or was it the way Angelica had made her father into a man who always let her have her way, never stood up to her, never contradicted her?

The door bell chimed. Then there was a friendly little rap on the wood.

Marie opened the front door. Father was standing on the step. He was wearing his grey suit, a white shirt and a new tie, green with red stripes. He smelt of after-shave. Mother would have given him after-shave for Christmas. So would Rosemary. And probably the same brand – if Marie knew Rosemary and her mother – a brand father wasn't allergic to.

'Your father's skin is very sensitive.' This was one of mother's key phrases. She said it at least once a day. At the same time she would coo and gently pet his sensitive face. This was mother's way of paying court to the man to whom she never listened.

'Come in, come in,' Marie said.

She pulled her father through the door and into her hall. She kissed him.

'I'm sorry, I'm late,' he apologised.

Her father's front right tooth, like hers, overlapped the left. He whistled when he spoke. He might follow Angelica's orders, but secretly, Marie had always believed, he was on her side. In all the years she had known him, he had never once shouted at her, or corrected her in public. Now he smiled at her, and her anger evaporated.

'I got entangled with Rosemary and the kids and Terry,' father explained.

Marie knew this was a fib yet she heard herself saying, 'It doesn't matter. I'll get my coat.'

But instead of going to the back of the hall to get her coat, she went into the living room. Her father followed behind. It was as if they wanted to stay there, together, and not rush away.

Justin had heard his grandfather coming in. He was sitting looking down at the ground with a shy expression on his face.

As the adults came towards him, he slowly rotated on the linoleum floor until he was facing the wall.

'Come on Justin, say hello, it's grandad.'

Justin dropped his head forward until his chin rested on his chest.

'You're a shy boy today,' her father whistled gently. 'You can't be a shy boy on Christmas Day.'

'He'll be all right once we get to the house,' she said, and then she added, 'I expect.'

IV

She re-did her lipstick and found her coat. Then the three of them went out to the car. Her father had put one of Rosemary's child seats in the back. He was thoughtful like that.

They set off. The streets of west Belfast were empty, just one row of low houses after another, crouched under a low grey sky. The only points of colour were the fairy lights on Christmas trees glimmering behind the net curtains of parlour windows. Marie was glad she had left her own lights on at home, making their own small contribution towards lessening the gloom.

The McAlister family house was detached. It was not far from the motorway and Dunmurry where her father worked. It was a private house, not a Housing Executive house; her father had made his first down payment in 1969; twenty-five years on and it was his.

The front door was on the latch. They went through. Inside the hall all the coats were thrown higgledy-piggledy into the huge Silver Cross pram. This had been Marie and Rosemary's pram when they were babies, and now her mother kept the pram for her daughters to wheel around the grandchildren when they visited. Except they always had their buggies, and so they never did.

Marie put her head around the door into the living room. Her father's younger, bachelor brother, Uncle Patrick, was there, along with Terry. They were drinking beer and watching *Back to the Future 2*. Rosemary's twins were on the floor, staring at the screen.

Her father led Justin towards the Christmas tree – as in her house it was in the front window – and Marie slipped out of the room and down to the kitchen. She found her mother kneeling in front of the oven. She was basting a turkey which was lying in the old black roasting pan, the one Angelica said imparted a special quality to whatever was cooked in it. She always used it at Christmas.

'Hello,' said mother. 'Happy Christmas.' She stood and closed the oven door with a bang.

Mother was wearing a white fluffy mohair sweater with sequins sewn into it, and an apron over the top.

'What kept you?' asked her mother.

The picture on the apron showed a fat man drinking beer, while the wife, trussed in short skirt and suspenders, was bent over a sink of dishes.

'What kept me! Nothing kept me. I was waiting for dad. What kept him?'

'Oh, sorry you had to wait! We were only cooking for twelve.'

Angelica puffed her chest forward and pointed at the legend below the picture: *The only one who does any work in the house is the poor woman who has to wear this.*

'Your good sister's present,' said her mother, and she pointed at Rosemary, who at that moment was slipping the trifle into the refrigerator.

'Happy Christmas,' Marie called to her sister, and that was when she heard a voice say, 'Hey! Don't forget about me!'

It was Veronica, hidden in the armchair behind the door.

Veronica had looked after Marie and Rosemary when they were children. This made her an Honorary Grandmother. She always came at Christmas.

'Happy Xmas,' said Veronica standing.

Veronica wore a worsted suit with what looked like a dog collar. Somehow, Veronica always managed to look like a priest, and to sound like one as well.

As Veronica's thin arms folded around her shoulders, Marie heard her mother saying, 'I cannot tell you how tired I am! I doubt I'd have managed without my two redoubtable helpers here.'

Marie felt her face reddening. Only two minutes in the house, and already her mother was complaining that she hadn't helped.

'So what'll you have?' mother was asking now, slurring like a drunk, her standard act when she offered anyone drink. 'G&T? Bush on the rocks? What's your Christmas tipple?'

'Ah, Angelica,' tittered Veronica. A fellow Pioneer, she loved this performance.

'Sherry, Budweiser . . . hic!'

The annoyance which Marie felt at the pose, and the bad temper she already felt because she was the last to have been collected, were now two streams inside her, rushing together to make something bigger.

'You know, I was waiting at least two hours for dad to lift me,' she said. 'I've been up since seven. I don't have a car, and taxis on Christmas Day, as you may have noticed, are not exactly cheap or plentiful.'

'Oh boy,' said Angelica, this time in her appalling John Wayne drawl, 'you sound as though you really could do with a drink. And a double, I should say.'

'Just a glass of wine, please,' said Marie.

V

Her father and Terry carried the table through from the living room and set it up in the kitchen. Marie fetched the table cloth from the hot press upstairs. It was still wrapped in the paper in which it had come back from the laundry. When Marie unfolded the cloth and spread it across the table, the kitchen was filled for a moment with the wonderful smell of starched linen.

Marie set out the place mats, the good ones with the pictures of Ben Nevis, Edinburgh New Town and Balmoral, and Rosemary fetched the canteen with the good, heavy cutlery. Rosemary and Marie had given the canteen to their parents on their twenty-fifth wedding anniversary. Rosemary was richer and had borne the bulk of the cost.

The sisters set the knives and forks and spoons around the place mats. Then they fetched the good china and the Waterford glass from the cabinet in the front room. Rosemary filled the cruets with salt and pepper. Marie mixed mustard up in an egg-cup, then decanted it into the little blue mustard dish which was part of the salt and pepper set.

As she worked, Marie found herself hoping that by immersing herself in the physical, the intense annoyance that smouldered inside like a hot coal, would simply die, go out.

It was not a theory – this had happened to her before in situations like this – but unfortunately, this time, when the table was finished, she found the anger was still burning inside her.

'Can I do anything else?' she called across.

Her mother was pouring boiling water out of the kettle into the saucepan of Brussels sprouts.

'What else can I do?' she repeated, and then Marie drained her glass.

There were wreaths of steam rising around Angelica's face and her high piled hair. For a moment, it looked to Marie as if her mother was on fire.

'Can you clear the ashtrays and empty the beer cans from the front room? It's probably a pigsty by now.'

Marie decided to fetch the ashtrays first. They were heavy, made of cut glass, and they were crammed with butts.

She carried them back to the pedal bin in the kitchen. She lifted the lid with the foot pedal, and was about to tip the butts away, when she saw the greasy cellophane that smelt of fish, in which a whole smoked salmon had come wrapped.

'Are we having smoked salmon?' she called over to her mother.

She tipped the ashtrays. The debris tumbled in, some of the grey ash sticking to the cellophane and forming a coating on it, like city snow.

'No,' her mother replied blithely.

'Oh.'

'I'm afraid we had that earlier. When Rosemary and Terry came. The kids were so hungry, they practically devoured the wrapping.'

Marie re-filled her wine glass, and the little voice inside her head said, You don't need another drink! It won't help things.

She ignored the voice and carried the drink through to the front room. She sat down on the sofa beside her brother-in-law.

'Terry.'

'Marie,' he acknowledged her.

On the television, the hero of Back to the Future 2 was at a dance in the open air, somewhere in the American mid-west, sometime in the middle of the last century.

'Are you hungry?' she said.

'Starving,' said Terry. 'The smell of that turkey and bacon is practically driving me up the walls.'

'It's been a long day,' said Marie, innocently.

'You're telling me. I've been here practically all day.'

Terry used 'practically' a lot, but even for him, twice in a row was excessive.

'I've had five wee cans of Tennents,' he continued, 'which I don't really like, and my head's swimming.'

'Did you have nothing else at all?'

'We had smoked salmon,' he said, and then he quickly added, 'Did we leave you any?'

'No.'

Terry looked over at the television and Marie looked as well. On the screen she saw there was a car flying through the air. Marie recognised it as a De Lorean.

'When did you get here?' she asked.

'When? I don't know. It must have been . . . What time did I get here, Pat?' he called over to her uncle.

Pat was on the floor assembling a Brio wooden train set. The twins were beside Pat. They were each sucking on a little wooden Brio man.

'I can't remember. I was here with Veronica a bit before you. Was that ten, ten-thirty?' Pat shouted back.

'So you came, you had smoked salmon and what?' Marie asked lightly.

'Scrambled egg. Coffee,' continued Terry. 'Since then, that's it. The day's vanished like a puff of smoke. Disappeared into thin air.'

Her glass was empty. She excused herself and went out into the hall. She found Justin on the stairs. He was clutching a teddy bear and a Coke bottle with a straw in it.

'Granny gave me a Coke,' he explained, pointing to the kitchen from where he had just come.

'And where are you going now?'

Her son sucked on the green straw sticking out of the bottle.

There was a faint bubbling sound. Marie could hear the older children squealing in the playroom upstairs.

'I'm going to see them,' said Justin.

He stared at her. He was dark skinned, with olive black eyes. There was no other child like him in Belfast, at least that she knew of. Sometimes, in the street, strangers would stop and stare at him. On rare occasions, strangers would even come over and say, 'Such a child. I've never seen a child with that colouring.'

And it was true; no child was like Justin.

Marie put her glass down on the table beside the telephone, and climbed up the stairs. She sat down, pulling her skirt over her knees, and then lifted Justin onto her lap.

'I love you,' she said, and buried her face in his neck. He smelt of himself, and shampoo, but mostly he smelt of Coca-Cola.

'I love you,' Marie said. 'Do you love me?'

He twisted playfully on her lap as he tried to escape from her. 'Don't tickle me,' he cried, by which he meant the exact opposite. 'Don't tickle me.'

'I'm going to blow on your tummy.'

'No, no, no,' he laughed, 'and I promise, I promise to be good.'

She set him back on the stairs.

'Now be good when you get up to the big children,' she said.

Justin continued to climb, clutching his teddy bear and his bottle. Marie went back down to the hall, found her glass and went into the kitchen.

She found her mother there alone. Rosemary and Veronica, she guessed, were upstairs with her father and Justin and the older children in the playroom. Marie poured herself a third glass of wine.

'You didn't tell me you were all having breakfast.'

'I'm amazed you and Rosemary didn't see how dusty the glasses were when you brought them down from the front room?' her mother replied briskly.

Angelica had washed them all, and the wet glasses were arranged upside-down on the draining board.

'They weren't fit to be used in the state they were in.'

Mother might be getting her retaliation in first, Marie thought, but she wasn't going to let herself be deterred.

'Why wasn't I invited for breakfast?'

'Sometimes,' said Angelica, 'I wonder if you two girls have eyes in your heads at all. The glasses were filthy.'

'You haven't answered my question.'

Her mother slipped past and put a dry glass at the head of the table, where her father sat.

'I don't understand you,' Marie heard herself continuing. 'I am up at home. You are all down here. Why didn't you send dad to come and get me?'

Mother went back to the sink, picked up a second glass and began to dry it.

'You might think, Marie, that the whole world revolves around you,' she said, 'but I'm sorry, it doesn't.'

The next glass squeaked as Angelica wiped it fiercely with the cloth.

'You had everyone up for smoked salmon,' said Marie, 'while I was left sitting at home.'

'Look, you don't like being *alone*,' said Angelica forcefully, 'it's down to you to do something about it. It's not for any of us.'

'What!'

'Pick up the phone, Marie. Get a taxi. Ask a friend to lift you.'

'Mother. Christmas Day. No taxis. Friends busy. With families. Marie at home awaits collection. But all McAlister family here.'

'You're being ridiculous,' said Angelica, and she glared furiously at her daughter.

'I would have liked to have been asked.'

'If you can't be *alone*, that's your problem,' hissed her mother, 'and lower your voice, please, it's Christmas Day.'

There was that 'alone' word again. It was Angelica's code for separated, of course, and in time, inevitably, it would become code for divorced.

A couple of weeks before Christmas, she remembered, her mother had asked about her plans for the future, and Marie had said it was her and Paul's intention to formalise their separation with a divorce. Mother had received the news silently, since when the subject had never been mentioned, or even alluded to until now. But that was it, wasn't it? That was the seed from which all this had come. Angelica couldn't countenance her divorcing. Catholics did not do that.

'What is it?' Marie heard herself saying, the level of her voice rising but what the hell. 'What is it about me? Why is it that I don't get the same treatment as everyone else in this family? Why for Rosemary, one set of rules, and breakfast and smoked salmon, and for me, another?'

'It's been fair play in this house,' said her mother grimly, 'from the moment you were born, to the moment you walked out that door, went to Leicester and embarked on your life. Since when . . .' and at that Angelica suddenly closed her mouth.

'Since when?' Marie shouted. 'Since when? Go on.' She was as much delighted as she was angry by her mother's slip. 'Yes. Since when, what?'

'I don't want to have an argument with you. It's Christmas Day,' her mother cut Marie short.

'Since when – what?'

'Since when,' said her mother, 'you've made your bed, and a

fine frigging mess you've made of it too. Now, you learn to lie in it, my girl. It's hard, I know, to be alone. I'm sorry for you, but there's nothing I can do about it.'

Her mother picked up another glass and began to dry it furiously.

Marie took a huge gulp of wine. To hell with abstinence and caution. And her mother was right, damn her. She was somewhat to blame for what happened. And now her husband was seeing another woman who was giving him what Marie had not.

Of course, Paul hadn't told her this directly, but she knew him that well, she could tell just from the way he said 'Hello,' and 'Goodbye' to her when he rang on Saturday nights to speak to Justin, and again when he had rung that very Christmas morning, she could tell he was seeing another woman . . .

But, she told herself, that was not what they were discussing, she and mother, and as a matter of fact they never would. Nor would they ever discuss the way she had felt quite revolted by her husband after Justin's birth, and had never been able to shake off that feeling of disgust, and was now sorry about that, very sorry, in fact was disgusted with herself.

Marie's mind was racing. Wine had that effect. Focus! she commanded herself. She took another drink.

'Has it ever occurred to you,' shouted Marie, 'that when you chose not to have me up for breakfast, it's not just me you're punishing – because I'm not like Rosemary, with a husband and a house and four children, and doubtless a fifth and a sixth on the way – you are also punishing a three-year-old boy!

'Justin didn't have anything to do with what went wrong. Justin is an innocent. He needs to be loved as much as Sinead and Michael upstairs and the twins down there in the front room, but you don't love him like them because what I've done is wrong according to what you believe, and what the

Church says. You love Justin less than them because I'm going to be divorced.'

Her mother's face had been darkening and shrinking as Marie spoke and now, as she finished, Marie braced herself.

'How dare you,' she heard her mother shouting back at her, 'how dare you say that! How dare you say I feel any less for one child than another. I've spent as much on his Christmas present, as I have on the other children's. I've changed his nappy, just like the other children. I cuddle him, just like the other children. You are a stupid, ridiculous, spoilt little girl.'

Marie heard the door open, which she guessed was her father coming in. She turned and she saw that indeed it was him. He had heard their voices in the playroom upstairs. Now he was coming to make the peace.

Marie turned back to Angelica. A Waterford cut glass was in her mother's hand. Her mother turned the glass against the cloth angrily. The glass shrieked and then exploded. A glass fragment scored across her mother's palm. It cut her from one corner right across to the other. A huge spurt of blood sprang out from the huge slit, and plopped down onto the linoleum floor.

'Look! what you've made me do with your stupid rowing,' her mother shouted, and Marie knew she had lost the argument. 'You've made me break one of my best Waterford glasses.'

Her father rushed her mother to the sink. He turned on the cold tap and he thrust Angelica's hand into the streaming water.

'That was one of a set they don't make any more. I won't get a replacement, you know.'

'I'm sorry,' Marie heard herself saying, 'I'm very sorry about your glass.'

'Not now,' said her father, with what, for him, was uncommon brusqueness. 'It's Christmas. Let your mother be.'

In the twenty-three years she had known him, this was the closest her father had ever come to rebuking her. The failure to invite her to breakfast might have been negligent, but this humiliation was crushing. Marie felt a pain in her Adam's apple.

'I'm going upstairs,' she said.

She went into the bathroom, not the toilet, and locked the door. She sat down on the edge of the bath. It was green, the colour of avocado. The room smelt of *Radox* and the *Cussons Imperial Leather* soap which mother favoured. It was the only soap to which her father was not allergic, or so Angelica claimed.

Marie felt something breaking inside her, and she let out a great rasping cry. Her tears followed, hot and salty.

A few minutes later she heard her Uncle Pat calling, 'Dinner. Come on everybody. Come and get it.'

She opened the door and called down, 'Just fixing my face.'

She waited until everyone had trooped through to the kitchen, then crept downstairs to her coat in the hall, retrieved her make-up bag from the pocket, and went back upstairs again to the bathroom.

VI

The turkey was on a platter on the breakfast counter and her father was using the electric carver to cut off thin slices of white meat.

Marie stood and watched while her mother scooted around the table, a white tea towel tied ostentatiously around her cut hand. Her mother was setting the crackers out. Angelica had two types of crackers. She had green and very solid-looking crackers from *Marks and Spencer*, and she had cheapos made of flimsy red crepe which she had bought in Royal Avenue, from a street vendor, one Saturday afternoon.

'Don't you think I'm marvellous to have the two types of cracker?' mother exclaimed as she flew past Marie. Angelica was blithe and cheerful as if nothing had happened, and before Marie could answer, her mother continued. 'The red ones will have keys and pens and rubbish which will keep the kids happy, and for us grown-ups, something with a little style. Thank you M and S.' She waved the green cracker she was holding before she plonked it down.

The huge picture window at the back of the kitchen was covered with condensation. Marie saw that someone had drawn a Christmas tree in the wet with a finger, and that darkness had fallen outside. She was holding yet another glass of wine, and now she took a drink. The wine was bitter. She could remember that she had taken a glass before they set the table, then a second and then a third, but after that she lost count.

Marie sat where she was told to sit. She ate the plate of food which was put in front of her. She pulled the crackers that were offered to her. She laughed at the jokes that came out of the crackers, when the older children read them out. She drank her wine, and held the glass out for more when it was empty . . .

Gradually, as late afternoon wore into evening, her hurt and anger became a pliant, fuzzy feeling. She had been slighted over the breakfast, she had been rebuked by her father, but none of this was going to trouble her any more. At least not for the rest of the day. The wine made sure of that.

When the plates were cleared away, and the children had gone off to play, Veronica told her story. She told it faithfully every Christmas Day. She was a stern and modest woman but on Christmas Day she couldn't stop herself rehearsing what she regarded as one of the finest moments, perhaps the finest moment in her otherwise loveless and miserable life.

One afternoon, sometime during the early seventies, two men had run into her house. They were carrying a bomb.

Veronica led them to her coal shed, made them lie down, and covered them over with coal.

Moments later, the soldiers who were in hot pursuit of the bombers were running all over Veronica's house.

'They're not here, whoever you're looking for,' she told the English Captain haughtily, 'and now kindly get out and let me get on with my baking.' She gestured at the flour and baking utensils which she had strewn, as a ploy, on the kitchen table. The soldiers apologised and left.

Five minutes later, two black-faced members of the IRA slunk out of her coal shed, muttered their thanks, and disappeared down to the Lagan. According to local lore, they supposedly threw the bomb into the river.

Everyone laughed at the story. Marie laughed as well. Veronica's tale of military stupidity and native Irish cunning was Christmas as much as the turkey and the crackers; they couldn't have Christmas without it. It was also, Marie recognised, the climax, the last obligation. Christmas Day was over now for her. She was free to go.

Half an hour later, she was in the front of the car, her father was at the wheel, and Justin was asleep in the child's seat in the back.

Everyone came out to the front door to wave her off, and then her father drove away down the street.

The traffic light ahead of them was red. Her father slowed and then halted. There was an army Land Rover parked against the bollard in the middle of the road. That first ceasefire Christmas, there were still soldiers around. As neither Marie nor her father had been speaking – they hadn't spoken properly since her father had reprimanded her – they were both grateful to have something to look at.

The back door of the Land Rover was open, and Marie saw

that there was a loop of silver tinsel hanging down inside the door.

She pointed. Her father nodded. He had seen it too.

There was a soldier on the bench inside and now he ran his finger along the tinsel, much as a child might; and then, suddenly realising he had been seen, he looked back at the pair of them in the car.

The soldier smiled and mouthed the season's greetings.

The traffic lights were turning. Marie raised an arm and waved expansively.

Then she saw that the most extraordinary look of surprise, mingled with alarm, had appeared on her father's face. He was horrified. And her mother, when she heard, would no doubt be horrified. As would Veronica. As would everyone else. You didn't wave at them.

But she had, and now the soldier waved back, his hand curling, his grin wide and surprised.

BRENDAN GRIFFIN

Cold Turkey

He remembers Christmas in the blue flash of walls new white-washed, the cobbling swept clean of dung, the smell of oozing ash logs in the fire. A Christmas Eve dinner of boiled fish and the bitter-sweet spoonful of mulled port. The silence and sad glances in the house when the postman went by at nightfall and brought no parcel from America. The Milky Way and streak of shooting stars when his grandmother led the family to Mass. The prodding and whacking of her cane in the church porch as she cleared a way through night-revellers loitering there. One year, the enamelled bucket on the kitchen floor and his father and uncle kneeling and pushing for their turn to vomit. They had waited until they got home from the village houses before disgorging themselves. That way their manhood – their capacity to hold drink – wouldn't be impeached. The uproar of their heaving off had frightened the children out of their sleep and down to the kitchen to see black torrents cascading from open mouths and lashing the bucket like horsetails. They watched petrified as spasms tore up the men's bodies as if something fearful had to be exorcised. Finally, the yells subsided to a spitting and the men sat white-faced and panting and rubbing water from their eyes. His mother laughed at them and grandmother scolded. 'Not used to it,' Mother said. 'Not able for it.' She was happy that her men weren't like others: inveterates who'd drain a firkin without throwing up. Father and uncle drank tea, then, and told of Christmas in the village. Of news and people they met. Of shops and bars crowded, young men and girls home from Birmingham talking loud and buying drink for all. Of windows all lit up, and sadly, they told of one more house which was, this year, in darkness. He remembers Christmas most vividly in the turkey fair on days of frost and silent mizzle. He remembers the day Christmas was lost; the fair day of his sinning.

A week or so before Christmas, a high-railed lorry from town drew into the shop yard at the cross and all the turkeys in the district were carted there and sold. It was a clamorous day: the trundle of horse and donkey carts on the four roads, the gobbling of turkeys gleaming black, bronze and white. Crimson of caruncle and blue of dewbill. A day like patron day. The school was closed and the wheel-of-fortune man set up his stall under canvas.

'You can pick, choose or select any prize at all you like on the board, on the board: Tickets two pence a piece. Now she's rolling, rolling, rolling on the Yankee bazaar.' He had delph on his board, china dogs and cats, framed pictures and soldiers beating drums. It was a day of first Craven A and first love as the young of the district gathered at the cross for fun and to earn a few shillings packing boxes in the shop. They wrapped cakes, candles and bottles of tawny wine in brown paper and the stronger ones loaded the provisions on the carts and wheeled sacks of bran and flour from the storehouse. They lifted out crates of stout and gallons of paraffin. It was the shop's busiest day; women bought for Christmas when they sold their turkeys and they settled old accounts. Between jobs, a boy and girl might go to the storehouse to pet and kiss against the piled sacks. Some might make bold enough to climb on ledges made where sacks were removed. Always they'd soon be disturbed by someone wheeling in a hand-barrow and they'd scamper, beating the dust of bran and Indian maize from their clothes. Scrapping also passed the time in the yard, playing Jew's harp or blowing a bugle won at the wheel-of-fortune stall; or skating on the sloping yard when there was frost.

He began carting turkeys when he was eleven. With his donkey and boxed cart he transported birds from farmhouses deep in fields and from roadside cottages. A widow or old person mightn't be up to the job of loading, a bachelor might be too shy to be seen at the fair, people with large flocks needed a second cart for transport. Beforehand he'd have found out where he was needed and he had work from first light until dark. And, even though they always complained of poor prices and being cheated in weight, his clients paid him generously for the scratches he suffered at the work. At the end of a day he'd have more than he got on Confirmation day, more than he'd make a whole Autumn picking blackberries and more than his troupe would collect on a long traverse on Wren-day. And he'd meet Lisa at the cross and talk to her while he waited his turn to unload. As he made his rounds, he anticipated the evening when he finished. He'd buy her a few tickets, a chocolate bar in the shop and they'd go into the storehouse and high on the sacks.

Maybe it was because of Lisa and because he wanted to buy her more, that on his third year carting he devised a scheme to swindle the turkeyman. Maybe it was the first prompting of avarice. In the months before, he had set himself trials of risk and danger to steel his nerves. Climbing to the top of the high crane that dredged the river, scaling the wall into Goodman's garden to take plums from trees outside the kitchen window, crossing a field close to Goodman's bull. He knew that all he needed on a turkey day was nerve.

His turn came in the line to the turkey lorry. The handler jumped into his cart, grabbed turkey after turkey, and with dexterous twists of hands and arms tied the legs with yellow twine and interlocked the wings.

Another man on a weighing platform took each bird from the handler and slid the hook of his scales under the twine.

'Whose?' the man weighing called.

'Lily Croom,' the woman standing by answered.

'Lily Croom. Hen thirteen and a half,' the man weighing shouted, and squeezed the turkey into the lorry through a square cut in the side.

'Lily Croom. Hen thirteen and a half,' a third man repeated. He sat on an orange box and wrote in a ledger.

'Heavier than that,' Lily Croom objected. 'Rogue. You didn't let the full weight rest on the scales.'

'Live weight, missus,' chanted the man weighing. 'Top prices paid today. And this little bantam here is well stuffed with spuds. Cock sixteen pounds.'

'Cock sixteen,' the clerk repeated and recorded.

When his cart was emptied of Lily Croom's turkeys, he moved it towards the back of the lorry to make way for the next cart. He waited while Lily Croom went to the clerk, got a chit from him and went to the cab of the lorry where a fourth man – the boss – sat with a satchel of cash. She came, grumbling, back to the young carter, gave him five shillings and wished him a happy Christmas.

Traffic in the yard was one way. Between the side of the storehouse and the roadside wall there was room only for the lorry and one line of carts. All carts leaving had to go through the shopowner's haggard, into one of the fields and from there out a gate to the road. The carter had taken account of this when laying his plan. He had, also, taken Sonny Haley for granted.

Sonny's job on the lorry was to pack the frightened birds into compartments. He had to lift some of them over his head and throw them into higher compartments. His hands and face were streaked with bleeding scratches and he was daubed with filth. Nobody in the district would do such work but Sonny, or bear the stench. At times during the day he might be heard cursing and screaming in the lorry, at other times he'd whistle or trill out some old song. He was a few years older than the carter and had spent a year or two at reformatory school. Even though his father gave him many a good kicking, he mitched and thieved and slept drunk on the side of the road. The turkey fair brought him a day's pay before Christmas.

'Sonny,' the carter called up at the back of the lorry.

Sonny slid open a hatchboard.

'Joseph Dalton, boy,' he whined. 'I'm torn asunder and the shit is piercin' me. They're chock-full of it. Bring me out a pint of wine.'

'Throw me down a few turkeys,' Joseph Dalton said.

'Get me wine,' Sonny said. 'I'm as dry as a Pharaoh.'

'You can have plenty of wine if you throw me down a few birds,' Joseph said.

'How's that, boy?'

'I'll sell 'em and divide with you.'

'Sell 'em to who?'

'To the turkey man.'

'He's only after buying 'em.'

'He'll buy 'em again.'

'Fire my bricks. Are you in earnest? Hi, boy, you'd have me before the judge again.'

'The job is oxo,' Joseph said. 'Throw 'em down quick. I'll say they belong to Chrissie Owens.'

'Chrissie Owens is dead.'

'The turkey man doesn't know that.'

'Frig it, boy,' Sonny said. 'You'll soon be in front of the judge.'

'Make a shape. Throw down a few,' Joseph urged.

'Here so,' Sonny said, lifting the turkeys nearest to him and dropping them into the cart. 'You can rip the cords and unravel the wings yourself.' He dropped six turkeys. By now these ones were stunned to silence. They settled at once in the cart and closed their eyes. 'That'll do you,' Sonny said. 'If you're not baulked and jailed I'll be waiting for my divide when I finish here. And if you attempt any trick-o'-the-loop on me, last of your gruel is ate.'

Joseph walked beside the cart through the haggard and into the field. Instead of turning to the road he guided the donkey down a dirt track towards a copse. He'd have to delay there before again joining the line of carts to the lorry. Time to untie the legs and unfold the wings. Smooth the feathers a bit. Even though the turkeys flapped them when loosened, the wings didn't rest snugly into the sides and he hoped that the handler wouldn't notice this. He rubbed the legs trying to erase the marks of the tying and he thought out answers to explain the birds' dishevelled appearance.

He sucked toffee while the donkey champed grass frosted in the shade. The copse had settled in winter stillness and smoked dun and purple in the depths of briar, hazel and blackthorn. The sun struck on patches and released a fragrance held back from Autumn in mildewed blackberries and wrinkled sloes. Racing thoughts dizzied him as he gazed into the copse. He'd be caught out; the consequences were unthinkable. He was cruel putting the turkeys, in their pitiable state, through a second ordeal. He'd let them loose here. He'd take them back to Sonny. Say there was a hitch. Chrissie Owens was watching him. And the holy time of year that was in it! Grievous matter, perfect knowledge, full consent loomed from his catechism. Confession, contrition, restitution.

In the hot blurring and throbbing of his eyes Rourke stood in front of him. He was the shopowner's farm-hand and he carried a knife from a day's crowning. He grunted, looking at the turkeys and then at Joseph.

'Twill freeze again,' he said, pointing the knife to the glowering sky. 'Crowds at the fair, I suppose.'

'Thronged,' Joseph said and played at fixing his braces on his shoulders.

Rourke laughed, drawing his own conclusion to explain the turkeys' and Joseph's presence at the copse.

'Ah, good man,' he said. 'No matter where or when or how busy you are, always go when it starts to come. That's if you don't want to be plagued with piles or constipation like I am.'

'True,' Joseph said.

'And you're not the first and only man to make it here,' Rourke said. 'Hurted looking craythurs,' he said, pointing to the turkeys. 'Whose are they?'

'Lily Croom's,' Joseph said.

'So. Another Christmas on top of us,' Rourke commented as he trudged away.

Joseph at once turned the donkey round and led it to the road. He didn't know how long he'd been at the copse but he didn't want to stay there any longer. He joined the line at the lorry and waited his turn, trying to block more racing thoughts.

'You made a quick voyage this time,' someone said to him and he nodded.

'Whose?' the man weighing called.

'Chrissie Owens,' Joseph said, his heartbeat choking down his voice and furring it.

'Chrissie Owens. Hen twelve!'

'They look a bit debauched,' the handler said. 'More like old cormorants the way the wings hang. Did you have to chase 'em cross country?'

'Old bat let 'em out this morning,' Joseph said. 'Forgot the day. They flew up trees and on top of the house.'

'Well, their flying days are gone,' the handler said, folding the wings of the next turkey and passing it down to the platform.

'Chrissie Owens. Four cocks, two hens,' the clerk said when the cart was emptied. Joseph stood in front of him, straining his mind to stop himself from running away.

'Seventy eight pounds at tenpence ha'penny. Twenty nine pounds at one and two.' The clerk did his reckoning, sing-song. 'Five pound two and a penny to Chrissie Owens. Say five pound two and trupence.'

He tore out the chit and Joseph took it to the cab to collect.

'Five pound, two and trupence,' the cashier said paying out. 'Now don't go and lose it on the poor woman.'

He felt a heat in the release of tension and a softening of his legs as he folded the pounds over the silver and put them in a pocket separate from his earnings. Something shuddered in him, a dark thing that sullied his day and all of Christmas.

Sonny had been looking out for him through the slats.

'Did you get the money?'

'I did.'

'Pull up here, so, and I'll throw down a few more.'

'No more,' Joseph said wearily.

'Frig it, boy. What's up with you? I want the price of a bike. Pull up quick. They'll be going away soon with the load.'

The lorry had to be emptied twice each fair day. Sonny ate and rested while the turkeys were taken to a compound in town. They'd be left there fasting until it was time to kill them.

'I have to make a long round before dark,' Joseph said.

'Six more! Six more!' Sonny pleaded. 'I account that might make up the price of a bike.'

'You'll have to wait until next year,' Joseph said.

Sonny was about to drop a turkey anyway, when he spotted Rourke up the haggard, preparing the animals' night fodder, throwing turnips and mangolds into the pulper.

'Now 'twill *have* to be next year,' Sonny whinged. 'Give me my divide. I want to get wine.'

'Later on,' Joseph said. 'Too risky now.' He climbed into the cart and went on his last round. But his pleasure was clouded and the sweetest part of fair-day in other years was soured. That was going home and reckoning his earnings. Thinking about what he'd buy. A new razor strop or flashlamp for his father, a glitter brooch for Grandmother's scarf. A gramophone record for his mother – always a record for her. Something rattly or cuddly for baby, new pencils or jotters for his brothers and sisters. He'd thought about what he might buy Liza, about a suitable opportunity and place to give it to her, something to say when giving it. Tonight his mind dwelt only on the press of the turkey-man's money on his groin.

He emptied his pockets in his bedroom and put his dirty clothes in a tub outside the back door.

This year no running to his mother with smiles and proud spreading of his earnings in her lap. To see the wonder on her face and hear her acclaim him and say, 'Poor boy, I suppose it was hard earned.' He washed and dabbed the scratches with iodine and put the money of his crime in a pocket of his clean trousers. He left his earnings on the mantelpiece except for a shilling. This would be for spending at the cross and he put it into a separate pocket.

*   *   *

Cold Turkey

Lisa danced in the shop yard with three other girls. They moved out of pools of darkness on to bars of light thrown through the shop windows. Lisa's sister played a mouth organ and an older boy squeezed a flashing accordion; they practised their Wren-day routine. Old men stood around, leaning on their bicycles, and women, when their shopping was done, complained that it was the worst fair ever and that there was no profit anymore in feeding a few turkeys. They recalled old days of the goose fairs and the long lines of carts stretching back the four roads. And all the young men and women who'd sing and dance there and earthen jars of porter brought from the shop. Soon, they were thinking there would be no fair at all.

Lisa flirted with the accordion player. The wheel-of-fortune man shouted, 'For the last time, before I finish here, conclude and go, get your tickets and I'll roll her, roll her on the Yankee bazaar!'

Joseph spent his shilling on tickets and gave them to Liza. She smiled and nodded towards the storehouse where a lamp had been lighted.

'By and by, maybe,' she whispered and joined the dance again.

In the shadows close to the shop wall, Sonny, still bloodied and stinking, grabbed him by the throat.

'I'll paste you, sowdog! Where's my divide? You squandered it all on women, did you?'

'I have it here for you,' Joseph said, putting a hand in his pocket.

'How much?'

'Your fair half.' He gave all the money to Sonny, feeling he had got rid of something repulsive.

'No tricking, boy,' Sonny threatened. 'How much?'

'It might buy the bike,' Joseph said.

Sonny let go his throat and moved into the light to look at the money.

'Pounds! A fist full of pounds,' he yelled. 'And to think that the bugger of a turkey-man only gave me a ten-shilling note!'

The wheel-of-fortune man called a number. Liza shrieked and dashed to the stalls. The others followed to see her take her pick. But Joseph stood nursing his guilt. Estranged from the raucous night, he went home, and in his sleep he was slinking through the haggard and blanched field where heifers coughed against the hedge. In the depths of the copse he thought he might retrieve something belonging to Christmas. He searched for something cocooned, in swaddling of grey filament and hanging among the sticks as in an Indian burial ground.

WILLIAM TREVOR

The Time of Year

All that autumn, when they were both fourteen, they had talked about their Christmas swim. She'd had the idea: that on Christmas morning when everyone was still asleep they would meet by the boats on the strand at Ballyquin and afterwards quite casually say that they had been for a swim on Christmas Day. Whenever they met during that stormy October and November they wondered how fine the day might be, how cold or wet, and if the sea could possibly be frozen. They walked together on the cliffs, looking down at the breaking waves of the Atlantic, shivering in anticipation. They walked through the misty dusk of the town, lingering over the first signs of Christmas in the shops: coloured lights strung up, holly and Christmas trees and tinsel. They wondered if people guessed about them. They didn't want them to, they wanted it to be a secret. People would laugh because they were children. They were in love that autumn.

Six years later Valerie still remembered, poignantly, in November. Dublin, so different from Ballyquin, stirred up the past as autumn drifted into winter and winds bustled around the grey buildings of Trinity College, where she was now a student. The city's trees were bleakly bare, it seemed to Valerie; there was sadness, even, on the lawns of her hall of residence, scattered with finished leaves. In her small room, preparing herself one Friday evening for the Skullys' end-of-term party, she sensed quite easily the Christmas chill of the sea, the chilliness creeping slowly over her calves and knees. She paused with the memory, gazing at herself in the looking-glass attached to the inside of her cupboard door. She was a tall girl, standing now in a white silk petticoat, with a thin face and thin long fingers and an almost classical nose. Her black hair was as straight as a die, falling to her shoulders. She was pretty when she smiled and she did so at her reflection, endeavouring to overcome the melancholy that visited her at this time of year. She turned away and picked up a green corduroy dress which she had laid out on her bed. She was going to be late if she dawdled like this.

The parties given by Professor and Mrs Skully were renowned neither for the entertainment they provided nor for their elegance. They were, unfortunately, difficult to avoid, the Professor being persistent in the face of repeated excuses – a persistence it was deemed unwise to strain.

Bidden for half-past seven, his History students came on bicycles, a few in Kilroy's Mini, Ruth Cusper on her motor-cycle, Bewley Joal on foot. Woodward, Whipp and Woolmer-Mills came cheerfully, being kindred spirits of the Professor's and in no way dismayed by the immediate prospect. Others were apprehensive or cross, trying not to let it show as smilingly they entered the Skullys' house in Rathgar.

'How very nice!' Mrs Skully murmured in a familiar manner in the hall. 'How jolly good of you to come.'

The hall was not yet decorated for Christmas, but the Professor had found the remains of last year's crackers and had stuck half a dozen behind the heavily framed scenes of Hanover that had been established in the hall since the early days of the Skullys' marriage. The gaudy crêpe paper protruded above the pictures in splurges of green, red and yellow, and cheered up the hall to a small extent. The coloured scarves and overcoats of the History students, already accumulating on the hall-stand, did so more effectively.

In the Skullys' sitting-room the Professor's record-player, old and in some way special, was in its usual place: on a mahogany table in front of the French windows, which were now obscured by brown curtains. Four identical rugs, their colour approximately matching that of the curtains, were precisely arranged on darker brown linoleum. Rexine-seated dining-chairs lined brownish walls.

The Professor's History students lent temporary character to this room, as their coats and scarves did to the hall. Kilroy was plump in a royal-blue suit. The O'Neill sisters' cluster of followers, jostling even now for promises of favours, wore carefully pressed denim or tweed. The O'Neill sisters themselves exuded a raffish, cocktail-time air. They were twins from Lurgan, both of them blonde and both favouring an excess of eye-shadow, and lipstick that wetly gleamed, the same shade of pink as the trouser suits that nudgingly hugged the protuberances of their bodies. Not far from where they now held court, the rimless spectacles of Bewley Joal had a busy look in the room's harsh light; the complexion of Yvonne Smith was displayed to advantage. So was the troublesome fair hair of Honor Hitchcock, who was engaged to a student known as the Reverend because of his declared intention one day to claim the title. Cosily in a corner she linked her arm with his, both of them seeming middle-aged before their time, inmates already of a draughty rectory in Co. Cork or Clare. 'I'll be the first,' Ruth Cusper vowed, 'to visit you in your parish. Wherever it is.' Ruth Cusper was a statuesque English girl, not yet divested of her motor-cycling gear.

The colours worn by the girls, and the denim and tweed, and the royal blue of Kilroy contrasted sharply with the uncared-for garb of Woodward, Whipp and Woolmer-Mills, all of whom were expected to take Firsts. Stained and frayed, these three hung together without speaking, Woodward very tall, giving the impression of an etiolated newt, Whipp small, his glasses repaired with Sellotape, Woolmer-Mills forever launching himself back and forth on the balls of his feet.

In a pocket of Kilroy's suit there was a miniature bottle of vodka, for only tea and what the Professor described as 'cup' were served in the course of the evening. Kilroy fingered it, smiling across the room at the Professor, endeavouring to give the impression that he was delighted to be present. He was a student who was fearful of academic failure, his terror being that he would not get a Third: he had set his sights on a Third, well aware that to have set them higher would not be wise. He brought his little bottles of vodka to the Professor's parties as an act of bravado, a gesture designed to display jauntiness, to show that he could take a chance. But the chances he took with his vodka were not great.

Bewley Joal, who would end up with a respectable Second, was laying down the law to Yvonne Smith, who would be grateful to end up with anything at all. Her natural urge to chatter was stifled, for no one could get a word in when the clanking voice of Bewley Joal was in full flow. 'Oh, it's far more than just a solution, dear girl,' he breezily pronounced, speaking of Moral Rearmament. Yvonne Smith nodded and agreed, trying to say that an aunt of hers thought most highly of Moral Rearmament, that she herself had always been meaning to look into it. But the voice of Bewley Joal cut all her sentences in half.

'I thought we'd start,' the Professor announced, having coughed and cleared his throat, 'with the *Pathétique*.' He fiddled with the record-player while everyone sat down, Ruth Cusper on the floor.

He was a biggish man in a grey suit that faintly recalled the clothes of Woodward, Whipp and Woolmer-Mills. On a large head hair was still in plentiful supply even though the Professor was fifty-eight. The hair was grey also, bushing out around his head in a manner that suggested professorial vagueness rather than a gesture in the direction of current fashion. His wife, who stood by his side while he placed a record on the turntable, wore a magenta skirt and twin-set and a string of jade beads. In almost every way – including this lively choice of dress – she seemed naturally to complement her husband, to fill the gaps his personality couldn't be bothered with. Her nervous manner was the opposite of his confident one. He gave his parties out of duty, and having done so found it hard to take an interest in any students except those who had already proved themselves academically sound. Mrs Skully preferred to strike a lighter note. Now and again she made efforts to entice a few of the girls to join her on Saturday evenings, offering the suggestion that they might listen together to Saturday Night Theatre and afterwards sit around and discuss it. Because the Professor saw no point in television there was none in the Skullys' house.

Tchaikovsky filled the sitting-room. The Professor sat down and then Mrs Skully did. The doorbell rang.

'Ah, of course,' Mrs Skully said.

'Valerie Upcott,' Valerie said. 'Good evening, Mrs Skully.'

'Come in, come in, dear. The *Pathétique*'s just started.' She remarked in the hall on the green corduroy dress that was revealed when Valerie took off her coat. The green was of so dark a shade that it might almost have been black. It had large green buttons all down the front. 'Oh, how really nice!' Mrs Skully said.

The crackers that decorated the scenes of Hanover looked sinister, Valerie thought: Christmas was on the way, soon there'd be the coloured lights and imitation snow. She smiled at Mrs Skully. She wondered about saying that her magenta outfit was nice also, but decided against it. 'We'll slip in quietly,' Mrs Skully said.

Valerie tried to forget the crackers as she entered the sitting-room and took her place on a chair, but in her mind the brash images remained. They did so while she acknowledged Kilroy's winking smile and while she glanced towards the Professor in case he chose to greet her. But the Professor, his head bent over clasped hands, did not look up.

Among the History students Valerie was an unknown quantity. During the two years they'd all known one another she'd established herself as a person who was particularly quiet. She had a private look even when she smiled, when the thin features of her face were startled out of tranquillity, as if an electric light had suddenly been turned on. Kilroy still tried to take her out, Ruth Cusper was pally. But Valerie's privacy, softened by her sudden smile, unfussily repelled these attentions.

For her part she was aware of the students' curiosity, and yet she could not have said to any one of them that a tragedy which had occurred was not properly in the past yet. She could not mention the tragedy to people who didn't know about it already. She couldn't tell it as a story because to her it didn't seem in the least like that. It was a fact you had to live with, half wanting to forget it, half feeling you could not. This time of year and the first faint signs of Christmas were enough to tease it brightly into life.

The second movement of the *Pathétique* came to an end, the Professor rose to turn the record over, the students murmured. Mrs Skully slipped away, as she always did at this point, to attend to matters in the kitchen. While the Professor was bent over the record-player, Kilroy waved his bottle of vodka about and then raised it to his lips. 'Hullo, Valerie,' Yvonne Smith whispered across the distance that separated them. She endeavoured to continue her communication by shaping words with her lips. Valerie smiled at her and at Ruth Cusper, who had turned her head when she'd heard Yvonne Smith's greeting. 'Hi,' Ruth Cusper said.

The music began again. The mouthing of Yvonne Smith continued for a moment and then ceased. Valerie didn't notice that, because in the room the students and the Professor were shadows of a kind, the music a distant piping. The swish of wind was in the room, and the shingle, cold on her bare feet; so were the two flat stones they'd placed on their clothes to keep them from blowing away. White flecks in the air were snow, she said: Christmas snow, what everyone wanted. But he said the flecks were flecks of foam.

He took her hand, dragging her a bit because the shingle hurt the soles of her feet and slowed her down. He hurried on the sand, calling back to her, reminding her that it was her idea, laughing at her hesitation. He called out something else as he ran into the breakers, but she couldn't hear because of the roar of the sea. She stood in the icy shallows and when she heard him shouting again she imagined he was still mocking her. She didn't even know he was struggling, she wasn't in the least aware of his death. It was his not being there she noticed, the feeling of being alone on the strand at Ballyquin.

'Cup, Miss Upcott?' the Professor offered in the dining-room. Poised above a glass, a jug contained a yellowish liquid. She said she'd rather have tea.

There were egg sandwiches and cakes, plates of crisps, biscuits and Twiglets. Mrs Skully poured tea, Ruth Cusper handed round the cups and saucers. The O'Neill sisters and their followers shared an obscene joke, which was a game that had grown up at the Skullys' parties: one student doing his best to make the others giggle too noisily. A point was gained if the Professor demanded to share the fun.

'Oh, but of course there isn't any argument,' Bewley Joal was insisting, still talking to Yvonne Smith about Moral Rearmament. Words had ceased to dribble from her lips. Instead she kept nodding her head. 'We live in times of decadence,' Bewley Joal pronounced.

Woodward, Whipp and Woolmer-Mills were still together, Woolmer-Mills launching himself endlessly on to the balls of his feet, Whipp sucking at his cheeks. No conversation was taking place among them: when the Professor finished going round with his jug of cup, talk of some kind would begin, probably about a mediaeval document Woodward had earlier mentioned. Or about a reference to *panni streit sine grano* which had puzzled Woolmer-Mills.

'Soon be Christmas,' Honor Hitchcock remarked to Valerie.

'Yes, it will.'

'I love it. I love the way you can imagine everyone doing just the same things on Christmas Eve, tying up presents, running around with holly, listening to the carols. And Christmas Day: that same meal in millions of houses, and the same prayers. All over the world.'

'Yes, there's that.'

'Oh, I think it's marvellous.'

'Christmas?' Kilroy said, suddenly beside them. He laughed, the fat on his face shaking a bit. 'Much over-rated in my small view.' He glanced as he spoke at the Professor's profile, preparing himself in case the Professor should look in his direction. His expression changed, becoming solemn.

There were specks of dandruff, Valerie noticed, on the shoulders of the Professor's grey suit. She thought it odd that Mrs Skully hadn't drawn his attention to them. She thought it odd that Kilroy was so determined about his Third. And that Yvonne Smith didn't just walk away from the clanking voice of Bewley Joal.

'Orange or coffee?' Ruth Cusper proffered two cakes that had been cut into slices. The fillings in Mrs Skully's cakes were famous, made with Trex and castor sugar. The cakes themselves had a flat appearance, like large biscuits.

'I wouldn't touch any of that stuff,' Kilroy advised, jocular again. 'I was up all night after it last year.'

'Oh, nonsense!' Ruth Cusper placed a slice of orange cake on Valerie's plate, making a noise that indicated she found Kilroy's attempt at wit a failure. She passed on, and Kilroy without reason began to laugh.

Valerie looked at them, her eyes pausing on each face in the room. She was different from these people of her own age because of her autumn melancholy and the bitterness of Christmas. A solitude had been made for her, while they belonged to each other, separate yet part of a whole.

She thought about them, envying them their ordinary normality, the good fortune they accepted as their due. They trailed no horror, no ghosts or images that wouldn't go away: you could tell that by looking at them. Had she herself already been made peculiar by all of it, eccentric and strange and edgy? And would it never slip away, into the past where it belonged? Each year it was the same, no different from the year before, intent on hanging on to her. Each year she smiled and made an effort. She was brisk with it, she did her best. She told herself she had to live with it, agreeing with herself that of course she had to, as if wishing to be overheard. And yet to die so young, so pointlessly and so casually, seemed to be something you had to feel unhappy about. It dragged out tears from you; it made you hesitate again, standing in the icy water. Your idea it had been.

'Tea, you people?' Mrs Skully offered.

'Awfully kind of you, Mrs Skully,' Kilroy said. 'Splendid tea this is.'

'I should have thought you'd be keener on the Professor's cup, Mr Kilroy.'

'No, I'm not a cup man, Mrs Skully.'

Valerie wondered what it would be like to be Kilroy. She wondered about his private thoughts, even what he was thinking now as he said he wasn't a cup man. She imagined him in his bedroom, removing his royal-blue suit and meticulously placing it on a hanger, talking to himself about the party, wondering if he had done himself any damage in the Professor's eyes. She imagined him as a child, plump in bathing-trunks, building a sandcastle. She saw him in a kitchen, standing on a chair by an open cupboard, nibbling the corner of a Chivers' jelly.

She saw Ruth Cusper too, bossy at a children's party, friendlily bossy, towering over other children. She made them play a game and wasn't disappointed when they didn't like it. You couldn't hurt Ruth Cusper; she'd grown an extra skin beneath her motor-cycling gear. At night, she often said, she fell asleep as soon as her head touched the pillow.

You couldn't hurt Bewley Joal, either: a grasping child, Valerie saw him as, watchful and charmless. Once he'd been hurt, she speculated: another child had told him that no one enjoyed playing with him, and he'd resolved from that moment not to care about stuff like that, to push his way through other people's opinion of him, not wishing to know it.

As children, the O'Neill sisters teased; their faithful tormentors pulled their hair. Woodward, Whipp and Woolmer-Mills read the Children's Encyclopaedia. Honor Hitchcock and the Reverend played mummies and daddies. 'Oh, listen to that chatterbox!' Yvonne Smith's father dotingly cried, affection that Yvonne Smith had missed ever since.

In the room the clanking of Bewley Joal punctuated the giggling in the corner where the O'Neill sisters were. More tea was poured and more of the Professor's cup, more cake was handed round. 'Ah, yes,' the Professor began. '*Panni streit sine grano.*' Woodward, Whipp and Woolmer-Mills bent their heads to listen.

The Professor, while waiting on his upstairs landing for Woolmer-Mills to use the lavatory, spoke of the tomatoes he grew. Similarly delayed downstairs, Mrs Skully suggested to the O'Neill sisters that they might like, one Saturday night next term, to listen to Saturday Night Theatre with her. It was something she enjoyed, she said, especially the discussion afterwards. 'Or you, Miss Upcott,' she said. 'You've never been to one of my evenings either.'

Valerie smiled politely, moving with Mrs Skully towards the sitting-room, where Tchaikiovsky once more resounded powerfully. Again she examined the arrayed faces. Some eyes were closed in sleep, others were weary beneath a weight of tedium. Woodward's newt-like countenance had not altered, nor had Kilroy's fear dissipated. Frustration still tugged at Yvonne Smith. Nothing much was happening in the face of Mrs Skully.

Valerie continued to regard Mrs Skully's face and suddenly she found herself shivering. How could that mouth open and close, issuing invitations without knowing they were the subject of derision? How could this woman, in her late middle age, officiate at student parties in magenta and jade, or bake inedible cakes without knowing it? How could she daily permit herself to be taken for granted by a man who cared only for students with academic success behind them? How could she have married his pomposity in the first place? There was something wrong with Mrs Skully, there was something missing, as if some part of her had never come to life. The more Valerie examined her the more extraordinary Mrs Skully seemed, and then it seemed extraordinary that the Professor should be unaware that no one liked his parties. It was as if some part of him hadn't come to life either, as if they lived together in the dead wood of a relationship, together in this house because it was convenient.

She wondered if the other students had ever thought that, or if they'd be bothered to survey in any way whatsoever the Professor and his wife. She wondered if they saw a reflection of the Skullys' marriage in the brownness of the room they all sat in or in the crunchy fillings of Mrs Skully's cakes, or in the Rexine-seated dining-chairs that were not comfortable. You couldn't blame them for not wanting to think about the Skullys' marriage: what good could come of it? The other students were busy and more organised than she. They had aims in life. They had futures she could sense, as she had sensed their pasts. Honor Hitchcock and the Reverend would settle down as right as rain in a provincial rectory, the followers of the O'Neill sisters would enter various business worlds. Woodward, Whipp and Woolmer-Mills would be the same as the Professor, dandruff on the shoulders of three grey suits. Bewley Joal would rise to heights, Kilroy would not. Ruth Cusper would run a hall of residence, the O'Neill sisters would give two husbands hell in Lurgan. Yvonne Smith would live in hopes.

The music of Tchaikovsky gushed over these reflections, as if to soften some harshness in them. But to Valerie there was no harshness in her contemplation of these people's lives, only fact and a lacing of speculation. The Skullys would go on ageing and he might never turn to his wife and say he was sorry. The O'Neill sisters would lose their beauty and Bewley Joal his vigour. One day Woolmer-Mills would find that he could no longer launch himself on to the balls of his feet. Kilroy would enter a home for the senile. Death would shatter the cotton-wool cosiness of Honor Hitchcock and the Reverend.

She wondered what would happen if she revealed what she had thought, if she told them that in order to keep her melancholy in control she had played about with their lives, seeing them in childhood, visiting them with old age and death. Which of them would seek to stop her while she cited the arrogance of the Professor and the pusillanimity of his wife? She heard her own voice echoing in a silence, telling them finally, in explanation, of the tragedy in her own life.

'Please all have a jolly Christmas,' Mrs Skully urged in the hall as scarves and coats were lifted from the hat-stand. 'Please now.'

'We shall endeavour,' Kilroy promised, and the others made similar remarks, wishing Mrs Skully a happy Christmas herself, thanking her and the Professor for the party, Kilroy adding that it had been most enjoyable. There'd be another, the Professor promised, in May.

There was the roar of Ruth Cusper's motor-cycle, and the overloading of Kilroy's Mini, and the striding into the night of Bewley Joal, and others making off on bicycles. Valerie walked with Yvonne Smith through the suburban roads. 'I quite like Joal,' Yvonne Smith confided, releasing the first burst of her pent-up chatter. 'He's all right, isn't he? Quite nice, really, quite clever. I mean, if you care for a clever kind of person. I mean, I wouldn't mind going out with him if he asked me.'

Valerie agreed that Bewley Joal was all right if you cared for that kind of person. It was pleasant in the cold night air. It was good that the party was over.

Yvonne Smith said good-night, still chattering about Bewley Joal as she turned into the house where her lodgings were. Valerie walked on alone, a thin shadow in the gloom. Compulsively now, she thought about the party, seeing again the face of Mrs Skully and the Professor's face and the faces of the others. They formed, like a backdrop in her mind, an assembly as vivid as the tragedy that more grimly visited it. They seemed like the other side of the tragedy, as if she had for the first time managed to peer round a corner. The feeling puzzled her. It was odd to be left with it after the Skullys' end-of-term party.

In the garden of the hall of residence the fallen leaves were sodden beneath her feet as she crossed a lawn to shorten her journey. The bewilderment she felt lifted a little. She had been wrong to imagine she envied other people their normality and good fortune. She was as she wished to be. She paused in faint moonlight, repeating that to herself and then repeating it again. She did not quite add that the tragedy had made her what she was, that without it she would not possess her reflective introspection, or be sensitive to more than just the time of year. But the thought hovered with her as she moved towards the lights of the house, offering what appeared to be a hint of comfort.

JOHN B. KEANE

The Woman Who
Hated Christmas

Polly Baun did not hate Christmas as some of her more uncharitable neighbours would have people believe. She merely disliked it. She was once accused by a local drunkard of trying to call a halt to Christmas. She was on her way out of church at the time and the drunkard, who celebrated his own form of mass by criticising the sermon while he leaned against the outside wall of the church, was seen to push her on the back as she passed the spot where he leaned. As a result Polly Baun fell forward and was rendered immobile for a week. She told her husband that she had slipped on a banana skin because he was a short-tempered chap. However, he found out from another drunkard who frequented the same tavern that Polly had been pushed. When he confronted her with his findings she reluctantly conceded that the second drunkard had been telling the truth.

'You won't do anything rash!' she beseeched him.

'I won't do anything rash,' Shaun Baun promised, 'but you will have to agree that this man's energies must be directed in another direction. I mean we can't have him pushing women to the ground because he disagrees with their views. I mean,' he continued in what he believed to be a reasonable tone, 'if this sort of thing is allowed to go on unchecked no woman will be safe.'

'It doesn't worry me in the least,' Polly Baun assured him.

'That may be,' he returned, 'but the fact of the matter is that no woman deserves to be pushed to the ground.'

Polly Baun decided that the time had come to terminate the conversation. It was leading nowhere to begin with and she was afraid she might say something that would infuriate her husband. He flew off the handle easily but generally he would return to his normal state of complacency after a few brief moments.

As Christmas approached, the street shed its everyday look and donned the finery of the season. Polly Baun made one of her few concessions to Christmas by buying a goose. It was a young goose, small but plump and, most importantly, purchased from an accredited goose breeder. It would suit the two of them nicely. There were no children and there would be no Christmas guests and Polly who was of a thrifty disposition judged that there would also be enough for Saint Stephen's Day. She did not need to be thrifty. The hat shop behind which they lived did a tidy business. The tiny kitchen at the rear of the shop served a threefold purpose all told. As well as being a kitchen it was also a dining area and sitting-room. They might have added on but Polly failed to see the need for this. She was content with what she had and she felt that one of the chief problems with the world was that people did not know when they were well off.

'They should be on their knees all day thanking God,' she would tell her husband when he brought news of malcontents who lived only to whine.

Shaun Baun sought out and isolated his wife's attacker one wet night a week before Christmas. The scoundrel was in the habit of taking a turn around the town before retiring to the pub for the evening. Shaun Baun did not want to take advantage of him while he might be in his cups and besides he wanted him sober enough to fully understand the enormity of his transgressions.

'You sir!' Shaun Baun addressed his victim in a secluded side street, 'are not a gentleman and neither are you any other kind of man. You knocked my wife to the ground and did not bother to go to her assistance.'

'I was drunk,' came back the reply.

'Being drunk is not sufficient justification for pushing a woman to the ground.'

'I was told,' the drunkard's voice was filled with fear, 'that she hates Christmas.'

'That is not sufficient justification either,' Shaun Baun insisted. The drunkard began to back off as Shaun Baun assumed a fighting pose.

'Before I clobber you,' Shaun Baun announced grimly, 'I feel obliged to correct a mistaken impression you have. My wife does not hate Christmas as you would infer. My wife simply discourages Christmas which is an entirely different matter.' So saying Shaun Baun feinted, snorted, shuffled and finally landed a nose-breaking blow which saw the drunkard fall to the ground with a cry of pain. At once Shaun Baun extended a helping hand and brought him to his feet where he assured him that full retribution had been extracted and that the matter was closed.

'However,' Shaun Baun drew himself up to his full height which was five feet one and a half inches, 'if you so much as look at my wife from this day forth I will break both your legs.'

The drunkard nodded his head eagerly, earnestly indicating that he had taken the warning to heart. He would, in the course of time, intimidate other women but he would never thereafter have anything to do with Polly Baun. For her part Polly would never know that an assault had taken place. Shaun would never tell her. She would only disapprove. She would continue to discourage Christmas as was her wont and, with this in mind, she decided to remove all the chairs from the kitchen and place them in the backyard until Christmas had run its course. If, she quite rightly deduced, there were no chairs for those who made Christmas visits they would not be able to sit down and, therefore, their visits would be of short duration.

On the day before Christmas Eve the hat shop was busy. Occasionally when a purchase was made the wearer would first defer to Polly's judgement. This, of course, necessitated a trip to the kitchen. The practice had been in existence for years. Countrymen in particular and confirmed bachelors would make the short trip to the kitchen to have their hats or caps inspected. On getting the nod from Polly Baun they would return to the shop and pay Shaun Baun for their purchases. Sometimes Polly would disapprove of the colour and other times she would disapprove of the shape. There were times when she would shake her head because of the hat's size or because of its rim or because of its crown. Shaun Baun's trade flourished because his customers were satisfied and the shy ones and the retiring ones and the irresolute ones left the premises safe in the knowledge that they would not be laughed at because of their choice of headgear.

As time passed and it became clear that the union would not be blessed with children Polly Baun became known as the woman who hated Christmas. Nobody would ever say it to her face and certainly nobody would say it to her husband's face. It must be said on behalf of the community that none took real exception to her stance. They were well used to Christmas attitudes. There was a tradesman who resided in the suburbs and every year about a week before Christmas he would disappear into the countryside where he rented a small cabin until Christmas was over. He had nothing personal against Christmas and had said so publicly on numerous occasions. It was just that he couldn't stand the build-up to Christmas what with the decorations and the lighting and the cards and the shopping and the gluttony to mention but a few of his grievances.

There was another gentleman who locked his door on Christmas Eve and did not open it for a month. Some say he simply hibernated and when he reappeared on the street after the prescribed period he looked as if he had. He was unshaven and his hair was tousled and his face was gaunt as a corpse's and there were black circles under his eyes.

Then there were those who would go off the drink for Christmas just because everybody else was going on. And there were those who would not countenance seasonal fare such as turkeys or geese or plum pudding or spiced beef. One man said he would rather an egg and another insisted that those who consumed fowl would have tainted innards for the rest of their days.

There were, therefore, abundant precedents for attitudes like Polly Baun's. There were those who would excuse her on the grounds that maybe she had a good and secret reason to hate Christmas but mostly they would accept what Shaun said, that she simply discouraged it.

There had been occasions when small children would come to the door of the kitchen while their parents searched for suitable hats. The knowing ones would point to where the silhouette of the woman who hated Christmas was visible through the stained glass of the doorway which led from the shop to the kitchen. One might whisper to the others as he pointed inwards 'that's the woman who hates Christmas!' If Polly Baun heard, she never reacted. Sometimes in the streets, during the days before Christmas, she would find herself the object of curious stares from shoppers who had just been informed of her pet aversion by friends or relations. If she noticed she gave no indication.

Shaun Baun also felt the seasonal undercurrents when he visited his neighbourhood tavern during the Christmas festivities. He drank but little, a few glasses of stout with a friend but never whiskey. He had once been a prodigious whiskey drinker and then all of a sudden he gave up whiskey altogether and never indulged again. No one knew why, not even his closest friends. There was no explanation. One night he went home full of whiskey and the next night he drank none. There was the inevitable speculation but the truth would never be known and his friends, all too well aware of his fiery temper, did not pursue the matter. Neither did they raise the question of his wife's Christmas disposition except when his back was turned but like most of the community they did not consider it to be of any great significance. There was, of course, a reason for it. There had to be if one accepted the premise that there was a reason for everything.

On Christmas Eve there was much merriment and goodwill in the tavern. Another of Shaun Baun's cronies had given up whiskey on his doctor's instructions and presumed wrongly that this might well have been the reason why Shaun had forsaken the stuff. Courteously but firmly Shaun informed him that his giving up whiskey had nothing to do with doctors, that it was a purely personal decision. The night was spoiled for Shaun Baun. Rather than betray his true feelings on such an occasion he slipped away early and walked as far as the outermost suburbs of the town, then turned and made his way homewards at a brisk pace. Nobody could be blamed for thinking that here was a busy shopkeeper availing himself of the rarer airs of the night whereas the truth was that his mind was in turmoil, all brought on by the reference to whiskey in the public house. Nobody knew better than Shaun why he had given up whiskey unless it was his wife.

As he walked he clenched and unclenched his fists and cursed the day that he had ever tasted whiskey. He remembered striking her and he remembered why and as he did he stopped and threw his arms upwards into the night and sobbed as he always sobbed whenever he found himself unable to drive the dreadful memory away. He remembered how he had been drinking since the early afternoon on that fateful occasion. Every time he sold a hat he would dash across the roadway to the pub with the purchaser in tow. He reckoned afterwards that he had never consumed so much whiskey in so short a time. When he closed the shop he announced that he was going straight to the public house and this despite his wife's protestations. She begged him to eat something. She lovingly entreated him not to drink any more whiskey, to indulge in beer or stout and he agreed and kissed her and then hurried off to surfeit himself with more whiskey. He would later excuse himself on the grounds that he was young and impetuous but he would never be able to excuse the use of his fist in that awful moment which would haunt him for the rest of his life. An oncoming pedestrian moved swiftly on to the roadway at the sight of the gesticulating creature who seemed to rant and rave as he approached. Shaun Baun moved relentlessly onward, trying to dispel the memory of what had been the worst moment he had ever experienced but he still remembered as though it had happened only the day before.

He had left the pub with several compatriots and they had gone on to an after-hours establishment where they exceeded themselves. Shaun had come home at seven o'clock in the morning. He searched in vain for his key but it was nowhere to be found. He turned out his pockets but the exercise yielded nothing. Then he did what his likes had been doing since the first key had been mislaid. He knocked gently upon the front window with his knuckles and when this failed to elicit a response he located a coin and used it to beat a subdued tattoo on the fanlight and when this failed he pounded upon the door.

At length the door was opened to him and closed behind him by his dressing-gowned, bedroom-slippered wife. It took little by way of skill to evade his drunken embrace. She passed him easily in the shop and awaited him with folded arms in the kitchen.

A wiser woman would have ushered him upstairs, bedded him safely down and suspended any verbal onslaught until a more favourable time. She did not know so early in her married days that the most futile of all wifely exercises is arguing with a drunken husband.

She began by asking if he saw the state of himself which was a pointless question to begin with. She asked him in short order if he knew the hour of the morning it was and was he aware of the fact that he was expected to accompany her to mass in a few short hours. He stood silently, hands and head hanging, unable to muster a reply. All he wished for was his bed; even the floor would have satisfied him but she had only begun. She outlined for him all the trouble he had caused her in their three years of marriage, his drinking habits, his bouts of sickness after the excesses of the pub, his intemperate language and, worst of all, the spectacle he made of himself in front of the neighbours. Nothing remarkable here, the gentle reader would be sure to say, familiar enough stuff and common to such occasions in the so-called civilised countries of the world but let me stress that it was not the quality of her broadsides but the quantity. She went on and on and on and it became clear that she should have vented her ire piecemeal over the three years rather than hoard it all for one sustained outburst.

Afterwards Shaun Baun would say that he did what he did to shut out the noise. If there had been lulls now and then he might have borne it all with more patience but she simply never let up. On the few occasions that he nodded off she shouted into the more convenient ear so that he would splutter into immediate if drunken wakefulness. Finally, the whole business became unbearable. Her voice had reached its highest pitch since the onslaught began and she even grew surprised at the frenzy of her own outpourings.

Could she but have taken a leaf out of the books of the countless wives in the neighbourhood who found themselves confronted with equally intemperate spouses she would have fared much better and there would be no need for recrimination on Christmas morning. Alas, this was not her way. She foolishly presumed that the swaying monstrosity before her was one of a kind and that a drastic dressing-down of truly lasting proportions was his only hope of salvation.

Whenever he tried to move out of earshot she seized him firmly by the shoulders and made him stand his ground. Drunk and incapable as he was he managed to place the table between them. For awhile they played a game of cat and mouse but eventually he tired and she began a final session of ranting which had the effect of clouding his judgment such was its intensity. He did not realise that he had delivered the blow until she had fallen to the ground.

Afterwards he would argue with himself that he only meant to remove her from his path so that he could escape upstairs and find succour in the spare bedroom. She fell heavily, the blood streaming from a laceration on her cheekbone. When he attempted to help her he fell awkwardly across her and stunned himself when his forehead struck the floor. When he woke he saw that the morning's light was streaming in the window. The clock on the kitchen mantelpiece confirmed his worst fears. For the first time in his life he had missed mass. Then slowly the events of the night before began to take shape. He prayed in vain that he had experienced a nightmare, that his wife would appear any moment bouncing and cheerful from last mass. He struggled to his feet and entered his shop.

The last of the mass-goers had departed the street outside. Fearing the worst he climbed the stairs to the bedroom which they had so lovingly shared since they first married. She lay on the bed her head propped up by bloodstained pillows, a plaster covering the gash she had suffered, her face swollen beyond belief. Shaun Baun fell on his knees at the side of the bed and sobbed his very heart out but the figure on the bed lay motionless, her unforgiving eyes fixed on the ceiling. There would be no Christmas dinner on that occasion. Contritely, all day and all night, he made sobbing visitations to the bedroom with cups of coffee and tea and other beverages but there was to be no relenting.

Three months would pass before she acknowledged his existence and three more would expire before words were exchanged. Two years in all would go unfleetingly by before it could be said that they had the semblance of a relationship. That had all been twenty-five years before and now as he walked homewards avoiding the main streets he longed to kneel before her and beg her forgiveness once more. Every so often during the course of every year in between he would ask her to forgive the unforgivable as he called it. He had never touched her in anger since that night or raised his voice or allowed his face to exhibit the semblance of a frown in her presence.

When he returned she was sitting silently by the fire. The goose, plucked and stuffed, sat on a large dish. It would be duly roasted on the morrow. As soon as he entered the kitchen he sat by her side and took her hand in his. As always, he declared his love for her and she responded, as always, by squeezing the hand which held hers. They would sit thus as they had sat since that unforgettable night so many years before. There would be no change in the pattern. They would happily recall the events of the day and they would decide upon which mass they would attend on the great holy day. She would accept the glass of sherry which he always poured for her. He would pour himself a bottle of stout and they would sip happily. They would enjoy another drink and another and then they would sit quietly for awhile. Then as always the sobbing would begin. It would come from deep within him. He would kneel in front of her with his head buried in her lap and every so often, between great heaving sobs, he would tell her how sorry he was. She would nod and smile and place her hands around his head and then he would raise the head and look into her eyes and ask her forgiveness as he had been doing for so many years.

'I forgive you, dear,' she would reassure him and he would sob all the more. She would never hurt him. She could not find it in her heart to do that. He was a good man if a hotheaded one and he had made up for that moment of madness many times over. All through the night she would dutifully comfort him by accepting his every expression of atonement. She always thought of her father on such occasions. He had never raised his voice to her or to her mother. He had been drunk on many an occasion, notably weddings and christenings, but all he ever did was to lift her mother or herself in his arms. She was glad that she was able to forgive her husband but there was forgiveness and forgiveness and hers was the kind that would never let her forget. Her husband would never know the difference. She would always be there when he needed her, especially at Christmas.

ELIZABETH BOWEN

The Tommy Crans

Herbert's feet, from dangling so long in the tram, had died of cold in his boots; he stamped the couple of coffins on blue-and-buff mosaic. In the Tommy Crans' cloak-room the pegs were too high – Uncle Archer cocked H.M.S. *Terrible* for him over a checked ulster. Tommy Cran – aslant meanwhile in the doorway – was an enormous presence. 'Come on, now, come!' he exclaimed, and roared with impatience. You would have said he was also arriving at the Tommy Crans' Christmas party, of which one could not bear to miss a moment.

Now into the hall Mrs Tommy Cran came swimming from elsewhere, dividing with curved little strokes the festive air – hyacinths and gunpowder. Her sleeves, in a thousand ruffles, fled from her elbows. She gained Uncle Archer's lapels and, bobbing, floated from this attachment. Uncle Archer, verifying the mistletoe, loudly kissed her face of delicate pink sugar. 'Ha!' yelled Tommy, drawing an unseen dagger. Herbert laughed with embarrassment.

'Only think, Nancy let off all the crackers before tea! She's quite wild, but there are more behind the piano. Ah, is this little Herbert? Herbert . . .'

'Very well, thank you,' said Herbert, and shook hands defensively. This was his first Christmas Day without any father; the news went before him. He had seen his mother off, very brave with the holly wreath, in the cemetery tram. She and father were spending Christmas afternoon together.

Mrs Tommy Cran stooped to him, bright with a tear-glitter, then with a strong upward sweep, like an angel's, bore him to gaiety. 'Fancy Nancy!' He fancied Nancy. So by now they would all be wearing the paper caps. Flinging back a white door, she raced Herbert elsewhere.

The room where they all sat seemed to be made of glass, it collected the whole daylight; the candles were still waiting. Over the garden, day still hung like a pink flag; over the trees like frozen feathers, the enchanted icy lake, the lawn. The table was in the window. As Herbert was brought in a clock struck four; the laughing heads all turned in a silence brief as a breath's intake. The great many gentlemen and the rejoicing ladies leaned apart; he and Nancy looked at each other gravely.

He saw Nancy, crowned and serious because she was a queen. Advanced by some urgent pushing, he made his way round the table and sat down beside her, podgily.

She said: 'How d'you do? Did you see our lake? It is all frozen. Did you ever see our lake before?'

'I never came here.'

'Did you see our two swans?'

She was so beautiful, rolling her ringlets, round with light, on her lacy shoulders, that he said rather shortly: 'I shouldn't have thought your lake was large enough for two swans.'

'It is, indeed,' said Nancy; 'it goes round the island. It's large enough for a boat.'

They were waiting, around the Christmas cake, for tea to be brought in. Mrs Tommy Cran shook out the ribbons of her guitar and began to sing again. Very quietly, for a secret, he and Nancy crept to the window; she showed how the lake wound; he could guess how, in summer, her boat would go pushing among the lily leaves. She showed him their boat-house, rusty-red from a lamp inside, solid. 'We had a lamp put there for the poor cold swans.' (And the swans were asleep beside it.) 'How old are you, Herbert?'

'Eight.'

'Oh, I'm nine. Do you play brigands?'

'I could,' said Herbert.

'Oh, I don't; I'd hate to. But I know some boys who do. Did you have many presents? Uncle Ponto brought me a train; it's more suitable for a boy, really. I could give it to you, perhaps.'

'How many uncles—?' began Herbert.

'Ten pretence and none really. I'm adopted, because mummy and daddy have no children. I think that's better fun, don't you?'

'Yes,' replied Herbert, after consideration; 'anybody could be born.'

All the time, Nancy had not ceased to look at him seriously and impersonally. They were both tired already by this afternoon of boisterous grown-up society; they would have liked to be quiet, and though she was loved by ten magic uncles and wore a pearl locket, and he was fat, with spectacles, and felt deformed a little from everybody's knowing about his father, they felt at ease in each other's company.

'Nancy, cut the cake!' exclaimed Mrs Tommy, and they all clapped their hands for Nancy's attention. So the coloured candles were lit, the garden went dark with loneliness and was immediately curtained out. Two of the uncles put rugs on and bounded about the room like bears and lions; the other faces drew out a crimson brand round the silver teapot. Mrs Tommy could not bear to put down the guitar, so the teapot fell into the hands of a fuzzy lady with several husbands who cried 'Ah, don't, now!' and had to keep brushing gentlemen's hands from her waist. And all the others leaned on each other's shoulders and laughed with gladness because they had been asked to the Tommy Crans'; a dozen times everyone died of laughter and rose again, redder ghosts. Teacups whizzed down a chain of hands. Now Nancy, standing up very straight to cut the cake, was like a doll stitched upright into its box, apt, if you should cut the string at the back, to pitch right forward and break its delicate fingers.

'Oh dear,' she sighed, as the knife skidded over the icing. But nobody heard but Herbert. For someone, seeing her white frock over that palace of cake, proposed 'The health of the bride'. And an Uncle Joseph, tipping the tea about in his cup, stared and stared with juicy eyes. But nobody saw but Herbert.

'After tea,' she whispered, 'we'll go and stand on the lake.' And after tea they did, while the others played hide and seek. Herbert, once looking back through a window, saw uncles chasing the laughing aunts. It was not cold on the lake. Nancy said: 'I never believed in fairies – did you either?' She told him she had been given a white muff and was going to be an organist, with an organ of her own. She was going up to Belfast next month to dance for charity. She said she would not give him the train after all; she would give him something really her own, a pink glass greyhound that was an ornament.

When Uncle Archer and Herbert left to walk to the tram terminus, the party was at its brightest. They were singing 'Hark the herald' around the drawing-room piano: Nancy sat on her Uncle Joseph's knee, more than politely.

Uncle Archer did not want to go home either. 'That was a nice little girl,' he said. 'Eh?'

Herbert nodded. His uncle, glad that the little chap hadn't had, after all, such a dismal Christmas, pursued heartily: 'Kiss her?' Herbert looked quite blank. To tell the truth, this had never occurred to him.

He kissed Nancy later; his death, even, was indirectly caused by his loss of her; but their interchanges were never passionate, and he never knew her better than when they had been standing out on the lake, beyond the cheerful windows. Herbert's mother did not know Uncle Archer's merry friends: she had always loved to live quietly, and, as her need for comfort decreased, she and Herbert saw less, or at least as little as ever of Uncle Archer. So that for years Herbert was not taken again across Dublin to the house with the lake. Once he saw Nancy carry her white muff into a shop, but he stood rooted and did not run after her. Once he saw Mrs Tommy Cran out in Stephen's Green throwing lollipops to the ducks: but he did not approach; there was nothing to say. He was sent to school, where he painfully learnt to be natural with boys; his sight got no better; they said he must wear glasses all his life. Years later, however, when Herbert was thirteen, the Crans gave a dancing-party and did not forget him. He danced once with Nancy; she was silenter now, but she said: 'Why did you never come back again?' He could not explain; he trod on her toes and danced heavily on. A Chinese lantern blazed up, and in the confusion he lost her. That evening he saw Mrs Tommy in tears in the conservatory. Nancy clung, pressing her head, with its drooping pink ribbons, to Mrs Cran's shoulder; pressing, perhaps, the shoulder against the head. Soon it was all right again and Mrs Tommy led off in 'Sir Roger', but Nancy was like a ghost who presently vanished. A week afterwards he had a letter:

Please meet me to tea at Mitchell's; I want your advice specially.

She was distracted: she had come in to Dublin to sell her gold wrist-watch. The Tommy Crans had lost all their money – it wasn't fair to expect them to keep it; they were generous and gay. Nancy had to think hard what must they all do. Herbert went round with her from jeweller to jeweller: these all laughed and paid her nothing but compliments. Her face, with those delicate lovely eyebrows, grew tragic under the fur cap; it rained continuously; she and Herbert looked with incredulity into the grown-up faces: they wondered how one could penetrate far into life without despair. At last a man on the quays gave her eight-and-six for the watch. Herbert, meanwhile, had spent eight shillings of his pocket-money on their cab – and, even so, her darling feet were sodden. They were surprised to see, from the window, Tommy Cran jump from an outside car and run joyfully into the Shelbourne. It turned out he had raised some more money from somewhere – as he deserved.

So he sold the house with the lake and moved to an ornamental castle by Dublin Bay. In spite of the grey scene, the transitory light from the sea, the terrace here was gay with urns of geraniums, magnificent with a descent of steps – scrolls and whorls of balustrade, all the grandeur of stucco. Here the band played for their afternoon parties, and here, when they were twenty and twenty-one, Herbert asked Nancy to marry him.

A pug harnessed with bells ran jingling about the terrace. 'Oh, I don't know, Herbert; I don't know.'

'Do you think you don't love me?'

'I don't know whom I love. Everything would have to be different. Herbert, I don't see how we are ever to live; we seem to know everything. Surely there should be something for us we don't know?' She shut her eyes; they kissed seriously and searchingly. In his arms her body felt soft and voluminous; he could not touch her because of a great fur coat. The coat had been a surprise from

Tommy Cran, who loved to give presents on delightful occasions – for now they were off to the Riviera. They were sailing in four days; Nancy and Mrs Tommy had still all their shopping to do, all his money to spend – he loved them both to be elegant. There was that last party to give before leaving home. Mrs Tommy could hardly leave the telephone; crossing London, they were to give yet another party, at the Euston Hotel.

'And how could I leave them?' she asked. 'They're my business.'

'Because they are not quite your parents?'

'Oh, no,' she said, eyes reproachful for the misunderstanding he had put up, she knew, only from bitterness. 'They would be my affair whoever I was. Don't you see, they're like that.'

The Tommy Crans returned from the Riviera subdued, and gave no more parties than they could avoid. They hung sun-yellow curtains, in imitation of the Midi, in all the castle windows, and fortified themselves against despair. They warned their friends they were ruined; they honestly were – and there were heartfelt evenings of consolation. After such evenings, Mrs Tommy, awaking heavily, whimpered in Nancy's arms, and Tommy approached silence. They had the highest opinion of Nancy, and were restored by her confidence. She knew they would be all right; she assured them they were the best, the happiest people; they were popular – look how Life came back again and again to beg their pardon. And, just to show them, she accepted Jeremy Neath and his thousands. So the world could see she was lucky; the world saw the Tommy Crans and their daughter had all the luck. To Herbert she explained nothing. She expected everything of him, on behalf of the Tommy Crans.

The two Crans were distracted by her apotheosis from the incident of their ruin. They had seen her queen of a perpetual Christmas party for six months before they themselves came down magnificently, like an empire. Then Nancy came to fetch them over to England, where her husband had found a small appointment for Tommy, excuse for a pension. But Tommy would not want that long; he had a scheme already, a stunner, a certainty; you just wrote to a hundred people and put in half a crown. That last night he ran about with the leaflets, up and down the uncarpeted castle stairs that were his no longer. He offered to let Herbert in on it; he would yet see Herbert a rich man.

Herbert and Nancy walked after dark on the terrace: she looked ill, tired; she was going to have a baby.

'When I asked you to marry me,' he said, 'you never answered. You've never answered yet.'

She said: 'There was no answer. We could never have loved each other and we shall always love each other. We are related.'

Herbert, a heavy un-young young man, walked, past desperation, beside her. He did not want peace, but a sword. He returned again and again to the unique moment of her strangeness to him before, as a child, she had spoken. Before, bewildered by all the laughter, he had realised she also was silent.

'You never played games,' he said, 'or believed in fairies, or anything. I'd have played any game your way; I'd have been good at them. You let them pull all the crackers before tea: now I'd have loved those crackers. That day we met at Mitchell's to sell your watch, you wouldn't have sugar cakes, though I wanted to comfort you. You never asked me out to go round the island in your boat; I'd have died to do that. I never even saw your swans awake. You hold back everything from me and expect me to understand. Why should I understand? In the name of God, what game are we playing?'

'But you do understand?'

'Oh, God,' he cried in revulsion. 'I don't want to! And now you're going to have a stranger child.'

Her sad voice in the dark said: 'You said then, "Anybody could

be born!'' Herbert, you and I have nothing to do with children –
this must be a child like them.'

As they turned back to face the window, her smile and voice
were tender, but not for him. In the brightly lit stripped room the
Tommy Crans walked about together, like lovers in their freedom
from one another. They talked of the fortune to be made, the child
to be born. Tommy flung his chest out and moved his arms freely
in air he did not possess; here and there, pink leaflets fluttered
into the dark. The Tommy Crans would go on for ever and be
continued; their seed should never fail.

LYNN DOYLE

A Bowl of Broth

An easygoing, pleasant manner of dealing with his fellow-creatures will take a man further in the world than a kind heart, especially in this island of ours, said Mr Patrick Murphy; an' an unkept promise of a ten-bob-note will earn more gratitude than the gift of a shilling. Mr Robin Tanner, who made his money in Belfast during the first Great War, an' came down to Ballygullion afterwards an' bought the Forred estate, was one of the easygoing, pleasant kind. The kindness didn't go very deep; not that he was bone-selfish, but because his father had laid the foundations of his fortune for him, an' he'd never had to work or thole. He was easy with everybody in his ways an' speech. People liked him well enough, but didn't remember him long after he'd gone by.

The Forred estate was made up of a Big House, with woods an' marshes, an' a stretch of moorland lying across the road to nowhere, but reaching to the wee hills before the mountains riz. There was a good home farm, but Mr Tanner didn't care whether it made money or not. All he wanted was plenty of shooting an' fishing, so that he could invite to his house, an' entertain, the real big-bugs, an' learn in time to be a big-bug himself.

Mr Scotter, the previous proprietor, had preserved the game reasonably strict. It was easy enough to do, on account of the wild part of the estate lying, mostly, away from the labourable land. But Mr Tanner wanted every game bird an' beast for himself. There was a by-road, not 'on the County', that ran from the back of the Big House through the scroggy marshy land along the moor, an' then turned away from it an' in among some very hungry farming land. It was a handy entrance for anybody looking for a quick shot, or setting a trap or two unbeknownst. Mr Tanner was no sooner settled in the Big House than he closed the road.

But, forbye closing the road, he closed the only cottage on it, a decent, well-built, four-roomed cottage, where old Mrs Hannah Gillin lived. This was a sore blow to the old body. Her husband had been a labourer on the home farm in Mr Scotter's time, with a little bit of poaching winked at, as well. She herself had been a kind of stand-by for the Big House any time there happened to be extra work, owing to company. The pair of them did not-badly for themselves, an' brought up two children, both of whom died young. There was a delicacy in the father's family. He himself died before he was sixty. The old woman made out a fair living by her lone, what with work at the Big House, an' raising fowl, an' getting an odd kindness from Mrs Scotter an' the young ladies. But the Scotters went; an' she was given notice to quit, an' cut off from the Big House. She moved to a hovel of a two-roomed cottage outside the borders of the demesne, though still in rough damp country; an' there she struggled to live.

She didn't live well. The fowl she could manage as well as ever, but she was a bad hand, as you would expect, at keeping down rats. Then, the town of Ballygullion was a long way off. She wasn't always strong enough to travel; an' the local small farmers would give her little for eggs an' chickens; for they looked to be making a bit of profit for themselves. The odd jobs she got from them out-of-doors, or from their wives, in-doors, were badly paid. But she an' her man had saved a little money; an' she hained that, an' eked out her other earnings with it, all the more carefully as it drew to an end.

It came to an end at last; an' then, to put the thing in plain speech, she must, for a while, have near starved. But nobody knew that; for she made no sign. She had a cheerful, half-humorous way with her, though her heart might be aching. An' she was shy an' proud. Though more than one farmer's wife gave her little obligements of clothes, an' even food, from time to time, it be't to be done as a present an' not as charity. The people in the Big House never knew of her difficulty, or no doubt they would have done something. Mrs Tanner was even more uppish than her man, but she had more thought for her poorer fellow-beings. Old Mrs Gillin didn't know that; an' if she had known she'd maybe still have said nothing. She had no spite or grudge against the Tanner family, or against anybody in the world. But in her heart she thought she hadn't got fairplay about the cottage.

There came a Christmas when she was nearly at the end of her tether; hardly a bite of food in the house. Coming up to the holiday she had visited her farming friends in the hope of a little present or two. And she did get presents, only they were nearly all bits of clothes. A loaf and a donkey-load of turf were the best she got in the way of food an' firing. The hens were all gone, long before. What broke her heart altogether was that she didn't get even a grain of tea, though she had only a bare half-spoonful left. With a loaf in the house she couldn't starve outright, but there came on her a craving for something warm an' heartening on Christmas night.

The more she thought the more she saw that a good bowl of

broth was the best thing for her to aim at. At any rate it would be warm an' filling. Meat she couldn't beg for, without giving away the completeness of her poverty; but she could get the rest of the materials for the asking, if she pretended at each house that she was short of only the one thing. So on Christmas Eve she went to bed with everything in the house to make a bowl of broth. She said that to herself; but there was a great vacancy in her heart, an' in the pot, for a good big lump of any kind of flesh, from a rabbit up. She skinned the thought over as well as she could, warmed herself at a good fire, ate a slice of bread washed down with hot water an' a colouring of milk, an' went to bed. We'll not think too much of what her feelings were, for they can't have been very high.

On Christmas morning she lay in bed to keep warm, for she had no clothes that she considered she could go to church in. In the afternoon she got up to make her broth. She took another slice of bread for breakfast, an' plain water to it, because she wanted to save her grain of tea an' wee sup of milk for a wind-up of the feast she meant to treat herself to in the evening. An', as she was putting the little pot on the fire there came a great bang an' clatter on the outside door of the kitchen, as if something heavy had fallen against it. When she ran to the door, here was Mr Tanner leaning against the frame of it an' holding on to keep himself from falling. He was in his shooting rig-out with a wee canvas bag on his back, an' a gun in his hand. His stockings an' knickerbockers were all clabbered with thick mud, an' one side of his jacket; an' his hat was gone. He looked at her in a dazed way:

'The ditch fell with me,' says he. 'Let me sit down a while, for my head is turning round.'

When the old woman fetched him in an' sat him on a chair she saw that one side of his head was bruised, an' bleeding a little. She washed it with a rag, all the time him paying little or no attention to her, but sitting there with his eyes closed. Then he began to come round a bit.

'I'm wet,' says he, 'an' cold. Have you any whiskey?'

'I have not,' says she, 'but I could make you a drop of tea.'

An' as she spoke, it went through her like a stoon to think that one-half of her Christmas party was gone with the breath of her mouth. But she wouldn't go back on her word.

'Sit there,' says she, 'till I fetch a live sod of turf up the room. I'll have a good fire for you in no time at all; an' you can sit at it an' dry yourself. I'll fetch the tea in to you.'

When she brought him the tea he was hunched down in the wooden armchair, looking more stupid than sleepy. He pulled himself together when he saw her. She watched him drinking the tea, standing close to him for fear he'd drop the mug; for crockery was getting scarce with her, too.

Half-dazed an' all as he was he didn't think much of the tea.

'That's poor stuff,' says he. 'Could you not have put in another spoonful?'

She thought the less of him for saying that, not because it was ungrateful of him, but because she thought if he had been real gentry, an' not a Belfast upstart, he wouldn't have known so much about how tea was made.

'It's all I have in the house,' says she, a trifle short. But he didn't seem to heed her.

'I'm cold,' he says, half to himself; 'cold and wet. I'll get my death.' An' with that he began to shiver, an' his teeth chattered.

She looked at him, all uneasy; an' then she went an' fetched off her bed the only pretence of a warm blanket that she had, an' wrapped it round him from the neck to the knees.

'Sit, now,' she says, 'an' sleep, an' dry yourself; an' after a little I'll bring you something that'll warm the cockles of your heart. Only don't be impatient, for it'll take some while.'

By this time she had forgot all about herself, thinking of the state the man was in, an' him maybe taking pneumonia; an' a notion had come into her head of an old housekeeper. She went over to the game-bag, that had fallen on the ground. There was something in it, she knew. The broth she was making for herself would be a poor brash of vegetables, at the best; but what if she could put a wild duck into it, or a partridge, or a hare? A bowl of that would be something-like, an' would put warmth an' heart into him. Her memory stirred at the thought. It was as if her own man had come back. Many an' many a time she had watched him being brought-round again by a bowl of broth after a cold clarty day's work in the rain; an' her standing by with her belly empty except for a splash of tea, and a mouthful of dry bread.

When she opened the game-bag an' shook it, there tumbled out a hen-partridge, young an' plump; nothing else. But it was plenty. In ten minutes or so – for she worked furious, an' tore feathers an' skin off the bird – the pieces of it were in the broth. For the best part of an hour she went back an' forrard between the wee pot an' the sick man. He had dropped into an uneasy sleep; but was still shivering, whiles. At last she could thole no longer, but ran an' poured about half the broth into a bowl, an' went into the room to him.

'Here,' says she, 'wake up, an' put that into you. Blow on the spoon at first, for the broth is hot.'

He sat up with a start an' another shiver; an' when he saw the steaming broth he just put out his hands, an' got to work with the iron spoon. When he had finished, he sat up straight an' held out the empty bowl.

'Have you any more of that?' he asks. 'It's great stuff.'

There came another clutch at her heart as she went for the second half of the broth; but when she looked at the remains of the partridge her spirits riz a little, an' she thanked her

Maker that there hadn't been time to boil the whole good out of the bird.

Mr Tanner supped the second bowl of broth near as greedy as the first, an' half-held out the bowl again.

'I suppose you haven't any more to spare?' he asked, a little bit awkward.

'I haven't any more at all,' says she, simply.

He turned a trifle red at that, an' said nothing. Then he stood up on his feet. He was looking more like his natural self again, an' his courage had come back. A spark of decency had come back to him, as well. He felt that it wouldn't do to offer the old woman money; but he didn't know what to say to her. At last, in a clumsy way, he began to praise her broth. He had never tasted the like of it in his whole life before, he said, not even of late years, when his wife had a professed cook. It was going through him that moment like new life. He felt he'd be able to walk home by himself. Would she mind telling him what it was made with?

The question was a facer for the old woman; but she didn't dare to say anything about the partridge. So she told him all the other things that were in the broth, flour, an' oatmeal, an' cabbage, an' brussels-sprouts, an' turnips, an' carrots, an' a stalk or two of celery, an' a sup of milk. She had kind neighbours, she said, an' each of them had given her some wee thing.

An', being a man, he believed it all, an' swore she had worked a miracle. His own cook was a bungler an' a waster compared with her. She must come up to the Big House kitchen some day soon, an' show the woman how to make broth. An' all poor Mrs Gillin could answer to this proposal was to say that she was afraid it would be of no use, because things never tasted the same when they were cooked on a range.

Mr Tanner was well enough content to let it pass at that, an' stood up to go. An' as he straightened himself a bit in his clothes

an' began to look round for his gun, Mrs Gillin bethought herself
for the first time of the empty game-bag, an' the sight nearly left
her eyes. Why had she not told him about the partridge! He had
supped the broth of it an' surely he wouldn't grudge her the
carcase. But she had lied to him about the broth. And he was
uppish, an' mightn't like being made a fool of by a person of
her class.

'I'll get the bag for you, sir,' says she, an' runs into the kitchen
before him. When he came out of the room she hung the bag on
his back, an' put the gun in his hand. An' as she watched him go
up the remnants of the old closed road she hoped he'd never come
back, or if he did that it wouldn't be till she had devoured the
solid end of the partridge for her supper that night.

Mr Tanner made his way home, feeling a deal better than he
thought he'd feel in so short a time after the accident. He was a
selfish man, as all rich people are; but it was through thoughtlessness
more than ill-nature. An', as he turned over in his mind all that
had happened in Mrs Gillin's cottage, he saw that she had been
by-ordinary kindly an' Christian to him, she a poor creature that
was near the point of starvation an' yet had given up to him in his
misfortune her grain of tea an' every mouthful of the broth that,
very likely, was to make the big end of her Christmas meal. An',
being in that frame of mind, he was struck with compassion as he
went past the good dry cottage he had put her out of, to sink her
in what was little better than a swamp. He made up his mind that
he would reinstate her an' give her a few shillings a week to keep
her eye on poachers; for he felt that she could be depended on.

But he knew he would first of all have to prepare his wife for
this move. She was come of more quality than he was, an' hated
a poacher by instinct, the way a cat hates a rat. So when he got
home, an' the first fuss an' wonder was died, an' the wife an' he
sat down to talk the whole adventure over, he came out very strong

about the kindness of the old woman, an' how she had given him her Christmas dinner. Above all he came out powerful about the quality of the broth, how hot an' rich an' tasty it was, an' how – here he made a mistake – he had never got anything like it in his own house, though it was made of nothing but a gather-up of vegetables.

His wife took particular notice of this last part – for she was no fool – an' began to cross question him about the broth; what exactly was in it, an' how it tasted. An' the further she went with the examination the more she grew suspicious.

'Did this wonderful broth taste anything like the game soup we had for dinner the day before yesterday – that you liked so much?' she asked him.

'The very thing!' says he, slapping his leg. 'That must have been why I liked it so much. But her's was richer an' better altogether,' he put in, sticking to his point.

'And made of very much the same ingredients, no doubt,' says his wife, very dry. 'It's no wonder you can't tell claret from Burgundy, when you don't know the difference between a vegetable soup and one reeking with your own game birds, that you reared! And you tell me you want to put this old plausible rascal in among them again. She can't hold a gun,' says she, 'but evidently she can get somebody to hold one for her.'

He looked at her with his jaw dropping.

'I declare I never thought of that,' he says. 'Game it must have been that gave the body and flavour. That ends her so far as the cottage is concerned. But, all the same,' he says, 'we must do some trifle for her. The poor creature wet for me the only grain of tea she had in the house.'

'What's that?' said his wife, very sharp. Then he told her about the tea.

An' it went to the marrow of her. For a cup of tea makes sisters of all weemin, whether they're high-up or low-down.

'Robin,' says she, 'the old creature has a great heart, even if she is an associate of poachers. And we won't condemn her unheard. What have you in your bag?'

'The divil a thing but one partridge,' says he. 'I was too cold to shoot,' he puts in, excusing himself. 'This is a bitter day, out.'

'Has she firing?' asks his wife.

'She has,' he answered: 'for she made me a roaring fire of turf an' sticks.'

'Very well,' says she. 'I'll have a good parcel of tea an' sugar an' eatables made up for her, an' I'll bring it to her myself. I'll bring the partridge, too. When I get there I'll ask to see her larder – if she has such a thing – an' her cooking-utensils. An' if I find nothing that she isn't lawfully entitled to, I'll give her the partridge, an' tell her about the cottage and the rest of it. But not otherwise, mark you! Fetch me the bag. It's still on the hall table.'

He brought the bag. She opened it an' turned it upside-down on the hearth. It was the right place, too; for there fell out a little sod of grassy, poor turf. He looked at her, an' she looked at him; an' then they both began to laugh, but a little shamefaced.

'Now isn't she the great, antic old woman,' says he, at the last. 'Did I say one word too much about her?'

'You didn't say enough,' says she. 'Ring for the housekeeper; and bring me my fur coat.'

HUGO HAMILTON

Nazi Christmas

It began with the man in the fish shop saying 'Achtung!' and all the customers turning around to look at us. Even the people outside under the row of naked turkeys and hanging pheasants stared in through the window. We were exposed. Germans. War criminals using Ireland as a sanctuary. There was a chance they might have overlooked the whole thing if it wasn't for the man in the fish shop trying out some more of his German. All the stuff he had picked up from films like *Von Ryan's Express* and *The Great Escape*.

'Guten Morgen,' he said leaning over the counter, then leaning back with an explosive laugh that acted as a trademark for his shop. Our mother was shy of these friendly, red-faced Irishmen. She smiled at all the people in the shop and they smiled back silently. That was the thing about Ireland. They were all so friendly.

'We haff ways of making you talk,' he said to us whenever we refused to perform for the benefit of his customers and say a few words of German. Like our mother, we were too shy and unable to respond to these contortions of language.

'Halt! We must not forgetten der change.' There was something about us that made people laugh, or whisper, or stop along the street quite openly to ask the most bizarre questions; something that stuck to us like an electronic tag.

It was as though the man in the fish shop had let out this profane secret about us. The word was out. Our assumed identity as Irish children was blown. Everywhere we went, the German past floated on the breeze after us. 'Heil Hitler!' we heard them shout, on the way to Mass, on the way to school, on the way back from the shops. Our mother told us to ignore them. We were not Nazis.

When we were on our own they jumped out behind us or in front of us howling their warcries. It was all 'Donner und Blitzen', and 'Achtung! Get the Krauts'. We lacked the Irish instinct for blending in with the crowd, that natural expertise of human camouflage. It didn't help that Eichmann went on trial for war crimes when I was around five years old. So I was called Eichmann, or sometimes Göring. My older brother usually went under Hitler or Himmler, and the greeting 'Sieg Heil!' was generally accompanied by a neat karate chop on the back of the neck.

It didn't help either that on those shopping trips into town before Christmas, our mother talked to us in German on the bus. Just when we began to enjoy the comfort of anonymity, she would say 'Lass das sein' ('Stop that') in a harsh German tone and the passengers would turn around to stare again. But once we saw the lights in the city and the vast toy departments it was easy to forget. On the way home she told stories and sang Christmas songs like 'O Tannenbaum' with the shopping bags stacked on the seats beside us and the winter sky lighting up pink beyond the roofs of the houses. It was a sign that the angels were baking. And at home there was always the smell of baking.

When we got home there were sweets laid out in the hallway, on the stairs, sometimes across our pillows at night, and when we asked how they got there she said: 'the angels'. She made 'marzipan potatoes', small marzipan marbles coated with cinnamon. On the morning of the sixth of December we came down to find a plate for each of us filled with sweets and a glazed 'Männeken' – a little man with raisin eyes that lasted for ever. The St Nicholas plates stood on the Truhe in the hall, a large oak trunk made in 1788 to store vestments. It was part of her heirloom from Kempen. Everything inside our house was German.

Everything outside was Irish, or imported from Britain. The other houses all had coloured fairy-lights on Christmas trees in the windows. We envied those coloured lights. At the same time we knew we were the only house with real candles, almost like a sign to the outside, a provocation. Most of our clothes and our toys came in parcels from German relatives.

The snow seemed to be a German invention too. Thick flakes fell in Ireland that Christmas and made our mother think of home. There was never any snow again at Christmas; perhaps afterwards in January but never on Christmas Day itself. Somehow Ireland had committed itself more towards the milder Mediterranean climate. With the undercurrent of the Gulf Stream, people here had grown a variety of palm tree that leaned towards the tropical; palm trees that formed the centrepiece of front gardens and patios. Guest houses along the coast expanded the subtropical illusion by hanging nameplates like Santa Maria or Stella Maris from their palms.

Snow was another import which remained mostly in the imagination, on Christmas cards, on top of Christmas cakes, in the form of cotton wool on the roof of the crib. But that year the snow was real; full white snow that took away the seaside appearance and transformed the streets into a fairy-tale of winter. It was our Christmas. Our father put on his favourite Christmas record of the Cologne Children's Choir and the house was filled with the bells of Cologne Cathedral ringing out across the sea to

Dublin. There was the taste of German food, pretzels and *Lebkuchen* and exotic gifts from Germany.

We might as well have been in Kempen where our mother came from, kneeling in front of the crib as we prayed and sang in German with the white candles reflected in my father's glasses and the smell of pine merging with the smell of *Glühwein* in the front room.

Later, we went out to build a snowman in the front garden and it was only when we entered a snowball fight with other children in the street that we realised we were back in Ireland; where children had scooped snow from the low walls or where the cars had skidded and exposed the raw street underneath. We went from one garden to the next looking for new untouched sheets of snow, where the street was still under a dream. And when all the other children disappeared inside for Christmas dinner, we decided to go to the football field to see how deep the snow was there.

It seemed like a good idea until we were ambushed in the lane by a gang of boys we had never seen before. Amelia and I ran away into the field through the opening in the barbed-wire fence, but they had caught Karl and pushed him against the wall. One of them held a stick across his neck. 'You Nazi bastard,' they said.

Amelia and I shouted to let him go. She threatened to tell on them but it was a frail plea. We were trapped.

'Get them,' one of them said and three or four of the boys ran into the field after us. There was no point in screaming for help either because nobody would hear.

'You Nazi bastard,' they said again to Karl. Then they twisted his arm up behind his back and made him walk towards the field where Amelia and I had already been caught behind a line of eucalyptus trees. One of them was forcing snow up Amelia's jumper and she was whining with the effort to fight him off.

Karl said nothing. He had already put into action his plan of inner defiance and was determined to give them nothing but silence, as though they didn't exist, as though they would soon get tired and go away. Amelia stopped resisting and they stopped putting snow under her jacket because she wasn't contributing to the fun. We were told to line up with our backs against the wall of the football field.

The leader of the gang had no fear of the cold. While the other boys blew into their cupped red hands for warmth, he calmly picked up more snow and caked it into a flat icy disc in his palms. We kept repeating in our heads the maxims our mother had taught us: 'The winner yields. Ignore them.' I tried to look as though standing against the wall was exactly what I wanted to be doing at that very moment.

'What will we do with these Nazi fuckers?' the leader asked, holding his stony white disc up to our faces. 'Put them on trial,' somebody said.

They formed a circle around us and discussed how they would proceed with this. There was no point in thinking of escape. One of the boys was pushing a discoloured piece of brown snow towards Karl with the tip of his shoe, whispering to him: 'I'm going to make you eat that.' Amelia started crying again but Karl told her to be quiet.

'OK, Nazi,' the leader said. 'What have you got to say for yourselves?'

'Don't indulge them,' Karl said to us. 'Don't indulge them,' they all mocked and for some of them it was the sign to start speaking in a gibberish of German. 'Gotten, blitzen . . . Himmel.' Another boy started dancing around, trampling a circle in the snow with 'Sieg Heils' until Amelia could no longer contain a short, nervous smile. For the leader it was a sign to hurl his snowball. It hit me in the eye with a flash of white; a hard lump of icy stone that immediately made me hold my face. I was close to tears but I didn't want to let Karl down and give them the satisfaction.

'The Nazi Brothers,' he then announced. 'Guilty or not guilty?'

'Guilty,' they all shouted and they laughed and collected more snow. The trees were being pushed by the wind. Above the white landscape of the football field the sky was darkening and it looked as though it would snow again. Low on the grey sky there were flashes of white or silver seagulls.

'We have to go home now,' Amelia said with a sudden burst of self-righteousness as she moved forward to go. But she was held back. 'You're going nowhere, you SS whore.'

All of it meant little to us. It was as though the terms were being invented there and then, as though they came from somebody's perverse imagination. One of them said something about concentration camps, and gas chambers. Whenever I asked my mother about the Nazis I saw a look in her eyes somewhere between confusion and regret.

'Execute them,' they all shouted. They were looking for signs that one of us might break. The only hope for us was that they might get bored with it all. That they too might be numb with the cold.

The sentence became obvious as they quietly began an industry of snowball-making. Somebody mentioned the 'firing squad'. Some of them laughed and Amelia once more began to cry. They crouched down and collected mounds of snowballs, enough to start another war. Somebody reminded everyone to pack them hard. One of them included the discoloured piece of snow in his armoury and when they all had heaps of white cannonballs ready beside their feet, we waited for the order and watched the leader of the gang mutely raise his hand.

It seemed like an endless wait in which it was possible to

think of all kinds of random, irrelevant things like Christmas cake, and marzipan potatoes and the peculiar skull-shaped design of the plum pudding as well as other even more irrelevant things like the three little dials of the gas meter under the stairs, until the hand eventually came down and the piercing shout brought with it a hail of blinding white fire. Karl put his hands up to his eyes. 'It's only snow.'

CANON SHEEHAN

Frank Forrest's Mince-Pie

I

'I declare, Frank,' said Mrs Forrest, 'that is the fourth mince-pie you have eaten this evening. I am afraid, my boy, they will make you ill, so put away this one until tomorrow.'

Frank knew not how to disobey his beloved mother; so he promptly took up the delicacy, and placed it in the cupboard. It was Christmas Eve. Presently a feeble, timid knock was heard; and, as cook was ever so busy preparing tarts and pies for the morrow, Frank ran to the door and opened it. A gust of sleety wind nearly lifted him from his feet, and a few snowflakes fell softly on the floor, and melted slowly on the carpet in the hall.

'Something for the children,' said a weak, faltering voice; and Frank saw before him a pale, delicate woman shivering in the icy wind. She had a child in her arms, looking sickly, and the snow had made a little crown for his head on the cloak which his mother had wrapped around him. She held another child by the hand, and its little rags flapped and fluttered, as the cruel storm tossed them, and pierced the little limbs with its icy needles.

'Stop a moment,' said Frank, who was a rough, brusque,

manly lad, but had tender feelings, though he was unconscious of possessing them. In a few moments he returned with the following miscellany, several buns, scraps of cold meat, a paper of tea, a paper of soft sugar, a bunch of raisins, a wooden monkey on a stick, a battered doll, and, crowning all, his own mince-pie which he had put away for the morrow.

'God bless you, dear,' said the woman, as she opened her apron and wrapped up all these treasures; and a smile flashed across her face and lighted up her eyes, as if an angel had rushed by and touched and transfigured her.

Nine o'clock came, and Frank sat by his bedroom fire, watching the flames dancing and leaping, and gambolling around the bars. Then, slowly and reluctantly, he pulled off one shoe after another, and soon found himself nestling in his little cot, listening to the wild storm that shook the windows, and wondering where were the children resting whom he had seen that afternoon. Softly sleep stole upon him, and he closed his eyes in the peaceful slumber of boyhood.

Boom – boom – boom. It was the great Cathedral bell swinging out the midnight hour, and sending its welcome tones on the wings of the storm. Frank started up.

Ding-dong, ding-dong, ding-dong; and mingling their sweet silvery notes with the deep booming, the joybells pealed out rapturously the Christmas chimes. Frank heard the hall-door open and shut, and he knew that mother was going through the storm to the midnight Mass. He rubbed his eyes, and looked around. Heigho! what's this? He rubbed his eyes again, then started up and leaned on his elbow. No doubt about it. There, in his own chair, opposite the fire, was a little old man, not a bit bigger than Frank himself. He held his hands before the fire, and Frank could see their dark shadows distinctly before the red embers. For a moment the boy was astonished, but presently the boyish daring and courage came back, and he shouted cheerily:

'Hallo! old fellow, a happy Christmas!'

The stranger rose slowly, then came to the bedside, his two hands folded behind his back, and bending over the boy, he exclaimed, half-seriously, half-jestingly:

'Ah! you bad boy!'

'I am not a bad boy,' said Frank, indignant at such an answer to his welcome, 'and you have no right to say so.'

'Where's my mince-pie?' said the old man, lifting up one finger, and shaking it warningly.

'I am sure,' said Frank, 'I don't know where's your mince-pie; but I gave mine to a poor woman.'

'Ah! you bad boy,' said the stranger again, as he slowly turned away and took up his seat by the fireplace.

But Frank knew that the old man did not mean what he said. Presently, his hand dived deep, deep down into his pocket, and he placed on the table, near Frank's collar and cuffs, the very identical mince-pie which Frank had given the poor woman at the door. There it was, with its mitred edge, its brown crust, and the five currants which Frank had ordered the cook to place crosswise on the top. The old man lifted off the crust and placed it gently beside him.

'He's going to eat it, the old glutton,' thought Frank; 'he surely stole it from the poor woman.' But no! he simply lighted a match on the coals, and swiftly passed it round the edge of the pie before him. A bright blue flame shot upwards, flickering and flashing in the darkness till it reached the ceiling. Then it assumed gradually the form of a house on fire. The windows were shown clearly against the dark walls by the terrible flames within, and Frank could see the little spurts of fire that broke from the slates on the roof. Now there was a rumbling and the confused murmur of many voices, and the tramping of many feet, and a noise like the roaring of the sea. Then there was a wild shout, and a tiny jet of water rose like a thread from the crowd and scattered its showers upon the fire. Another shout, and the boy's heart sank within him as he saw at the window of the burning house a young lad like himself, clad only in his night-dress, terror and agony on his face, and his arms flung wildly hither and thither. A cheer went up, and a ladder was planted firmly against the window, and a sailor lad swiftly ascended, and in a moment the little fluttering figure was grasped in the strong arms, and carried safely where gentle hands and warm hearts would protect him. Frank's heart was throbbing wildly, the perspiration stood out in beads on his forehead, when he heard the harsh voice of the old man:

'Shut your eyes!'

Frank shut them, but kept one little corner open, and he saw the old man quietly taking up the crust and place it in the pie, completely extinguishing this awful conflagration. And the Christmas bells were chiming.

'Shut your eyes!' said the old man again, quite angrily. And Frank shut them and kept them closed for a long time, as he thought.

'Look,' said the same voice.

Frank opened his eyes, fearing and wondering what new strange vision was going to burst on him. It was nothing terrible, however; but somehow the mince-pie had expanded and grown into a deep and broad valley, with rugged rocks and strange dark places, and black mountains huddled together, and tossed about as if by an earthquake. And from their midst rose a mighty peak, the base of which was clothed with fir trees, and farther up were black frowning rocks, and the top was crowned by a pinnacle of snow that shot up high into the air, and was lost beyond the ceiling of the little bedroom. At the base of the mountain was a village, and there was a bustle in the village, and the noise of many tongues.

In the street many mules were standing, laden with provisions, and three guides, tall and strong, and brown, strolled up and down, their alpenstocks in their hands, and huge coils of rope strung across their shoulders. Three young gentlemen stood apart, talking earnestly. They were young, scarcely more than boys, but there was vigour and courage in their looks, and gait and manner. They had not heard of the word 'Danger!' At last one separated from the rest, and walked away quite dejected and angry. The word was given, and the two gentlemen and their guides set out to scale the mountain. They were watched until they turned the spur of the hill. Then one ringing cheer, and they disappeared in the shadows of the mountains. The day wore on, and evening came. But before the twilight descended, Frank saw that people came from their houses with long telescopes, and levelled them at the snowy summit. Nothing was visible there, as Frank could see, but the cold, hard, glittering snow, shining pink and ruby from the reflections of the fire. Suddenly there was a shout: 'There they are!' Frank looked, and thought he saw five tiny black specks in the snow, linked together by a thread. Slowly these specks moved up the slippery surface until they were lost in the clouds. A few minutes later those same black specks reappeared, toiling down the steep side of the mountain of ice. Frank held his breath. They had already travelled down half the mountain, when the lowest figure on the rope fell, and one after another the brave climbers were tossed from cliff to cliff, from precipice to precipice, until they were lost in the black valleys beneath. A cry of horror had gone up from the village. Frank shut his eyes, and put his fingers in his ears. After a few moments he looked again, and saw lights flashing in the village, and dark figures hurrying to and fro, and he felt they were going out to seek for the dead bodies of the guides and the two gentlemen. Presently a bell began to toll, and Frank thought it too cheerful for a funeral; for now down the slope of the hill, in amongst the trees, out across the valley, he saw the lights shining, and slowly the procession entered the village. Mountaineers, with their heads bent down, carried on their shoulders a bier, and on the bier was something covered with a black cloth. Behind them came a young man, whom Frank recognised as the companion, who was left behind in the morning. He was weeping silently, now and again passing his handkerchief across his face.

For one moment he raised his head, and the red light of the torches fell upon him, and Frank saw that it was himself, and he felt himself choking at the thought of his narrow escape from a terrible death. He lay for a while thinking and thinking, when once more he saw the old man by the fire with the mince-pie on the table, but the vision of the valley was gone. But the Christmas chimes were ringing.

After a little while, once more the voice of the old man, now very gently and lovingly, said, 'Shut your eyes!' Frank closed his eyes sorrowfully, for he felt very sad and frightened, and he dreaded another terrible picture.

'Now,' said the old man, 'you may look!'

II

Timidly enough, Frank peered forth; but how his heart bounded with joy when he saw his own beautiful harbour painted in its richest colourings of blue and gold, the sunshine streaming over its surface, and the little waves dancing and leaping and flashing. He looked for a long time out over the waters, but he heard the noise of laughter and talking quite close at hand, and he saw just beneath him a large, beautiful boat, and somehow he thought that this boat was but his mince-pie lengthened out and decorated. It was heaving and rocking on the water, and it had the straightest mast and the whitest sail in the world. And in the stern Frank saw quite

a crowd of 'fair women and brave men', and he knew them all
as the friends of his boyhood, though they were changed. Stout
watermen in blue jerseys were lifting hampers over the gunwale,
and over all there was a something Frank never saw before. It was a
joy and a peace and a glory as if reflected from some light brighter
than the sunshine. But he himself was very sad. And they pitied
him, and said, 'Another time, Frank; don't grieve too much.' And
then the oars were planted firmly on the gravel, and the boat was
pushed away, and after a few strokes the sail was lifted, and the
breeze caught it and carried the gay barque like a bird over the
bright waters. Frank turned away sick and disappointed, but lo!
as he came along from the Admiralty Pier, he saw facing him the
poor woman whom he had relieved and her children. But she was
changed. She had on that strange look which passed across her face
when the angel touched her, and her child was bright and ruddy,
and held forth his hands to Frank, and the little girl, dressed ever
so beautifully, caught Frank and bent him down towards her, and
whispered something that Frank could not hear. But a strange
peace stole over his heart, and all the sorrow and disappointment
were gone.

But when the evening came and the lamp was lighted, and the
books were opened, the same sadness stole into his heart. Suddenly
there was a sharp ring, and a succession of knocks, and hurried
whisperings at the door, and he heard his mother's voice saying,
'My God!' and then the door of his room opened, and his mother
glided in, and her face was wet with tears, and Frank knew that the
gay barque of the morning was drifting out a sad wreck into the
high seas, and he knew also that his dear friends from whom he
had parted so sadly in the morning were now lying cold and still
on the sand and shingle down deep beneath the cold blue waters.
But mother came near him, and flung her arms round him, and
he heard her say:

'Why, Frank, you lazy boy, still in bed at eight o'clock Christmas morning. You promised to be first in the sacristy to bid Father Ambrose a happy Christmas; and now you must wait for High Mass, and there's a pile of Christmas Cards waiting for you.'

Frank lay still a moment, collecting his thoughts, doubting all things, thinking all things a dream. But there was the white light of the Christmas snow shining in his room, and there was the bell ringing for Mass, and drawing a long sigh, he exclaimed:

'O mother, I had such a dream.'

'Never mind, my boy,' said his mother; 'you can tell it by-and-by!'

And by-and-by, when the tables were cleared and they were sitting round the fire, and there was not a shadow of gloom on the gay little circle, Frank told his dream, his hand softly clasped by his mother. And when he had done, she smoothed away his fair locks from his forehead, and kissed him gently, and said:

'It was not a dream, Frank, but a vision of dangers from which the good God will preserve my boy for his kindness to the little ones of Christ.'

RITA KELLY

The Conifers

Pine-needles and putrefaction. An air heavy with decay, October decomposes itself in damp brown bracken. Gaping cones underfoot and exposed gnarled roots. And yet that sudden sense of shape, human maybe, passing among the trunks, their encrusted bark, that uncanny quiet. A twig, crunched underfoot? A scampering claw? Where? Perhaps a beak against the upper bark. The sound dissipates itself and all is enveloped in an unticked silence.

Somewhere in the upper branches it is late afternoon, a slant of sun and rainclouds gathering themselves out of the vacancy. That is but a surmise here in this green, resin-filled gloom. Sharp and pungent. We are such late-comers to the conifer centuries. Quietly, they pulse within, knots of vascular bundles swelling and contracting, passing the bitter sap up the channels to the topmost twigs. And tough little root-hairs pushing their way through the sour earth, through rock crevices, contorting themselves and perforating the clay to suck it dry.

On the bark, the fingers feel only the abrasion, yet they sense the tension, and the push up out of the gloom for that dismal bit of sunlight.

With Georg it was so different. Georg saw an unending area of Christmas trees, *Bäumchens*, little ones, and *kleinen Kerzlein, Lichter und die Geschenke*, little candles, lights and gifts. So that is what he saw, bright words, strange and so different in sound and meaning from the terms in the zoology books, trying to comprehend them and their length. Dr Bennett, encouraging as usual, 'Of course Alice, those awful Germanic conglomerates, but . . .'

So that is what Georg saw. So full of fancy and playful feeling. But did he see the hundreds of trees lying in the Market Street on Christmas Eve, enough to tire one of the idea for ever. Broken branches in the gutter, all wet and bedraggled. He only saw one tree, glistening in the light, and the wonder in the little eyes gathered about it. Hands clutching nightclothes, too surprised to touch the gifts, and the tiny imaginations overrun with a glow of possibility. Until the *Geschenke* are finally exposed and taken fondly back to bed. Georg could even hear the churchbells, and feel the flutter of snow-flakes. A sensation stamped within and carried through far-distant nightwatches, battened down in the hold of memory. Memory?

She saw the orphanage. She saw the Orphan Nun, long white habit and blue shawl, striding into the refectory on Christmas morning with an apple and a currant bun sent down from Reverend Mother. The bit of scraggy ivy about the picture of the Holy Family, the one with the woodshavings and the pale Christ with a chisel. And Georg could not feel the cold of the red tiles through the canvas shoes, scrubbed on Christmas Eve, knees still sore, and he never had to step out of the way as Thomas, that big black bully with the tight curls, came tearing along the tiles in hob-nailed boots, and bear the whimpering when Mary Josephine, the big orphan, came from peeling onions for the dinner, to hit him a clout in the lug. Bold stump.

Acrid, the resin comes through the bark in brown blobs. There is a wind soughing in the upper branches, lonesome and lost.

But this Georg, in his festive fancy, he could not see the bowl of red jelly sitting out on the windowsill, and he never got goosepimples watching it congeal. Nor did he hear the thin bell of the Nun's Chapel while scurrying into twos on the frozen gravel, trying not to look at the scab of ringworm on the head in front, there in spite of all Sister Paul's prodding with the needle, thin sticks of arms, the skin flaked and rough, a dab of antiseptic and a sting of steel before the shot of pain. Purple and pinched with the cold under the pink smock.

Nor did he claw up the beams of the Gallery slipping on the varnish above where Mary Josephine and the Organ Nun were bellowing and blowing *Adeste Fideles*, to catch a glimpse of the Nun's crib, with a star and decent-looking ivy, yellow straw glowing in the light and a cow with painted horns. Then there was the scraping and pulling and fingernails sunk in the back of the leg, get down out of that for the love of Jesus. And the dig in the ribs going out the Chapel door. Back to the smell of onions and the grease of boiled hens, the same hens that the big lads had thrown stones at when Sister Paul was not looking. And the red jelly and custard cut with a knife, the bowl flung spinning down the formica.

But Georg kept talking about *das Eis*, skating on the frozen lake with all the other children. And *die Schnee*, everywhere, covering fields and houses and yet more falling until the little village had become fairylike and foreign. And avalanches cascading from the roofs and smashing themselves on the snow-packed ground. And friends coming to visit, sitting about the fire near the Christmas tree, their voices sounding in a sleepy distance, overcome after the day's excitement, tired throbbing limbs, *die schöne Erschöpfung*, exquisite exhaustion.

The Conifers

He had never sat at the window, scratching the frost with a fingernail, ripping the frozen ramification to gain a glimpse of the garden, hoping that there just might be snow. Nothing, but greyness, raw flowerbeds and bits of withered grass. The high grey wall of the convent, a few sparrows skirting about the saint's statue, or a crow with watchful eye through the grass, he might find some of the Garden Nun's crumbs. While behind in the bleak interior an unending scamper of little feet on the bare floorboards, the creaking of the iron beds, rows and rows of them, clambering up and down and pitching pillows until the feathers flew. But snow, it never came, just when it was needed to give point to the evening and the watery tea and bit of marble cake, and Mary Josephine blowing carols and the Teddy Bears' Picnic on a rusted tin-whistle, even then it never snowed. But it came in March, and caught the exposed daffodil. It seeped, slush, through the canvas shoes, there were running noses, raw eyes, colds, more onions and coughing in the night.

And then there was the city, she had a mother there once, she never came, until she was nothing but the ghost of an idea there in the city where ships came, big ships swaying in the docks and seen from the convent bus when the orphans were brought to the sea for good clean air. Noses flattened to the glass, standing on the bus-seats, tired of the sea and the toffee-apples, watching the names of ships until the bus lurched round a corner banishing the strange names and flags.

But Georg came, so unexpectedly from behind the spruce. Had he been there all the time? He seemed to belong there, walking so silently on the pine-needles. A voice clear-cut and guttural in the silence, she was surprised when she found that she understood the words. Pine forest. Reminds him of home.

It had been a Saturday, the girls at the laboratory gone home for the weekend. Home? And Dr Bennett going fishing.

'What are you doing yourself, Alice, for the weekend?'

Friends. A forest above the sea, good clean air, walking and sitting and mind-wandering. No one in the laboratory but the mice and rabbits, scratching at their cages and sucking water from the drip. And the coloured charts of needles, births, deaths, and no reactions. No *Lichter und Geschenke*, no pied piper from a candlelit Hamelin for these proliferating scraps of biology. White and pink-eyed, clambering about each other in the heat, breeding and giving suck to the pink-fleshed things. No reaction. Pages and pages of no reaction, the needle ready, the little mouse wriggling between the fingers, the serum pushed in, subcutaneously, the long wait. No reaction. The immaculate white coats hanging behind the door, starched and ready. The eternal scratching and clawing at the cages, a smell of food and excrement, brown currants on the bedding, woodshavings and straw. These are the cribs, these are the currant buns sent down by the Holy Mother. The twitching of the rabbits, rheum coming from the eyes, all those eyes watching, the breathing in one's ears, as if one lived in a burrow, a layered dug-out. And the squeak of the mouse caught between the fingers, darting about the floor, too eager he dashed from his cage feeling the lid off. Contaminated. The needle again, no further purpose, but write under the lists of no reactions, day and date, mouse 41 died.

From the trees he came. And smiled, speaking as if he had been merely interrupted for a few moments. How very odd. Finding someone in this forest after all the Saturdays, time out of mind, pushing through the pines to the overhang to watch the wind-scratched surface of the sea, to listen to the dull reverberation on the unseen rocks below. Still, he led the way to the overhang as if he knew, and though he must have been sorely tired of the sea he waited and listened. Close, not a twitch, not even a pulse, but a warmth not of rabbits. Must have been an age, huddled on a mossed rock, just listening, secure in the sound of the distant turmoil and the receding hiss, regular and rhythmic. A melting of sensation, mind-wandering and warm. Then his voice, calling that name.

'Elschen.' So different from Alice, weird and tender.

'You must not sleep. Es wird auch kälter, it's getting colder too.'

What? What was it? Some strange voice disrupting the rhythm, dragging one back. Elschen. Strangely familiar, wafted up from the depths, that awful moment of wave-speech, naming. Elschen. No, I am not your Kindlein, you from the old city of legend and ditchwater and deadly fairytale, pushing out of the Elbe mouth, rising and falling, watching the droplets cling to the porthole, rocked in your bunk, full of memories which are not mine, edging west to unload your cargo, torn from the inwards of the earth, making the landfall between the long limbs of the bay, slipping in after dark, dwarfing the houses near the docks. Steel, you bring it battened down, sharp blue, as your eyes.

Es wird kälter. And so it does. Sea and sky and gathering raincloud, a funnel trailing smoke slips out of sight. First breath of breeze hums in the forest, tugs at her scarf, rattles the old cones, releasing the bitter spores.

BENEDICT KIELY

Homes on the Mountain

The year I was twelve my father, my mother, my brother and myself had our Christmas dinner in the house my godmother's husband had built high up on the side of Dooish Mountain, when he and she came home to Ireland from Philadelphia.

That was a great godmother. She had more half-crowns in her patch pockets than there were in the Bank of England and every time she encountered me which, strategically, I saw was pretty often, it rained half-crowns. Those silvery showers made my friend Lanty and myself the most popular boy bravados in our town. A curious thing was, though, that while we stood bobby-dazzler caramels, hazelnut chocolate, ice cream, cigarettes and fish and chips by the ton to our sycophants, we ourselves bought nothing but song-books. Neither of us could sing a note.

We had a splendid, patriotic taste in song-books, principally because the nearest newsagent's shop, kept by an old spinster in Devlin Street, had a window occupied by a sleeping tomcat, two empty tin boxes, bundles of pamphlets yellowed by exposure to the light, and all members of a series called Irish Fireside Songs.

The collective title appealed by its warm cosiness. The little books were classified into Sentimental, Patriot's Treasury, Humorous and Convivial, and Smiles and Tears. Erin, we knew from Tom Moore and from excruciating music lessons at school, went wandering around with a tear and a smile blended in her eye. Because even to ourselves our singing was painful, we read together, sitting in the sunshine on the steps that led up to my father's house, such gems of the Humorous and Convivial as: 'When I lived in Sweet Ballinacrazy, dear, the girls were all bright as a daisy, dear.' Or turning to the emerald-covered Patriot's Treasury we intoned: 'We've men from the Nore, from the Suir and the Shannon, let the tyrant come forth, we'll bring force against force.'

Perhaps, unknown to ourselves, we were affected with the nostalgia that had brought my godmother and her husband back from the comfort of Philadelphia to the bleak side of Dooish Mountain. It was a move that my mother, who was practical and who had never been far enough from Ireland to feel nostalgia, deplored.

'Returned Americans,' she would say, 'are lost people. They live between two worlds. Their heads are in the clouds. Even the scrawny, black-headed sheep — not comparing the human being and the brute beast — know by now that Dooish is no place to live.'

'And if you must go back to the land,' she said, 'let it be the land, not rocks, heather and grey fields no bigger than pocket handkerchiefs. There's Cantwell's fine place beside the town going up for auction. Seventy acres of land, a palace of a dwelling-house, outhouses would do credit to the royal family, every modern convenience and more besides.'

For reasons that had nothing to do with prudence or sense, Lanty and myself thought the Cantwell place an excellent idea. There were crab-apple trees of the most amazing fertility scattered all along the hedgerows on the farm; a clear gravel stream twisted through it; there were flat pastures made for football and, behind the house, an orchard that not even the most daring buccaneer of our generation had ever succeeded in robbing.

But there were other reasons – again nostalgic reasons – why my godmother's husband who was the living image of Will Rogers would build nowhere in Ireland except on the rough, wet side of Dooish, and there, on the site of the old home where he had spent his boyhood, the house went up. There wasn't a building job like it since the building of the Tower of Babel.

'Get a good sensible contractor from the town,' said my mother, 'not drunken Dan Redmond from the mountain who couldn't build a dry closet.'

But my godmother's husband had gone to school with Dan Redmond. They had been barefooted boys together and that was that, and there was more spent, according to my mother, on malt whiskey to entertain Dan, his tradesmen and labourers, than would have built half New York. To make matters worse it was a great season for returned Americans and every one of them seemed to have known my godmother and her husband in Philadelphia. They came in their legions to watch the building, to help pass the bottle and to proffer advice. The acknowledged queen of this gathering of souls fluttering between two worlds was my Aunt Brigid, my mother's eldest sister. She was tiny and neat, precise in her speech, silver-haired, glittering with rimless spectacles and jet-black beads. In the States she had acquired a mania for euchre, a passion for slivers of chicken jelled in grey-green soup, a phonograph with records that included a set of the favourite songs of Jimmy Walker, and the largest collection of snapshots ever carried by pack mule or public transport out of Atlantic City.

Then there was a born American – a rarity in our parts in those days – a young man and a distant relative. Generous and jovial, he kissed every woman, young or old, calling them cousin or aunt; but it was suspected among wise observers that he never once in the course of his visit was able to see the Emerald Isle clearly. For the delegation, headed by my Aunt Brigid, that met him in Dublin set him straight away on the drink and when he arrived to view the building site – it was one of the few sunny days of that summer – he did so sitting on the dickey seat of a jaunting car and waving in each hand a bottle of whiskey. The builder and his men and the haymakers in June meadows left their work to welcome him, and Ireland, as the song says, was Ireland through joy and through tears.

Altogether it was a wet season: the whiskey flowed like water, the mist was low over the rocks and heather of Dooish and the moors of Loughfresha and Cornavara, the mountain runnels were roaring torrents. But miraculously the building was done; the returned Americans with the exception of Aunt Brigid, my godmother and her husband, went westwards again in the fall; and against all my mother's advice on the point of health, the couple from Philadelphia settled in for late November. The house-warming was fixed for Christmas Day.

'Dreamers,' my mother said. 'An American apartment on the groundwalls of an old cabin. Living in the past. Up where only a brave man would build a shooting lodge. For all they know or care there could be wolves still on the mountain. Magazines and gewgaws and chairs too low to sit on. With the rheumatism the mountain'll give them, they'll never bend their joints to sit down so low.'

Since the damp air had not yet brought its rheumatism we all sat down together in the house that was the answer to the exile's dream. Lamplight shone on good silver and Belfast linen. My godmother's man was proud to the point of tears.

'Sara Alice,' he said to my mother.

Content, glass in hand, he was more than ever like Will Rogers.

'Sara Alice,' he said. 'My mother, God rest her, would be proud to see this day.'

Practicality momentarily abandoned, my mother, moist-eyed and sipping sherry, agreed.

'Tommy,' he said to my father, 'listen to the sound of the spring outside.'

We could hear the wind, the voices of the runnels, the spring pouring clear and cool from a rainspout driven into a rock-face.

'As far as I recollect that was the first sound my ears ever heard, and I heard it all my boyhood, and I could hear it still in Girard Avenue, Philadelphia. But the voices of children used to be part of the sound of the spring. Seven of us, and me to be the youngest and the last alive. When my mother died and my father took us all to the States we didn't know when we were going away whether to leave the door open or closed. We left it open in case a travelling man might pass, needing shelter. We knocked gaps in the hedges and stone walls so as to give the neighbours' cattle the benefit of commonage and the land the benefit of the cow dung. But we left the basic lines of the walls so that nobody could forget our name or our claim to this part of the mountain.'

'In Gartan, in Donegal,' said my father, 'there's a place called the Flagstone of Loneliness where Saint Colmcille slept the night before he left Ireland under sentence of banishment. The exiles in that part used to lie down there the day before they sailed and pray to the saint to be preserved from the pangs of homesickness.'

My Aunt Brigid piped in a birdlike voice a bit of an exile song that was among her treasured recordings: 'A strange sort of sigh seems to come from us all as the waves hide the last glimpse of old Donegal.'

'Our American wake was held in Aunt Sally O'Neill's across the glen,' said my godmother's husband. 'Red Owen Gormley lilted for the dancers when the fiddlers were tired. He was the best man of his time at the mouth music.'

'He was also,' said my father, 'the first and last man I knew who could make a serviceable knife, blade and haft, out of a single piece of hardwood. I saw him do it, myself and wild Martin Murphy who was with me in the crowd of sappers who chained these mountains for the 1911 Ordnance Survey map. Like most of us, Martin drank every penny and on frosty days he would seal the cracks in his shoes with butter – a trick I never saw another man use. It worked too.'

'Aunt Sally's two sons were there at our American wake,' said my godmother's husband. 'Thady that was never quite right in the head and, you remember, Tommy, couldn't let a woman in the market or a salmon in the stream alone. John, the elder brother, was there with Bessy from Cornavara that he wooed for sixty years and never, I'd say, even kissed.'

The old people were silently laughing. My brother, older than myself, was on the fringe of the joke. As my godmother came and went I sniffed fine cooking. I listened to the mountain wind and the noise of the spring and turned the bright pages of an American gardening magazine. Here were rare blooms would never grow on Dooish Mountain.

'All dead now I suppose,' my father said to end the laughing.

'Bessy's dead now,' said my Aunt Brigid. 'Two years ago. As single as the day she was born. Like many another Irishman, John wasn't overgiven to matrimony. But in the village of Crooked Bridge below, the postman told me that John and Thady are still alive in the old house on Loughfresha. Like pigs in a sty, he said. Pigs in a sty. And eight thousand pounds each, according to all accounts, in the Munster and Leinster Bank in the town.'

'God help us,' said my mother. 'I recall that house as it was when Aunt Sally was alive. It was beautiful.'

My father was looking out of the window, down the lower grey slopes of Dooish and across the deep glen towards Loughfresha and Cornavara.

'It won't rain again before dark or dinner,' he said. 'I haven't walked these hills since I carried a chain for His Majesty's Ordnance Survey. Who'd ever have thought the King of England would be interested in the extent of Cornavara or Dooish Mountain.'

'Get up you two boys,' he said, 'and we'll see if you can walk as well as your father before you.'

The overflow of the spring came with us as we descended the boreen. Winter rain had already rutted the new gravel laid by drunken Dan Redmond and his merry men. Below the bare apple-orchard the spring's overflow met with another runnel and with yet another where another boreen, overgrown with hawthorn and bramble, struggled upwards to an abandoned house.

'Some people,' said my father, 'didn't come back to face the mountain. Living in Philadelphia must give a man great courage.'

He walked between us with the regular easy step of an old soldier who, in days of half-forgotten wars, had footed it for ever across the African veldt.

'That was all we ever did,' he would say. 'Walk and walk. And the only shot I ever fired that I remember was at a black snake and I never knew whether I hit or missed. That was the Boer war for you.'

Conjoined, innumerable runnels swept under a bridge where the united boreens joined the road, plunged over rock in a ten-foot cataract, went elbowing madly between bare hazels down to the belly of the glen. White cabins, windows already lamp-lighted and candle-lighted for Christmas, showed below the shifting fringe of black grey mist.

'This house I knew well,' he said, 'this was Aunt Sally's. The Aunt was a title of honour and had nothing to do with blood relationship. She was stately, a widow, a great manager and aunt to the whole country. She had only the two sons.'

By the crossroad of the thirteen limekilns we swung right and descended the slope of the glen on what in a dry summer would have been a dust road. Now, wet sand shifted under our feet, loose stones rattled ahead of us, the growing stream growled below us in the bushes. To our left were the disused limekilns, lining the roadway like ancient monstrous idols with gaping toothless mouths, and as we descended the old man remembered the days when he and his comrades, veterans all, had walked and measured those hills; the limekilns in operation and the white dust on the grass and the roadside hedges; the queues of farm carts waiting for the loading. Fertilisers made in factories had ended all that. There was the place (he pointed across a field) where a tree, fallen on a mearing fence, had lain and rotted while the two farmers whose land the fence divided, swept away by the joy of legal conflict, had disputed in the court in the town the ownership of the timber. The case never reached settlement. Mountainy men loved law and had their hearts in twopence. And here was Loughfresha bridge. (The stream was a torrent now.) The gapped, stone parapet hadn't been mended since the days of the survey. And there was the wide pool where Thady O'Neill, always a slave to salmon, had waded in after a big fish imprisoned by low water, taken it with his bare hands after a mad struggle and, it was said, cured himself by shock treatment of premature arthritis.

Once across the bridge our ascent commenced. Black brooding roadside cattle looked at us with hostility. On a diagonal across a distant meadow a black hound-dog ran silently, swiftly up towards the mist, running as if with definite purpose – but what, I wondered, could a dog be doing running upwards there alone on a Christmas

Day. The thought absorbed me to the exclusion of all else until we came to the falling house of John and Thady O'Neill.

'Good God in heaven,' said my father.

For a full five minutes he stood looking at it, not speaking, before he led his two sons, with difficulty, as far as the door.

Once it must have been a fine, long, two-storeyed, thatched farmhouse, standing at an angle of forty-five degrees to the roadway and built backwards into the slope of the hill. But the roof and the upper storey had sagged and, topped by the growth of years of rank decayed grass, the remnants of the thatched roof looked, in the Christmas dusk, like a rubbish heap a maniacal mass-murderer might pick as a burial mound for his victims.

'They won't be expecting us for our Christmas dinner,' said my brother.

To reach the door we went ankle-deep, almost, through plashy ground and forded in the half-dark a sort of seasonal stream. One small uncurtained window showed faintly the yellow light of an oil-lamp.

Knock, knock, knock went my father on the sagging door.

No dogs barked. No calves or cocks made comforting farmhouse noises. The wind was raucous in the bare dripping hazels that overhung the wreck of a house from the slope behind. An evil wizard might live here.

Knock, knock, knock went my father.

'Is there anybody there said the traveller,' said my brother, who had a turn for poetry.

'John O'Neill and Thady,' called my father. 'I've walked over from the Yankee's new house at Dooish and brought my two sons with me to wish you a happy Christmas.'

He shouted out his own name.

In a low voice he said to us, 'Advance, friends, and be recognised.'

Homes on the Mountain

My brother and myself giggled and stopped giggling as chains
rattled and slowly, with a thousand creaks of aged iron and timber
in bitter pain and in conflict with each other, the door opened.
Now, years after that Christmas, I can rely only on a boyhood
memory of a brief visit to a badly lighted cavern. There was a
hunched decrepit old man behind the opening door. Without
extending his hand he shuffled backwards and away from us. His
huge hobnailed boots were unlaced. They flapped around him
like the feet of some strange bird or reptile. He was completely
bald. His face was pear-shaped, running towards the point at the
forehead. His eyes had the brightness and quickness of a rodent's
eyes. When my father said, 'Thady, you remember me,' he agreed
doubtfully, as if agreement or disagreement were equally futile.
He looked sideways furtively at the kitchen table half-hidden in
shadows near one damp-streaked yellow wall. For a tablecloth that
table had a battered raincoat and when our knock had interrupted
him Thady had, it would seem, been heeling over onto the coat
a pot of boiled potatoes. He finished the task while we stood
uncertainly inside the doorway. Then, as if tucking in a child for
sleep, he wrapped the tails of the coat around the pile of steaming
tubers. A thunderous hearty voice spoke to us from the corner
between the hearth and a huge fourposter bed. It was a rubicund
confident voice. It invited us to sit down, and my father sat on a
low chair close to the hearth-fire. My brother and myself stood
uncomfortably behind him. There was, at any rate, nothing for
us to sit on. The smoky oil-lamp burned low but the bracket that
held it was on the wall above the owner of the voice. So it haloed
with a yellow glow the head of John O'Neill, the dilatory lover
of Bessie of Cornavara who had gone unwed to the place where
none embrace. It was a broad, red-faced, white-haired head, too
large and heavy, it seemed, for the old wasted body.

'It's years since we saw you, Tommy,' said John.

201

'It's years indeed.'

'And all the wild men that had been in the army.'

'All the wild men.'

'Times are changed, Tommy.'

'Times are changed indeed,' said my father.

He backed his chair a little away from the fire. Something unpleasantly odorous fried and sizzled in an unlidded pot-oven. The flagged floor, like the roof, had sagged. It sloped away from the hearth and into the shadows towards a pyramid of bags of flour and meal and feeding stuffs for cattle.

'But times are good,' said John. 'The land's good, and the crops and cattle.'

'And the money plentiful.'

'The money's plentiful.'

'I'm glad to hear you say it,' said my father.

'The Yankee came back, Tommy.'

'He came back.'

'And built a house, I hear. I don't go abroad much beyond my own land.'

'He built a fine house.'

'They like to come back, the Yankees. But they never settle.'

'It could be that the change proves too much for them,' said my father.

Then after a silence, disturbed only by the restless scratching of Thady's nailed soles on the floor, my father said, 'You never married, John.'

'No, Tommy. Bessy died. What with stock to look after and all, a man doesn't have much time for marrying.'

'Thady was more of a man for the ladies than you ever were,' said my father to John.

Behind us there was a shrill hysterical cackle and from John a roar of red laughter.

'He was that. God, Tommy, the memory you have.'

'Memory,' said my father.

Like a man in a trance he looked, not at John or Thady, but into the red heart of the turf fire.

'There was the day, Thady,' he said, 'when Martin Murphy and myself looked over a whin hedge at yourself and Molly Quigley from Crooked Bridge making love in a field. Between you, you ruined a half-acre of turnips.'

The red laughter and the cackle continued.

'Tommy, you have the memory,' said John. 'Wasn't it great the way you remembered the road up Loughfresha?'

'It was great,' said my father. 'Trust an old soldier to remember a road.'

The odour from the sizzling pot-oven was thickening.

'Well, we'll go now,' said my father. 'We wouldn't have butted in on you the day it is only for old time's sake.'

'You're always welcome, Tommy. Anytime you pass the road.'

'I don't pass this road often, John.'

'Well, when you do you're welcome. Those are your two sons.'

'My two sons.'

'Two fine clean young men,' said John.

He raised a hand to us. He didn't move out of the chair. The door closed slowly behind us and the chains rattled. We forded the seasonal stream, my brother going in over one ankle and filling a shoe with water.

We didn't talk until we had crossed the loud stream at Loughfresha Bridge. In the darkness I kept listening for the haunted howl of the black hound-dog.

'Isn't it an awful way, Da,' I said, 'for two men to live, particularly if it's true they have money in the bank.'

'If you've money in the bank,' said my brother, who suffered from a sense of irony, 'it's said you can do anything you please.'

With a philosophy too heavy for my years I said, 'It's a big change from the house we're going to.'

'John and Thady,' said my brother, 'didn't have the benefit of forty-five years in Philadelphia.'

My father said nothing.

'What, I wonder,' I said, 'was cooking in the pot-oven?'

'Whatever it was,' said my brother, 'they'll eat it with relish and roll into that four-poster bed and sleep like heroes.'

The black brooding roadside cattle seemed as formidable as wild bison.

'Sixty years,' said my father to himself. 'Coming and going every Sunday, spending the long afternoons and evenings in her father's house, eating and drinking, and nothing in the nature of love transpiring.'

Like heroes, I thought, and recalled from the song-books the heroic words: 'Side by side for the cause have our forefathers battled when our hills never echoed the tread of a slave; in many a field where the leaden hail rattled, through the red gap of glory they marched to their grave.'

Slowly, towards a lost lighted fragment of Philadelphia and our Christmas dinner, we ascended the wet boreen.

'Young love,' soliloquised the old man. 'Something happens to it on these hills. Sixty years and he never proposed nothing, good or bad.'

'In Carlow town,' said the song-books to me, 'there lived a maid more sweet than flowers at daybreak; their vows contending lovers paid, but none of marriage dared speak.'

'Sunday after Sunday to her house for sixty years,' said the old man. 'You wouldn't hear the like of it among the Kaffirs. It's the rain and the mist. And the lack of sunshine and wine. Poor Thady, too, was fond of salmon and women.'

'For I haven't a genius for work,' mocked the Humorous and Convivial, 'it was never a gift of the Bradies; but I'd make a most iligant Turk for I'm fond of tobacco and ladies.'

To the easy amusement of my brother and, finally, to the wry laughter of my father I sang that quatrain. Night was over the mountain. The falling water of the spring had the tinny sound of shrill, brittle thunder.

After dinner my godmother's husband said, 'Such a fine house as Aunt Sally O'Neill kept. Tables scrubbed as white as bone. Dances to the melodeon. I always think of corncrakes and the crowds gathered for the mowing of the meadows when I recall that house. And the churning. She has the best butter in the country. Faintly golden. Little beads of moisture showing on it.'

'We'll have a game of euchre,' said my Aunt Brigid.

'Play the phonograph,' said my godmother's husband.

He loathed euchre.

So on the gramophone high up on Dooish, we heard that boys and girls were singing on the sidewalks of New York.

I wondered where the hound-dog could possibly have been running to. In a spooky story I had once read the Black Hound of Kildare turned out to be the devil.

My godmother asked me to sing.

'But I can't sing,' I said.

'Then what do Lanty and yourself do with all the song-books?'

'We read them.'

Laughter.

'Read us a song,' said my brother.

So, because I had my back to the wall and also because once when visiting a convent with my mother I had sung, by request,

'Let Erin Remember', and received a box of chocolates from the Reverend Mother, I sang: 'Just a little bit of Heaven fell from out the sky one day, and when the angels saw it sure they said we'll let it stay; and they called it Ireland.'

That spring, following my heralding of the descent from Elysium of the Emerald Isle, there was a steady downpour of half-crowns.

BRIAN LYNCH

Curtains for Christmas

Edward smiled across the Musak-enchanted room at Michael the porter. Michael, short, fat and hurrying, waggled his fingers at the ceiling as if incredulous of how busy they were, and went back to the reception desk.

'That's some bleedin' gocr,' he said to the bell-boy.

'Who is?'

'That Norman fella hasn't stopped at the gargle since he came.'

'What fella?'

'Edward. Mr Norman.'

'That fella. What about him?'

The bell-boy was the oldest man in the hotel. He was so old he remembered the Black and Tans, drunk all night, firing guns into the ceiling or at the chandeliers. There wasn't any carry-on like that nowadays.

They slumped together on the desk before the battling door which opened and closed windily on the parcel-laden crowds thronging through to the lounge and the bar. It was Christmas

Eve. Most of the people seemed to be sleep-walking, distracted, concentrating, yearning like animals for somewhere to sit and something to drink. Michael and the bell-boy watched them as if at some vast controlled experiment.

Edward was sitting in the lounge, alone, back to the unlit fire. He was watching and smiling. He knotted his square strong hands behind his close-cropped head and tilted on his chair. The light caught the bright gold of the sovereign signet-ring on his little finger and his tight blue sweater rode up, generously displaying the greyness of his belly hard enough with muscle, loose enough with all the pints of Smithwick's ale he'd been drinking, for – was it days or weeks or months?

The man sitting nearest looked at the belly and then at the face and then looked away again. His wife didn't notice, dazedly quick-sipping her hot whiskey like a flustered hen. Her fur hat with the flaps tied under the chin was crooked, thick feathers of hair escaping on all sides. Edward smiled. He knew and he listened. There was a sound in his head like the roaring of the sea on a distant beach.

The lounge of Flynn's Hotel was painted yellow. The carpet was brown, green and yellow. The curtains were red, the lightshades orange. Some of the older chairs were upholstered in green leather. The banquettes lining the walls were new, black plastic leather.

The waitresses, still dressed as if of old, in black with little white aprons, brought drinks, tea and coffee and sandwiches on silver trays. Some of the pots, jugs and bowls were battered silver. Some were stainless steel, narrowing towards the tops, the handles inset with dark simulated wood, Swedish by design. The high ceiling was hung with paper chains and bits of tinsel.

'Not a parish priest in sight,' Mr Grealy said to his married daughter as she joined him from her shopping. 'Place used to be thick with them. I remember you couldn't spit here once for fear of committing sacrilege!'

'How many pints of stout have you had?'

'This is my first glass.'

'Could I have a coffee, please?' she said to Mr Lawrence, the lounge manager.

'Certainly, madam. One coffee is it?'

They understood each other instantly. She paused and looked briefly to the left and right of her. There was only one of her.

'One coffee. With cream.'

He bowed. She put out a restraining hand, almost touching his arm but not quite.

'And a very small glass of water. I think I'm getting a cold.' She said this to her father. 'And I want to take one of these tablets.'

'Certainly, madam.'

He bowed again, sympathetically, and went away to return swiftly with coffee and a half-pint glass of water.

'This is not what I asked for!'

'One coffee and a glass of water, madam.'

'I asked for a small glass of water.'

'This is the smallest glass we have.'

'Do you call that a small glass?'

'Shall I change it for you, madam?'

'However,' she said, 'it'll do.'

She poured off water into her father's almost empty glass of stout.

'Now,' she said, 'if you could take that away and bring me another glass of stout. No, wait. And a ham sandwich, I think we'll do for the moment.'

Mr Lawrence brushed back the wings of his silvery hair with both hands, removed some empty cups and used plates, left the water and stout mixing sickeningly together, and resolved, smiling tightly, never to return.

Edward finished his ninth pint of Smithwick's, stretched, picked up the glass and went through to the bar for another. The three barmaids entwined at the cash-register like Graces disentangled themselves. Even standing up, Edward's sweater was too small and exposed a couple of inches of flesh, a belt above the thick belt of his jeans.

'Give us a smile, ducks,' he said. Edward was happy. Not to be happy was, he felt, a moral fault, but the fact that his experience in showing happiness had not guaranteed reciprocity in others added an edge to his good nature that his smiling only accentuated.

Edward felt someone behind him trying to get in at the bar. He flicked the pressure away with his hip. A small man, Brendan Hartigan, staggered slightly against the man next to him. Two of the barmaids saw the move.

'Could I have,' Brendan said, 'a hot whiskey please and a cup of coffee please.'

'No coffee in the bar. You'll have to go into the lounge for that.'

The girl who spoke had not taken her eyes off Edward flexing and cracking his muscle-bound fingers.

'Holy Jesus,' Brendan said under his breath and went back to Paula, surrounded by packages, heavily pregnant, sunk deep in the soft tweed of an undersprung armchair.

'We'll have to go into the god-damned lounge if you want coffee.'

He rewound the eight feet of his thick bright scarf around his neck in annoyance, as if going on a long cold journey. They threaded their way along the narrow bar, stood in the crowded lounge, spotted a couple leaving and squeezed past Mr Grealy to a vacant spot on the black plastic. The girl who was serving a ham sandwich and a glass of stout took their order.

All this time Mrs Winnie Ormsby had been descending the stairs. Now she stood in the door of the lounge. Mouth clamped shut, breathing hard through her nose, one hand pressed to her side, the other held a little in front of her. She started off again, thin legs wavering. Her turquoise skirt hung lopsidedly because the zip had caught in a clump of pink slip. Her bright red cardigan was wrongly buttoned. It was all due to her eye. A thick, loose wad of cotton wool, stuck to forehead and cheek with plaster, pressed against one lens of her spectacles, lifting the arm so that it didn't rest on her ear.

When she came in sight of the bar she held up the key of her room for identification until they gave her her large Scotch. Then she headed for her corner. An arm encircled her shoulders and turned her around.

'I have a party for there this minute,' said Mr Lawrence.

He put her gently on a stool in the middle of the room beside a tiny table.

'This is a mad country,' Mr Grealy's daughter said, turning back her gaze.

'Where do they get the money, that's what I want to know. Daddy, don't eat my crusts, you know I don't like it. Where do they get it? I've never seen a country where they could drink more than Ireland.'

'I couldn't say so.'

She dropped the second of her big Rubex tablets into the water and watched it fizz angrily.

'Is it any wonder we're in the state we're in? Nothing but bars and bars and more bars.'

'I hear the asylums are full of publicans.'

'And not from poverty. Not from poverty. Some of the people

211

wouldn't think twice about going out and spending ten pounds in one night on drink.'

'And more maybe.'

'And more. And not one of them would dream of spending ten pounds on dinner in a restaurant. That's what has the country the way it is. The people wouldn't dream of eating.'

Edward stood up, stretched again and went to the lavatory, smiling. Mr Lawrence, going about with his eyes lowered to avoid further orders, first felt a vice-like arm groping his shoulder and then looked up into a pair of gleaming red eyes.

'You're run off your feet, ducks,' Edward said.

'Thank you, Mr Norman,' said Mr Lawrence. 'Have one on me, have a brandy.'

'Thank you, sir, very pleased to, much obliged.'

A pound note was pressed into the breast pocket of his shiny evening jacket.

'Compliments of the season, sir.'

'Enough said.'

'Rotten crowd of bleeders, what?'

Mr Lawrence saw the face press closer and felt the hot breath on his nose. He lowered his eyes.

'Don't be like a blue-arsed fly then.' There was a ghastly pause.

'What you say, cock? Bleeding Irish, that's all they are. Here.'

Mr Lawrence saw another pound note crush down on the first one.'

'Have a brandy or something. On me.'

Edward took his arm away, cannoned into an ivory-faced man and burst out through the door.

Mrs Winnie Ormsby held her key over her head, turned towards the girls behind the bar, found it was her wrong eye and turned again. Mr Lawrence, raging with relief, came up behind and snatched the key from her hand which remained stiffly in the air.

'Now, then, Mrs Ormsby, what's this, what's this?'

'Here I am, love. Not there sweetheart, here.'

'You can put your hand down now, you silly old dear.'

Slowly she turned and wordlessly raised the glass that was clutched in her clubbed arthritic fingers.

'One of our oldest residents,' Mr Lawrence said. 'Faithful and true, right up to the end.'

'Couldn't I have another coffee and a hot whiskey, please?' Brendan said.

'And I'll have another coffee, Daddy, do you think you'll manage another glass of Guinness?'

'Yes, well, another glass of Guinness.'

Mr Grealy's daughter thrust the almost empty glass into Mr Lawrence's hand.

'There's no rush, madam,' Mr Lawrence said easily, smiling politely and putting the glass back on the table. The girl he called over took the order again.

Mr Lawrence hovered and then descended. There was, after all, one thing he should do straight away.

'Excuse me, sir,' he said to Mr Grealy, 'if you could just stand up for a moment.'

Obediently Mr Grealy stood up. Kneeling on the banquette, Mr Lawrence pulled the cord which drew the red mock-velvet curtains. Then brushing his hands together he withdrew.

Edward, coming back from the lavatory, bumped into him and said, 'Do you come here often, darling, or is it the mating season?' and went off, laughing, to order the next pint.

Paula shivered first. She pulled up the collar of her coat and sank down further on her heavy body. There's a draught,' she said.

'I feel it too,' Brendan said.

The lounge was more crowded now and warm, but they felt a cold thin shaft of air down their necks.

'Do you feel it too?' Mr Grealy's daughter asked.

Brendan twisted around and drew the curtain aside.

'It's the fan,' he said. 'See, the fan in the window. It's all right when the curtains are open, but now he's drawn them the draught comes down and gets under the edge.'

Mrs Ormsby spoke: 'My eye hurts,' she said. She meant her good eye.

'Call that man,' Mr Grealy's daughter instructed. Brendan called out, raising his hand like the timid schoolboy he once was. Mr Lawrence passed by. Eventually a girl came, but she said she'd have to speak to the manager.

'Please ask him to come in, like a good girl,' Mr Grealy's daughter said. Mr Lawrence came eagerly.

'Now, then, sir, it's not that bad, is it? A little draught, you say.'

'My wife is cold.'

'I'm very sorry sir, we have to think of the other customers.'

Brendan was lost and didn't know what to say. This was the sort of thing he hated. He felt that his head had grown huge and that everyone was looking at it.

'It's hurting that old woman's eye,' he said at last.

'Sure it has cotton wool over it,' Mr Lawrence said, chuckling. 'Walked into an open door, didn't we, Mrs Ormsby? Naughty thing. I'm sorry sir, perhaps you can find another seat.'

He disappeared. Brendan sank back. Mr Grealy turned the bottom of his glass through wet circles. The draught brought a tear to Mrs Ormsby's good eye. It trembled on the glaciated lip of her cheekbone. Mr Grealy's daughter's eye did not water. It gleamed. She beckoned over the girl.

'What's your name, pet?' she asked. The girl involuntarily

brought her hands together in front of her and her bowels turned over.

'Jacinta, miss, Jacinta Higgins, miss.'

'What's the manager's name, Jacinta?'

'Mr Lawrence, miss.'

'Good. Now Jacinta, run over to Mr Lawrence like a good girl and tell him I want to see him. This instant.'

'Can we go home now?' Mr Grealy asked, but it was already too late.

'Can I help you, madam?' inquired Mr Lawrence.

'Pull back the curtains please.'

'Excuse me, madam?'

'There is a draught here. Kindly draw the curtains.'

'The curtains? These curtains?' Mr Lawrence raised his shoulders and held both of his palms upwards like a priest before a congregation. 'I'm sorry, madam, very sorry, but it's dark now, you see, I must draw the curtains when it's dark.'

'There is a draught here,' Mr Grealy's daughter said. 'Don't you feel it?'

'I'm sorry, madam.'

'A wind, a breeze. Do you know what that is?'

'You don't have to explain it to me, madam, with respect. But I think you're exaggerating a little fresh air.'

'There is a gale coming through that window.'

'Look,' said Brendan, 'the curtains are lifting with it.' The curtains swayed slightly. The smile faded from Mr Lawrence's face.

'You're a man, aren't you, you're not hurt by a little fresh air, are you?'

'We would like the curtains drawn,' Mr Grealy's daughter said in an amused voice. Mrs Ormsby bent her head into her glass as if it were an asthmatic's mask.

215

'I'm terribly sorry, madam,' Mr Lawrence said, 'I would like to be of assistance, but I have my orders.'

'Orders, what orders?'

She slammed her glass down on the formica-topped table and the remains of her Rubex shot up into the air and dived back down again as soon as they could. A ghastly silence ensued. It was as if sound had been suddenly removed from the world. Mr Grealy's daughter spoke, conversationally: 'I said draw the curtains.' Then her voice swelled up again: 'Now draw them.'

'No need to raise your voice,' Mr Lawrence stood his ground. 'Orders are orders, after all, where would we be without them?'

'Look here,' Brendan cried. The blood rushing to his head seemed to drive him to his feet. He scrambled down the banquette. His elbow hit Mr Grealy on the temple and sent his glasses flying. Clawing at the curtains he tried to find the proper cords, but when he pulled nothing happened.

'Brendan,' he heard Paula scream. The next thing he knew his feet were flailing the air and his chest was being crushed by a mighty arm.

'Don't hit an old man,' Edward Norman's voice, warm and fermenting, said mildly in his ear. Brendan, in terror, feeling his rib-cage crack, gasping for breath, kicked out frantically. One heel caught Mr Grealy flush on his blue-red nose, bringing forth a gush of blood. The other heel caught Mr Grealy's daughter cleanly on the chin. Her arms went out wide and her chair went over backwards.

Paula's face came near and Edward pushed it away, he thought gently. Brendan attempted to turn. His elbow hit Edward's jaw. Edward felt a gold filling break off. Enraged, he whirled Brendan around and flung him from him across the room. Brendan's clutching hand held on to the curtain rod as if it were a last lifeline, as he flew through the air. He landed on a table full of glasses. The curtain rail, aluminium, with a terrible sound was torn off the wall and speared Mrs Ormsby directly in the middle of her forehead.

There was silence. No one said or did anything for a moment. Then, with a sigh, a large star-shaped piece of plaster fell from the ceiling on Edward Norman's cropped head.

Unharmed, Mr Lawrence stood knee-deep in the human wreckage, trying desperately to persuade himself that the rictus of pleasure on his face was the purest anguish. Desperately he rubbed his hands together as if he were trying to mould in the hairy cushioned pads of his palms an appropriate expression for his features.

'Orders, orders,' he said over and over with a frantic giggle. 'I have my orders.'

Edward stood stock still, head and shoulders sprinkled with plaster dust like theatrical snow, eyes fixed with dog-numb adoration on what he recognised at last was his master's voice. His master's voice, freed from the awful sanity of restraint, now rose to a piercing goatish bellow of the purest, most panic-stricken merriment.

Everyone who was capable of movement moved either towards the door, where a screaming cork of bodies clawed and clogged, or against any wall into which a back might transubstantiate. Even in this hubbub Edward began to hear another sound. At first it was like a low humming and he couldn't work out what was causing it, but as it increased to a loud drum solo and then to a terrible pounding which made the floor vibrate violently, his eyes were drawn from Mr Lawrence's howling mouth to his feet. Tiny feet they were and utterly immobile – except that is, for the heels which were beating up and down in a blurred joyous tattoo. In a moment they reached such a speed that, like the wheels of buckboard wagons in cowboy films, they seemed not to move at all and then to go backward to their motion. Most wonderful of all, this allowed Edward to see the heels of Mr Lawrence's boots were – what else? – Cuban.

Unheard, unseen, somewhere else, Paula began to moan. Something far more interesting was happening to her.

MAEVE BINCHY

Be Prepared

It was to be their last Christmas as a family, all of them together. Next year, Sean would be married, Kitty would be in Australia and it would only be the two of them, and Martin. So Nora decided that it would be something really special, something they would remember when Kitty was drinking beer from a can on Bondi Beach and Sean was dealing with his prissy in-laws. There was even an unworthy part of Nora that made her want this Christmas to be so good that they would remember it with longing for the rest of their lives and regret ever leaving the nest.

Everything she read in the papers said it was all about being prepared – buying the cooking-foil in September, writing the Christmas cards in October, testing the lights for the tree, measuring the oven, cleaning out the freezer in November. All of it very admirable, and particularly for a couple as busy as Nora and Frank. She was very pleased with her progress, she had even booked the window cleaners, got a box of fancy crackers and arranged for a neighbour's child to bring her a ton of holly and ivy. And then she got the news that Girlie was coming for Christmas.

Girlie was Frank's aunt. Eccentric was the kindest word you could find for her. Somewhere in her late sixties, maybe older; always vague about details like that, always diamond-sharp at remembering the things you want forgotten.

Girlie was based, loosely speaking, in New York. She was mainly to be found travelling the world on the decks of expensive ocean-going liners. She would send irascible postcards from Fiji or Bali, complaining that the food on board was inedible or was so good that everyone had put on twenty pounds since embarkation. Nothing anywhere ever seemed to be right or good.

Yet Girlie, whose late husband had left her a staggering insurance policy, sometimes saved everyone's lives. She sent them money just when they needed it for Sean and Kitty's school fees. She also sent a lecture about the appalling results of the Irish educational system that she saw all over the world, results that made her despair of the nation. She sent Sean a deposit for his house and Kitty a ticket to Australia that allowed her a few stop-offs so that she might see a bit of the world before she went to that godawful place. Girlie disliked Australia as much as Ireland and the United States and, in fact, everywhere she had ever been.

Martin wondered if she had forgotten about him. Nothing seemed to be rolling his way from Girlie. But then he was only fourteen, the others told him; his needs had not become significant. Martin felt his needs were very significant indeed, and he certainly wouldn't waste his money on getting a horrible little box of a house and marrying some awful prissy girl like Lucy, as his brother Sean was doing, and he wouldn't go the whole way to Australia to be free, like Kitty was doing. You could be free anywhere if you had a good bicycle and a tent and were allowed to stay out all night in summer. But Girlie hadn't seemed to understand this, even though he had written it cunningly to her in many different ways.

Frank said it was preposterous; this woman always laid down the law and she shouldn't get away with it. How dare she impose on them, this, their last family Christmas? She was his father's totally loopy sister who had cut off all connection with the family years ago and just communicated in barking postcards and air letters ever since.

'And very generous cheques,' Nora reminded him. Frank wasn't convinced. She only did what she wanted to do and people couldn't buy affection: he was very muttery and growly about it. But Nora was adamant. Girlie had never asked for anything before; this year, it would suit her to come to Ireland and be with family. It was the least they could do.

Frank said that not only could she afford to stay in the Shelbourne, she could afford to buy the Shelbourne – but that didn't seem to be the point. She was going to come in the middle of November and leave before the New Year.

The family met the news with characteristic rage. Kitty said that she was not going to give up her room; no way was she having that old bat living in there and poking around among her things. Her room was sacred; it had been hers for twenty years. Nora thought grimly about how eager Kitty was to abandon this room in order to go to uncharted lands in Australia but said nothing.

Sean said it wasn't fair for him to be asked to give up his room; he had so much to do, life was busy, he was at a hugely important, stressful period of his life. He couldn't let this mad aunt come and take up his space.

Nora did not mention that it would be difficult for Sean to bring Lucy in for the night so often if he had to sleep in the box room on the camp bed. Lucy didn't stay for breakfast and there was a family fiction that she wasn't there at all – which covered everyone's honour and allowed Nora to meet Lucy's mother's eye with something like equanimity.

Martin said glumly: 'I suppose it has got to be me.'

'We'll get you the bicycle,' said his father in gratitude.

'And can I sleep out in the Wicklow mountains and by the side of a lake in Cavan, when it's summer?' he asked.

'We'll see,' said his mother.

'That means no,' said Martin, who was a realist. 'What's she coming for anyway?' he grumbled. 'Is she dying or something?'

The others, too caught up in their own lives, had never asked. 'God, I hope not,' said Frank. 'Not here anyway.'

'Not before the wedding,' said Sean.

'I couldn't put off going to Australia for her funeral; I don't even know her,' said Kitty.

'We don't even know if there's anything at all wrong with her,' said Nora, alarmed that the family had the woman buried before she arrived. But to herself she wondered long and without any resolution what made this aficionado of all the cruise ships of the world come to a suburban house in Dublin for Christmas – and not for a traditional four or five days but for four or five *weeks*.

Girlie did not want to be met at the airport; she had arranged her own limousine. Nora and Frank wouldn't have known where you found a limousine but Girlie in America had no such problems.

She had discussed the upcoming divorce referendum with the driver and arrived at the house well versed in the arguments for each side. Barely were the greetings over than she asked if she might be told whether she was staying in a Yes or No household. They looked at her, a small, plump, over-made-up woman who could be any age between fifty and eighty. They raked her face, with its lines and its heavy-duty eyeliner. Which way would she swing? It was impossible to tell. So, reluctantly they told her the truth which was that she had hit a family of two Yesses and two Nos. Nora was a Yes because of all the women she met at work who should have had a second chance; Frank was a No because he felt that society followed the law and that the place would be like California in a matter of months. Sean was a No because he and Lucy were taking vows for life and not just until they had a falling out; Kitty was a Yes because she wanted freedom. Martin wouldn't have a vote for another four years.

Girlie asked Martin which way he would vote if he had one. Her small eyes had got piggy: he sensed a fight coming, whatever he said.

Martin was depressed by the whole thing – his poky bedroom, his clothes hanging on a rail borrowed from a shop, the roster of duties his mother had put up in the kitchen as part of Being Prepared.

'If I'm not old enough to have a vote and to stay out on a summer night in a tent, then I'm not old enough to have any kind of an opinion at all,' he said. And he imagined that she looked at him with some kind of respect, which was very different from the glares he was getting from the rest of the family who had recognised the mutinous rudeness in his tone.

She was, at the same time, much easier and much more difficult as a guest than they had thought. For one thing, she asked for an electric kettle and toaster in her bedroom and did not appear before lunch. This was a huge relief. She had retained the services of the limousine and went on outings on which she disapproved of everything that she saw. St Kevin was barking mad, a basket case, she said when she came back from Glendalough – but then, if you thought that it might be safe to criticise the Church on anything religious, you would be wrong. There was a conspiracy against all these unfortunate priests, none of them had ever done anything untoward; it was a plot to discredit them, that was all.

One day Ireland was a pathetic backwater, the next day it was a society based on worshipping money and more affluent than most of the EU from which it was demanding Hardship Money. One shopping day the place was gross with its conscious spending, the next day it was like a Soviet supply-hall in the worst years of the Cold War.

'She's not very sane, is she?' Frank whispered apologetically to Nora in bed.

'She's not consistent certainly,' Nora agreed.

Frank had always been kind to her relatives: she would put up with this disagreeable and unpredictable woman for a few short weeks. It was, however, making her plans to Be Prepared much more difficult. Who could Be Prepared when you had Girlie in the house? She had brought the limousine driver in last night and they had eaten all the brandy snaps that Nora had stored lovingly in a tin.

Girlie would, of course, buy something unexpected and generous herself in turn. A fleet of Chinese waiters came up and set out an elaborate banquet for them on a night that Nora had been going to serve an Irish stew. Nora and Frank didn't know you could do this sort of thing in Dublin. Girlie knew everything and enjoyed remarkably little.

Martin saw more of her than the others. Sean was out with Lucy's family discussing the calligraphy on the wedding invitations; Kitty was with her friends arranging to meet them in Manley, or Randwick or King's Cross and all talking as if they knew Sydney intimately.

Nora and Frank were at their work until late in the evening.

'What are all these lists?' Girlie asked Martin once, looking at a roster in the kitchen.

'It's the nights we each do the washing up,' Martin explained.

Girlie took a ruler and made a few measurements. In minutes, she had the right man in the right electrical store. It was never clear what she promised or gave, but he sent carpenters up to the house and the dishwasher was operational that evening.

Be Prepared

Everyone said they were delighted. But in fact Sean felt inadequate now because Lucy admired it so inordinately and he would never be able to afford one. Kitty thought they were all mad to be tied to possessions when everyone should be free. Frank was sad because that had been his Christmas surprise: he had ordered a much cheaper version and now he had to cancel it. And Nora was sorry because she knew all about the secret and wanted Frank to have the pleasure of giving it to the family.

But they were all grateful for the thought and the speed and the gesture and they warmed towards Girlie until she said that it was a relief to have one in the house because this way you really knew that the cups and glasses were clean.

And the referendum came and went, and when she was with Frank and Sean, Girlie said that they were typical men trying to hold back society and ride roughshod over women. And when she was with Nora and Kitty she said that they were selfish women advancing a world where no one would take care about the young.

To those who thought that the visit of President Clinton was over-hyped, she said they should be goddamn grateful that the good old US of A was going to rescue them from their silly bickerings; to those who praised the trip, she said they were easily swayed by a vote-catching exercise.

She was similarly different in her views about Finola Bruton's speech. It was either the most sensible thing said by a woman since time began or the most inappropriate bleating that had ever been heard. She took to reading the letters column in The Irish Times and would praise the side that appeared to have less support.

About herself and her lifestyle, she revealed little.

No amount of polite questioning about her late and extremely provident husband yielded anything.

'He was a man,' she would say and the family, feeling they

sensed a less-than-joyful marriage, tactfully asked no more. Girlie, however, had no such tact and reserve. She would ask the very questions that everyone had been skirting around. Like asking Sean: 'Are your in-laws putting too much pressure on you over this wedding? Why are you going along with it? Are you afraid of Lucy?'

Or Kitty: 'Aren't you only going to Australia on this open ticket because everyone else is? You really want to go for three months and then come back and settle down.'

Or to Nora: 'Your job sounds terrible. Don't tell me you're getting any satisfaction out of it. You're only doing it to keep up the mortgage on this place, aren't you?'

And to Frank: 'You're your father's son, Frank, that's for certain. He could never make a decision to save his life. You'd love a smaller place entirely but you have some notion that everyone wants this pile of red brick and that you owe it to them, and so you frown and wince over bills and estimates. I see you; you can't hide anything from Girlie.'

By the Friday before Christmas, Girlie had the household near a collective nervous breakdown. Only Martin remained outside her influence.

'Why aren't you sulking and flouncing with me the way everyone else is?' Girlie said to him, as she left the house to get into her limousine as usual.

'You haven't annoyed me like you've annoyed all of them,' he said simply.

'Do you want to come out for a drive with me?'

'No thank you.'

'Please?'

'No thank you, Girlie. I don't like shopping, I don't have any money left, I don't want you to give me money, and I won't tell you things about myself that will make you

226

know what's wrong and then torture me like you do the others.'

'I don't go shopping,' she said. 'Come on.'

Martin got into the car and they drove out to Wicklow Gap. As soon as they were miles from anywhere, the car stopped and the driver brought them white linen napkins, a box of smoked salmon sandwiches, and a bottle of wine.

'I don't drink,' he said.

'You do today,' said Girlie.

'Why did they call you Girlie?'

'I was the only girl in a family of six: they weren't very bright,' she said.

'Why are you so awful to them all? They're doing their best to give you a happy Christmas.'

'What I'm saying is true. You know that, don't you?'

'It might be,' he agreed.

'Well, don't you hate poisonous little Lucy, Sean's much too good for her, and Kitty as nervous as a cat about seeing the world, and your mother hates that damn job and your father's in a state of panic about the new roof he thinks the place needs . . .'

'Well why don't you give them money then, you've got lots of it?'

'Money wouldn't solve their problems, it has never solved a problem.' Girlie spoke very definitely.

'That's easy to say when you have it.' Martin was brave.

'No, it's true: if I gave Sean money he'd buy that horrible prissy little thing an even bigger ring, and Kitty would have to see the Kalahari desert as well as the Outback when all she wants to do is to have a laugh with her friends in the sun.

'Your father would get the roof done and worry about something else; your mother would give up work and feel guilty and beholden to me. Much better make them see what's wrong. What do you worry about, Martin?'

'I won't tell you.'

'Why not? I have been utterly honest with you.'

'OK, but you've got to answer a few questions first.'

'Shoot.'

He paused . . . Should he ask her about her husband? The one who left her all the money? Should he ask about how much she had left? Why she had come to visit them?

'Are you dying of something?' he asked suddenly, surprising himself.

'Yes,' she said.

Wicklow Gap looked beautiful as it always did. But, of course, he had never seen it from a heated limousine eating smoked salmon sandwiches and drinking white wine, and he never would again.

'I'm sorry,' he said.

'Sure,' said Girlie. 'Now tell me what's worrying you.'

He told her that next summer he would be fifteen and they wouldn't let him have a tent and come out to places like this and spend the night under the stars. They were afraid he'd get murdered or rheumatism or something.

She listened with interest and without comment. Then she gave back the glasses and the box of crumbs to the chauffeur and they drove to the shop in Dublin which sold the most expensive kind of tent in the world.

'They'll kill me for getting you on my side,' he said.

'I was always on your side,' said Girlie. She didn't need to tell him not to talk about their conversation.

Some things never need to be said.

It was a very strange Christmas. Nora said to Frank that a lot of this stuff about Being Prepared was for the birds. Look at all the great things that had turned out this year when they could prepare for damn all.

They had decided to put the house on the market. Sean and Lucy had postponed their wedding indefinitely. Kitty said she'd be back from Australia at Easter.

And Martin, he had been a positive saint with that dreadful old Girlie who had bought him an entirely inappropriate tent and said what did it matter if he got pneumonia from sleeping out of doors, weren't there antibiotics for it nowadays, which was actually true when you came to think of it.

'Do you think she liked it here? She's as odd as two left shoes,' Frank said.

'I think she liked it too much. We should be prepared, she may well come again next year,' Nora said.

And Martin just looked out the window into the garden and said nothing at all.

FRANK O'CONNOR

Christmas Morning

I never really liked my brother, Sonny. From the time he was a baby he was always the mother's pet and always chasing her to tell her what mischief I was up to. Mind you, I was usually up to something. Until I was nine or ten I was never much good at school, and I really believe it was to spite me that he was so smart at his books. He seemed to know by instinct that this was what Mother had set her heart on, and you might almost say he spelt himself into her favour. He spelt himself into her favour.

'Mummy,' he'd say, 'will I call Larry in to his t-e-a?' or: 'Mummy, the k-e-t-e-l is boiling,' and, of course, when he was wrong she'd correct him, and next time he'd have it right and there would be no stopping him. 'Mummy,' he'd say, 'aren't I a good speller?' Cripes, we could all be good spellers if we went on like that!

Mind you, it wasn't that I was stupid. Far from it. I was just restless and not able to fix my mind for long on any one thing. I'd do the lessons for the year before, or the lessons for the year after: what I couldn't stand were the lessons we were supposed to be doing at the time. In the evenings I used to go out and

230

play with the Doherty gang. Not, again, that I was rough, but I liked the excitement, and for the life of me I couldn't see what attracted Mother about education.

'Can't you do your lessons first and play after?' she'd say, getting white with indignation. 'You ought to be ashamed of yourself that your baby brother can read better than you.'

She didn't seem to understand that I wasn't, because there didn't seem to me to be anything particularly praiseworthy about reading, and it struck me as an occupation better suited to a sissy kid like Sonny.

'The dear knows what will become of you,' she'd say. 'If only you'd stick to your books you might be something good like a clerk or an engineer.'

'I'll be a clerk, Mummy,' Sonny would say smugly.

'Who wants to be an old clerk?' I'd say, just to annoy him. 'I'm going to be a soldier.'

'The dear knows, I'm afraid that's all you'll ever be fit for,' she would add with a sigh.

I couldn't help feeling at times that she wasn't all there. As if there was anything better a fellow could be!

Coming on to Christmas, with the days getting shorter and the shopping crowds bigger, I began to think of all the things I might get from Santa Claus. The Dohertys said there was no Santa Claus, only what your father and mother gave you, but the Dohertys were a rough class of children you wouldn't expect Santa to come to anyway. I was rooting round for whatever information I could pick up about him, but there didn't seem to be much. I was no hand with a pen, but if a letter would do any good I was ready to chance writing to him. I had plenty of initiative and was always writing off for free samples and prospectuses.

'Ah, I don't know will he come at all this year,' Mother said with a worried air. 'He has enough to do looking after steady boys who mind their lessons without bothering about the rest.'

'He only comes to good spellers, Mummy,' said Sonny. 'Isn't that right?'

'He comes to any little boy who does his best, whether he's a good speller or not,' Mother said firmly.

Well, I did my best. God knows I did! It wasn't my fault if, four days before the holidays, Flogger Dawley gave us sums we couldn't do, and Peter Doherty and myself had to go on the lang. It wasn't for the love of it, for, take it from me, December is no month for mitching, and we spent most of our time sheltering from the rain in a store on the quays. The only mistake we made was imagining we could keep it up till the holidays without being spotted. That showed real lack of foresight.

Of course, Flogger Dawley noticed and sent home word to know what was keeping me. When I came in on the third day the mother gave me a look I'll never forget, and said: 'Your dinner is there.' She was too full to talk. When I tried to explain to her about Flogger Dawley and the sums she brushed it aside and said: 'You have no word.' I saw then it wasn't the langing she minded but the lies, though I still didn't see how you could lang without lying. She didn't speak to me for days. And even then I couldn't make out what she saw in education, or why she wouldn't let me grow up naturally like anyone else.

To make things worse, it stuffed Sonny up more than ever. He had the air of one saying: 'I don't know what they'd do without me in this blooming house.' He stood at the front door, leaning against the jamb with his hands in his trouser pockets, trying to make himself look like Father, and shouted to the other kids so that he could be heard all over the road.

'Larry isn't left go out. He went on the lang with Peter Doherty and me mother isn't talking to him.'

And at night, when we were in bed, he kept it up.

'Santa Claus won't bring you anything this year, aha!'

'Of course he will,' I said.

'How do you know?'

'Why wouldn't he?'

'Because you went on the lang with Doherty. I wouldn't play with them Doherty fellows.'

'You wouldn't be left.'

'I wouldn't play with them. They're no class. They had the bobbies up to the house.'

'And how would Santa know I was on the lang with Peter Doherty?' I growled, losing patience with the little prig.

'Of course he'd know. Mummy would tell him.'

'And how could Mummy tell him and he up at the North Pole? Poor Ireland, she's rearing them yet! 'Tis easy seen you're only an old baby.'

'I'm not a baby, and I can spell better than you, and Santa won't bring you anything.'

'We'll see whether he will or not,' I said sarcastically, doing the old man on him.

But, to tell the God's truth, the old man was only bluff. You could never tell what powers these superhuman chaps would have of knowing what you were up to. And I had a bad conscience about the langing because I'd never before seen the mother like that.

That was the night I decided that the only sensible thing to do was to see Santa myself and explain to him. Being a man, he'd probably understand. In those days I was a good-looking kid and had a way with me when I liked. I had only to smile nicely at one old gent on the North Mall to get a penny from him, and I felt if only I could get Santa by himself I could do the same with him and maybe get something worthwhile from him. I wanted a model railway: I was sick of Ludo and Snakes-and-Ladders.

I started to practise lying awake, counting five hundred and then a thousand, and trying to hear first eleven, then midnight, from Shandon. I felt sure Santa would be round by midnight, seeing that he'd be coming from the north, and would have the whole of the south side to do afterwards. In some ways I was very farsighted. The only trouble was the things I was farsighted about.

I was so wrapped up in my own calculations that I had little attention to spare for Mother's difficulties. Sonny and I used to go to town with her, and while she was shopping we stood outside a toyshop in the North Main Street, arguing about what we'd like for Christmas.

On Christmas Eve when Father came home from work and gave her the housekeeping money, she stood looking at it doubtfully while her face grew white.

'Well?' he snapped, getting angry. 'What's wrong with that?'

'What's wrong with it?' she muttered. 'On Christmas Eve!'

'Well,' he asked truculently, sticking his hands in his trouser pockets as though to guard what was left, 'do you think I get more because it's Christmas?'

'Lord God,' she muttered distractedly. 'And not a bit of cake in the house, nor a candle, nor anything!'

'All right,' he shouted, beginning to stamp. 'How much will the candle be?'

'Ah, for pity's sake,' she cried, 'will you give me the money and not argue like that before the children? Do you think I'll leave them with nothing on the one day of the year?'

'Bad luck to you and your children!' he snarled. 'Am I to be slaving from one year's end to another for you to be throwing it away on toys? Here,' he added, tossing two half-crowns on the table, 'that's all you're going to get, so make the most of it.'

'I suppose the publicans will get the rest,' she said bitterly.

Later she went into town, but did not bring us with her, and returned with a lot of parcels including the Christmas candle. We waited for Father to come home to his tea, but he didn't, so we had our own tea and a slice of Christmas cake each, and then Mother put Sonny on a chair with the holy-water stoup to sprinkle the candle, and when he lit it she said: 'The light of heaven to our souls.' I could see she was upset because Father wasn't in – it should be the oldest and youngest. When we hung up our stockings at bedtime he was still out.

Then began the hardest couple of hours I ever put in. I was mad with sleep but afraid of losing the model railway, so I lay for a while, making up things to say to Santa when he came. They varied in tone from frivolous to grave, for some old gents like kids to be modest and well spoken, while others prefer them with spirit. When I had rehearsed them all I tried to wake Sonny to keep me company, but that kid slept like the dead.

Eleven struck from Shandon, and soon after I heard the latch, but it was only Father coming home.

'Hello, little girl,' he said, letting on to be surprised at finding Mother waiting for him, and then broke into a self-conscious giggle. 'What have you up so late?'

'Do you want your supper?' she asked shortly.

'Ah, no, no,' he replied. 'I had a bit of pig's cheek at Daneen's on my way up.' (Daneen was my uncle.) 'I'm very fond of a bit of pig's cheek ... My goodness, is it that late?' he exclaimed, letting on to be astonished. 'If I knew that I'd have gone to the North Chapel for midnight Mass. I'd like to hear the *Adeste* again. That's a hymn I'm very fond of – a most touching hymn.'

Then he began to hum it falsetto.

> *Adeste fideles*
> *Solus domus dagus.*

Father was very fond of Latin hymns, particularly when he had a drop in, but as he had no notion of the words he made them up as he went along, and this always drove Mother mad.

'Ah, you disgust me!' she said in a scalded voice, and closed the room door behind her. Father laughed as if he thought it a great joke; and he struck a match to light his pipe and for a while puffed at it noisily. The light under the door dimmed and went out but he continued to sing emotionally.

> Dixie medearo
> Tutum tonum tantum
> Venite adoremus.

He had it all wrong but the effect was the same on me. To save my life I couldn't keep awake.

Coming on to dawn, I woke with the feeling that something dreadful had happened. The whole house was quiet, and the little bedroom that looked out on the foot and a half of back yard was pitch-dark. It was only when I glanced at the window that I saw how all the silver had drained out of the sky. I jumped out of bed to feel my stocking, well knowing that the worst had happened. Santa had come while I was asleep, and gone away with an entirely false impression of me, because all he had left me was some sort of book, folded up, a pen and pencil, and a tuppenny bag of sweets. Not even Snakes-and-Ladders! For a while I was too stunned even to think. A fellow who was able to drive over rooftops and climb down chimneys without getting stuck – God, wouldn't you think he'd know better?

Then I began to wonder what that foxy boy, Sonny, had. I went to his side of the bed and felt his stocking. For all his spelling and sucking-up he hadn't done so much better, because, apart from a bag of sweets like mine, all Santa had left him was a popgun, one that fired a cork on a piece of string and which you could get in any huxter's shop for sixpence.

All the same, the fact remained that it was a gun, and a gun was better than a book any day of the week. The Dohertys had a gang, and the gang fought the Strawberry Lane kids who tried to play football in our road. That gun would be very useful to me in many ways, while it would be lost on Sonny who wouldn't be let play with the gang, even if he wanted to.

Then I got the inspiration, as it seemed to me, direct from heaven. Suppose I took the gun and gave Sonny the book! Sonny would never be any good in the gang: he was fond of spelling, and a studious child like him could learn a lot of spellings from a book like mine. As he hadn't seen Santa any more than I had, what he hadn't seen wouldn't grieve him. I was doing no harm to anyone; in fact, if Sonny only knew, I was doing him a good turn which he might have cause to thank me for later. That was one thing I was always keen on; doing good turns. Perhaps this was Santa's intention the whole time and he had merely become confused between us. It was a mistake that might happen to anyone. So I put the book, the pencil, and the pen into Sonny's stocking and the popgun into my own, and returned to bed and slept again. As I say, in those days I had plenty of initiative.

It was Sonny who woke me, shaking me to tell me that Santa had come and left me a gun. I let on to be surprised and rather disappointed in the gun, and to divert his mind from it made him show me his picture book, and cracked it up to the skies.

As I knew, that kid was prepared to believe anything, and nothing would do him then but to take the presents in to show Father and Mother. This was a bad moment for me. After the way she had behaved about the langing, I distrusted Mother, though I had the consolation of believing that the only person who could contradict me was now somewhere up by the North Pole. That gave me a certain confidence, so Sonny and I burst in with our presents, shouting: 'Look what Santa Claus brought!'

Father and Mother woke, and Mother smiled, but only for an instant. As she looked at me her face changed. I knew that look; I knew it only too well. It was the same she had worn the day I came home from langing, when she said I had no word.

'Larry,' she said in a low voice, 'where did you get that gun?'

'Santa left it in my stocking, Mummy,' I said, trying to put on an injured air, though it baffled me how she guessed that he hadn't. 'He did, honest.'

'You stole it from that poor child's stocking while he was asleep,' she said, her voice quivering with indignation. 'Larry, Larry, how could you be so mean?'

'Now, now, now,' Father said deprecatingly, ''tis Christmas morning.'

'Ah,' she said with real passion, 'it's easy it comes to you. Do you think I want my son to grow up a liar and a thief?'

'Ah, what thief, woman?' he said testily. 'Have sense, can't you?' He was as cross if you interrupted him in his benevolent moods as if they were of the other sort, and this one was probably exacerbated by a feeling of guilt for his behaviour of the night before. 'Here, Larry,' he said, reaching out for the money on the bedside table, 'here's sixpence for you and one for Sonny. Mind you don't lose it now!'

But I looked at Mother and saw what was in her eyes. I burst out crying, threw the popgun on the floor, and ran bawling out of the house before anyone on the road was awake. I rushed up the lane beside the house and threw myself on the wet grass.

I understood it all, and it was almost more than I could bear; that there was no Santa Claus, as the Dohertys said, only Mother trying to scrape together a few coppers from the housekeeping;

that Father was mean and common and a drunkard, and that she had been relying on me to raise her out of the misery of the life she was leading. And I knew that the look in her eyes was the fear that, like my father, I should turn out to be mean and common and a drunkard.

Acknowledgements

The editor and publishers are grateful for permission to include the following copyright stories in this anthology.

MAEVE BINCHY: 'Be Prepared', reprinted from the *Irish Times* by permission of the author and Christine Green, Authors' Agent.

ELIZABETH BOWEN: 'The Tommy Crans', © 1934 by Elizabeth Bowen, is reprinted by permission of Curtis Brown, London.

CLARE BOYLAN: 'The Miracle of Life'. First published in *Concerning Virgins* (Hamish Hamilton Ltd), © 1989 by Clare Boylan. Reprinted by permission of the author and Rogers, Coleridge & White Ltd.

PÁDRAIC BREATHNACH: 'The Snowman'. First published in *The March Hare* (Cló Iar-Chonnachta Teo). Reprinted by permission of the author and publishers.

Acknowledgements

LYNN DOYLE: 'A Bowl of Broth'. First published in *A Bowl of Broth* (Duckworth) and reprinted by permission of A.P. Watt Ltd on behalf of Mrs Wyn Fisher.

CARLO GÉBLER: 'Christmas'. First published in *W9 & Other Lives* (Lagan Press). Reprinted by permission of the author and Aitken & Stone.

BRENDAN GRIFFIN: 'Cold Turkey', reprinted from the *Irish Press New Irish Writing* by permission of the author.

HUGO HAMILTON: 'Nazi Christmas', reprinted from *Dublin Where the Palm Trees Grow* (Faber and Faber) by permission of the author.

JOHN B. KEANE: 'The Woman Who Hated Christmas', reprinted from *The Voice of an Angel* (Mercier Press) by permission of the author.

RITA KELLY: 'The Conifers', reprinted from *The Whispering Arch* (Arlen House) by permission of the author.

BENEDICT KIELY: 'Homes on the Mountain', reprinted from *A Journey to the Seven Streams* (Poolbeg Press) by permission of the author.

BRIAN LEYDEN: 'Christmas Promise', reprinted from *Departures* (Brandon Books) by permission of the author and publishers.

BRIAN LYNCH: 'Curtains for Christmas', reprinted from the *Irish Press New Irish Writing* by permission of the author.

BERNARD MacLAVERTY: 'A Present for Christmas', reprinted from *Secrets and Other Stories* (The Blackstaff Press) by permission of the publishers and the author.

FRANCIS MacMANUS: 'Family Portrait', reprinted from *Pedlar's Pack* (The Talbot Press).

COLUM McCANN: 'The Year of the Green Pigeons', reprinted from the *Irish Times* by permission of the author.

FRANK O'CONNOR: 'Christmas Morning', reprinted from *Collected Stories* (Macmillan) by permission of the Peters Fraser & Dunlop Group Ltd.

SEAN O'FAOLAIN: 'Two of a Kind', reprinted from *I Remember! I Remember!* (Jonathan Cape) © Sean O'Faolain 1961 by permission of Rogers, Coleridge & White Ltd.

TERRY PRONE: 'Butterfly Christmas', reprinted from *Blood Brothers, Soul Sisters* (Poolbeg Press) by permission of the author.

WILLIAM TREVOR: 'The Time of Year', reprinted from *Beyond the Pale and Other Stories* (The Bodley Head) by permission of the author.

While every effort has been made to trace all copyright holders, the publishers would be glad to hear from any who may have been omitted.

Biographical Notes

MAEVE BINCHY: Born in Co. Dublin, she is a history graduate of University College, Dublin, and was a teacher before joining the *Irish Times* in 1969. Her novels have gained worldwide popularity, been translated into many languages, and filmed. She has also written plays for the stage and TV, as well as four collections of short stories.

ELIZABETH BOWEN: Born Dublin, 1899, she spent most of her life in England. From 1952 until 1960 she lived in Bowen's Court, Co. Cork, which she inherited on her father's death in 1928. She wrote a great deal of non-fiction, ten novels and many short stories, and is regarded as one of the leading writers of the twentieth century. She died in 1973.

CLARE BOYLAN: Born Dublin, 1948, she turned from journalism to full-time creative writing in the early eighties, since when she has published four novels, three collections of short stories and a book about cats.

PÁDRAIC BREATHNACH: Born Moycullen, Co. Galway, he is a lecturer in Irish in Limerick. A novelist, essayist and short-story writer, he has also won the Butler Literary Award of the Irish-American Cultural Institute.

EDMUND DOWNEY: Born Waterford, 1856, the son of a ship owner, he was a well-known writer of sea stories towards the end of the nineteenth century.

LYNN DOYLE: Born Downpatrick, Co. Down, 1873. He wrote many plays but is best known for his collections of comic stories set in the fictional district of Ballygullion. He died in 1961.

CARLO GÉBLER: Born Dublin, 1954, he grew up in London and now lives in Enniskillen, Co. Fermanagh. He has written non-fiction, children's fiction, a collection of short stories and six novels.

BRENDAN GRIFFIN: Born Lixnaw, Co. Kerry, he is a teacher in Co. Dublin. His early stories were published in the Irish Press New Irish Writing.

HUGO HAMILTON: Born Dublin, 1953, of Irish-German parents, he has travelled extensively throughout Europe and his first three novels were set in Germany. A winner, in 1992, of the Rooney Prize for Irish Literature, he has also published a collection of short stories.

JOHN B. KEANE: Born Listowel, Co. Kerry, 1928, he is one of Ireland's leading playwrights. He has also published novels, short stories, an autobiography, humorous essays and poetry.

Biographical Notes

RITA KELLY: Born Co. Galway, 1953, her poetry and prose, in both Irish and English, have appeared in many periodicals and she has published a novel and a collection of short stories.

BENEDICT KIELY: Born Co. Tyrone, 1919, he taught for many years in the US, and now lives in Dublin. One of Ireland's leading short-story writers, he has also published a critical biography of William Carleton and many widely acclaimed novels.

BRIAN LEYDEN: Born Co. Roscommon, 1960. He has won the RTE Francis MacManus Short Story Award, published one story collection, written radio documentaries and devised and performed a one-man stage show on W.B. Yeats.

BRIAN LYNCH: Born Dublin, 1945, he is a TV playwright, poet and critic.

BERNARD MacLAVERTY: Born Belfast, 1945, he taught for some years in Scotland where he now lives. He has written two novels which became highly praised films, and four short-story collections.

FRANCIS MacMANUS: Born Kilkenny, 1909. A prolific writer of stories, essays, biography, history and novels, he became Features Director of Irish Radio in 1947. He died in 1965.

COLUM McCANN: Born Dublin, 1967. He won a *Sunday Tribune Hennessy Literary Award* in 1990, published a widely acclaimed short-story collection and a novel. He now lives in the USA.

FRANK O'CONNOR: Born Cork, 1903, he is acknowledged as one of literature's masters of the short story. He also wrote two novels, a biography of Michael Collins, two volumes of autobiography, travel books, translations of Irish poetry, and much criticism. He died in 1966.

SEAN O'FAOLAIN: Born Cork, 1900. Another acknowledged master of the short story, he was one of Ireland's most distinguished twentieth-century men of letters. Novelist, biographer, autobiographer, playwright, travel writer and critic, he was also the founder-editor of the mould-breaking monthly, *The Bell*. He died in 1991.

TERRY PRONE: Born Dublin, 1949. She is a leading communications expert and has written a number of books on the subject. She has also published a collection of short stories and a novel.

CANON SHEEHAN: Born Mallow, Co. Cork, 1852, he was ordained in 1875. One of the most popular Irish novelists of his day, *My New Curate* and *Glenanaar* are still widely read. He died in 1913.

WILLIAM TREVOR: Born in Mitchelstown, Co. Cork, 1928, he has written many novels and short stories and is widely recognised as one of the world's great short-story writers of today.